Jennifer McMurrain

Return to Quail Crossings
By Jennifer McMurrain

©2014 by Jennifer McMurrain

Cover Design: Brandy Walker
        www.sistersparrowgraphicdesign.com

Published by LilyBear House, LLC
        www.LilyBearHouse.com

ISBN: 978-1500858414

Also available in eBook publication

PRINTED IN THE UNITED STATES OF AMERICA

Dedication

To my parents, Randy and Cathy Collar, for making sure I always knew I could return home, no matter what.

Chapter One

Evalyn Brewer lurched forward as the bus rolled to a stop. With a heavy sigh, she stood and stretched her arms overhead.

"We'll be stopped for fifteen minutes to use the facilities and get some food. Next stop is two hours away," the bus driver sang out.

"That man is far too happy," she mumbled under her breath, trying not to inhale the strong exhaust from the bus.

"I know. He was actually whistlin' earlier. Nobody likes to drive a bus that much," came a scratchy voice from behind her.

Evalyn turned to see a tall, skinny man with a pointed nose, leaning on the bus seat behind her. She gave him a polite nod, tucking a strand of dark blonde hair behind her ear, before bending to gather her bundle and bag.

The man leaned over, his breath hot on the back of her neck, and whispered. "How 'bout you let me buy you lunch? Then we can sit together for a while and get to know each other better." His tongue flicked her ear.

Evalyn bolted up and slapped the man. "How dare you!"

The stranger grabbed his cheek and looked around at the other passengers. "I was just offerin' to buy the lady lunch," he explained. "Guess she ain't hungry."

He gave her an extra shove with his shoulder as he exited the bus. Evalyn scanned the other passengers, knowing her face was five shades of red, then turned back to her pack and hurried off the bus.

Keeping her bundle securely on the booth seat between the wall and herself, she ordered a bottle of milk and a ham sandwich at the roadside cafe. She was thankful the sandwich came quickly since her stomach was already growling at the smell of the chicken dinner special being served all around her. Her taste buds balked at the dry sandwich, wishing for chicken, but she reminded herself she had to watch what she spent, since she still had dinner and breakfast to purchase before getting back to Knollwood, Texas.

She had been hungry before. She had survived it then, and she would survive it now. Her time off the bus was almost over, but her backside still ached as she thought of the hours she had left. Another urge told her she should use the facilities before their departure.

The restrooms were at the back of the café; the only entrance was from the outside. After taking care of her needs, Evalyn hurried back toward the bus. Just as she rounded the corner a hand grabbed her, pulling her back and slamming her against the wall of the café.

She pulled her bundle close as the skinny man with the pointed nose stared down at her. "Think you can embarrass me like that and get away with it?"

"Let me go or I'll scream." She held the man's gaze, fighting the urge to vomit at his stench of tobacco, dirt, and bad hygiene.

"Oh, I'll make you scream all right." He grabbed both shoulders and pushed her toward the men's bathroom.

Evalyn let out a fierce roar as she pushed back with her body, frustrated that her hands were tangled in her bundle. She knew she couldn't let the man get her into the men's restroom. If he did, there would be little chance someone would hear her scream and come to her aid. She planted her feet and screamed louder.

"Shut up, you little hussy," the man snarled, "or I'll slap your face off."

A shadow loomed over the struggling pair for the briefest of seconds before the skinny man was lifted off Evalyn and thrown into the dirt. "You best git!" she heard the shadow say. "And I don't mean back to the bus. This is your stop."

The skinny man scrambled to his feet and ran down the street. Evalyn studied her unexpected hero. His shaggy black hair, in desperate need of a trim, fell into his eyes. He was tall and stocky, but she wasn't fooled. The man was built like an ox. Had she been the skinny man, she would have run too.

"Are you okay?" the man asked.

Evalyn nodded, but her heart was pounding so hard she could feel it in her ears. "I can't thank you enough, Mr...?"

The man extended his hand. "Robert Smith."

A cry rang out from Evalyn's bundle, and once again, she felt her cheeks flush. Robert's face softened. "Is your baby okay?"

Evalyn looked down at the baby girl cradled in a heavy blanket in her arms and gave the infant a little bounce.

"Oh, I think she's fine. Thanks to you, the man only had time to push me around a bit. She must've slept right through most of it." She started to the bus. "Thanks again, Mr. Smith. You really are a hero."

"Wait," Robert called out, "What's your name?"

Evalyn ignored Robert's question as she hurried toward the bus. She reached the door just as the driver called out, "Alllll aboooard!" He smiled as she entered, "I always wanted to work on the trains."

"That's nice," said Evalyn. Taking her seat in the middle of the bus and grabbing the milk bottle out of her bag, she fastened on a nipple and plopped it into the baby's mouth. Laying her head against the window, she tried to forget the scene that had just taken place. Lord knows what that man would have done to her if Mr. Smith hadn't shown up.

Suddenly she felt someone sit next to her. She knew she'd have to share a seat at some point. She'd been lucky up until then to have had one all to herself. Looking at her seat partner, she took in a short breath of air. "Mr. Smith?"

"You didn't answer my question, and please call me, Robert."

The bus pulled onto the highway as Evalyn looked around for an open seat. The bus was full. She'd have to share the bench seat with Mr. Smith.

"What question?" she asked, sighing. It was bad enough she had to share a seat, but it was obvious the man wanted to chat.

"I asked your name," he said.

"My name is Evalyn Brewer." She smiled at the baby. "And this is Joy."

Robert smiled at Evalyn. "That seems fittin'; I can tell she fills you with joy."

"Mr. Smith, I'm not sure you sittin' here is entirely appropriate given the circumstances. Would you mind tradin' seats with one of the other single ladies?" asked Evalyn.

"Given the circumstances, I believe it's entirely appropriate," said Robert. "This is not a part of the country through which a lady wants to travel alone. It isn't safe for you or your baby. I'll just sit with you as far as Knollwood, Texas. Then you're on your own. I won't take no for an answer"

"You're getting off in Knollwood?" Evalyn gasped.

Robert nodded. "Yes. Why? Do you know someone from there?"

Evalyn sat back in her seat. "You could say that."

"Who? I grew up there. In fact, I spent my whole life there up until about six years ago."

"Why are you going back?" asked Evalyn.

Robert hung his head. "My father passed about a year ago. I've had a pretty good job with the railroad and have finally saved up enough money to return to the homestead and make something' of it. Funny thing is, if you would've told me six years ago I'd be excited to return to Knollwood, I would've laughed at you. Now, I can't wait to get back."

"I know the feelin'," mumbled Evalyn.

"You know, you're really good at that."

Evalyn looked at Robert. "Good at what?"

"Avoiding my questions. Who do you know in Knollwood?" asked Robert, a slight grin causing his dimples to show.

The man had been very nice and Evalyn hadn't had anyone to talk to since she got on the bus in Los Angeles, California. Knollwood was a small town, so he was going to find out anyway. "James Murphy and Dovie Grant. They kind of adopted my siblings and me about five years ago."

"Well, ain't this a small world? Mrs. Grant was so good to my ma before she passed. It broke my heart to hear about her husband and child passin' in that car accident."

The mood grew heavy, and Evalyn looked down at Joy and tried to imagine living without her. It wouldn't be possible.

"So you're headed back there to see your family?" asked Robert. "I mean no disrespect when I say this, but I can't understand how your husband would let you and your daughter travel halfway across the country alone."

Evalyn shook her head as Joy finished her bottle. She propped the child up on her shoulder to burp. There was no hiding what was to come, so she might as well spit out the words. "I have no husband, Mr. Smith. I'm hopin' that I'll be able to raise Joy properly in Knollwood, and that my kin will take us both in, regardless of the situation.

Joy let out a hearty burp that sent giggles running through the bus. Evalyn cradled Joy on her lap.

"Mr. Murphy and Mrs. Grant wouldn't turn a rattlesnake away if it needed help," Robert said softly, smiling at Joy. "Your young'un is lucky to have them on her side."

"It's not my family I'm worried about," said Evalyn before laying her head on the back of the seat to rest. "You know how small towns are."

Chapter Two

Evalyn was surprised that Robert didn't wait for Joy and her when the bus stopped in Knollwood. He'd stuck to her like sweat on a dusty brow since the incident at the rest stop. Probably doesn't want to be associated with a woman who'd have a child out of wedlock, she thought. Not that she could blame him. Small towns were notorious for being fickle and, dare she say, judgmental. They'd either accept Joy as one of their own, or they'd both be outcasts for life. Not that it mattered. Evalyn had used the last of her money to buy milk for Joy. They had no place else to go.

On the bus she had played with the notion of telling everyone that Joy's father had died. But every time the thought came up, she remembered how she had almost lost her younger sister, Alice, five years ago during the horrific dust storm of Black Sunday. After that day, the thought of lying about the death of a loved one, left a bad taste in her mouth.

Wrapping Joy up tightly, Evalyn grabbed her bag and exited the bus. Knollwood hadn't changed much in the year and a half she'd been gone. It still had a bustling main street, complete with Knollwood Market, a feed store, Johnson's Drug Store, and Annette's Café. People went on about their daily life as if Evalyn had never left.

Goose bumps covered her body at the sight of her hometown, but she knew it wasn't from the weather. The early morning spring air still held a bit of a chill, but the day was going to be sunny and nice. The goose bumps were due to being nervous and excited at the same time.

"Evalyn, over here!"

Evalyn spun around, wondering who was calling her name. She hadn't told anyone she was coming. Her new life was about to begin. It was time to face it.

Her shoulders relaxed a bit when she saw it was Robert hailing her. But as the bus crowd disappeared into Johnson's Drug Store and Annette's Cafe, she was able to make out who was standing next to him. It was none other than Pastor Spaulding and his wife, Susan.

Evalyn shook her head at Robert. She knew her face displayed utter horror at the thought of talking with Pastor Spaulding. The last person she wanted to face right now was the leader of the church and his wife. They'd be so disappointed in her circumstances. Would they shun her from the church? She had hoped Dovie or James would be able to put in a good word around town before she had to face the church members.

Before she could flee, Robert hustled over. "Pastor Spaulding has agreed to give you a ride to Quail Crossings as he takes me to my homestead, Rockwood. I just hope I can get my pa's old truck to start once I get out there."

"I can't, Robert," said Evalyn. "That was really kind of you to find me a ride, but I have a lot of explainin' to do, and I'm not ready to do it with Pastor Spaulding."

Robert's eyes softened. "It'll be okay. How else are you gonna get there? Give the Spaulings a chance to understand before writing them off. Besides the longer you stay in town, the sooner the rumors will start."

She couldn't argue with that. Joy was sleeping soundly, but there was no telling how long that would last. She nodded and walked with Robert to the car.

"Evalyn," sang Mrs. Spaulding, giving Evalyn and Joy a gentle hug, "so glad you're home."

Pastor Spaulding opened the back door. "Why don't you and Susan ride in back and catch up? Your family will be so happy to see you. Are you goin' to Quail Crossings or to Bill's house, Quail Crossings, Jr.?"

Evalyn couldn't help but smile at Pastor Spaulding's joke. James Murphy had not only taken her family in six years ago, but he had also given her older brother, Bill, five acres of Quail Crossings for a house of their own. After Bill's wedding to Lou Anne Garber, Evalyn, her younger brother, Elmer, and Alice had decided to stay with Dovie Grant and James so the newlyweds could have their privacy. They had become so close, it just seemed natural for them to stay at Quail Crossings.

"If I know my family, they'll all be at Quail Crossings," Evalyn answered, smiling at the thought of her home. There was a time when she would have given anything to be in California. Now she was happy to be back.

Pastor Spaulding gave a quick nod and closed the door once Evalyn and Joy were seated. Susan motioned to Joy. "Do you mind if I hold her for a bit? You've had such a long journey, I'm sure you could use a break."

Evalyn hesitated. "I don't know. She's not used to strangers."

Pastor Spaulding laughed as Evalyn got into the car. "My Susan has never been a stranger to anyone."

Evalyn held on tightly. "I would hate for y'all to have to listen to her scream all the way to the farm."

"Why not lay her between us then?" asked Susan. "She'd probably enjoy stretchin' out."

Evalyn reluctantly laid the six month old baby between them. Feeling the freedom, Joy stretched her legs out and arched her back.

"She's adorable, Evalyn. Did I hear Robert say her name is Joy?" Susan tickled the baby under her neck, causing a big grin.

"Yes," said Evalyn.

"Well, it's a very fittin' name. I can see why you chose it. Dovie must be delighted."

Evalyn sighed. "Nobody knows."

"What did you say, dear?" asked Susan.

"She doesn't know about Joy," said Evalyn.

"Oh," said Susan, "well this will be a delightful surprise."

Evalyn turned her attention to the countryside. She just wanted to enjoy seeing home again and was glad Susan didn't pry further. Now wasn't the time to announce that she was returning home with an illegitimate baby.

The landscape had changed quite a bit from when the Brewers first moved to Knollwood. The drought had been thick, and the "Dirty Thirties" wasn't just a catchy nickname. Now the wheat grew again, and farmers terraced their land to keep from making the same mistakes. If only a bit of terraced land could fix her own mistakes, Evalyn thought.

"Here we are." Pastor Spaulding woke Evalyn from her daydream. "Good ol' Quail Crossings."

Evalyn took in her home. The two story brown house looked the same, but she could see that Dovie had put up some new blue curtains. The old white ones had seen too many dusters and looked tan, no matter how many washings they had. It was good to see Dovie lightening the place a bit.

The big barn still sat in the back, no doubt with Poppy in the stall waiting to be milked, and the horses, Tex and Pronto, keeping her company. Evalyn knew there would be at least a couple of pigs and maybe even some piglets. She wondered how many cattle James had in his herd this year and if Alice still talked to the chickens.

Pastor Spaulding stopped the car and Evalyn eased out and stretched her arms. She'd walk a thousand miles before ever wanting to sit in a car or bus again. It had been a long journey. She turned and leaned into the car to grab Joy.

"That is the biggest goose I've ever se … Evalyn, look out!" yelled Robert.

Evalyn's eyes grew wide as she realized her mistake. Before she could turn, the big goose dashed toward her and bit her right on the rump.

"Norman!" she screamed, slapping the goose off her behind. "Get off me!"

The goose hissed and lifted his wings as Robert hurried out of the car and placed himself between Evalyn and the bird. "Get back in the car, Evalyn, this goose is sick."

Evalyn pushed Robert to the side. "He's not sick. He's just being Norman. The ol' bird should've been dog bait years ago."

Placing two fingers in her mouth, Evalyn let out a loud whistle. Immediately, a black and white cow dog came running around the corner, nipping at Norman and chasing him back to the pond. "And that is Button, the only animal or person on this farm that Norman is afraid of."

"What on God's green Earth is all this commotion? Sounds like a hoedown on Harvest Night with all this ruckus."

Evalyn closed her eyes. It could only be one person, Dovie. Evalyn reached into the car once again and grabbed Joy, then turned to meet the closest thing she'd had to a mother over the past six years.

"Evalyn?" Dovie whispered.

"Hello, Dovie."

"Evalyn! You're home!" Dovie wrapped Evalyn up in a huge hug. "Why didn't you write? I would have come and picked you up at the station."

"Careful," said Evalyn, trying to back away but running into the car door. "I'm not alone."

She leaned forward and showed Dovie the baby. "Dovie, this is my daughter, Joy."

Dovie's hands found her apron as she started twisting it. "Your daughter?"

Evalyn nodded. "Would it be all right if we stayed with you?"

"Of course." Dovie smiled, and then looked at Robert. "You and your husband are always welcome here. You're family."

Evalyn shook her head. "No, Dovie, he's not ..."

Pastor Spaulding came around the car and patted Robert firmly on the back. "Well, Mr. Smith, you didn't tell me you and Evalyn were married. We just assumed y'all met on the bus."

"'Cause we ..." Evalyn started.

"I won't be stayin'." Robert offered his hand to Dovie, interrupting Evalyn. "But allow me to introduce myself since my wife has failed to do so. I'm Robert Smith. My parents own the Rockwood place. Well, at least they did before my pa passed."

"Oh, you can't be," said Dovie, laughing. "The Robert Smith I know is knee-high to a June bug."

"It's been a while, I know" said Robert, blushing. "But I'll be goin' up to my pa's place to get it ready for us while Evalyn and Joy stay here, if that's okay?"

"Of course," Dovie said again. "I was really sorry to hear about your pa."

"It's okay," said Robert. "Thank you."

"Nothing's okay," Evalyn interjected. "We are not ..."

"Would you please excuse us for a minute, Mrs. Grant? Evalyn and I are not seeing eye to eye on where they'll be stayin'. But Rockwood is no a place for a baby of mine right now."

Robert grabbed Evalyn's elbow and led her away from the crowd. "I think I have a way to help us both out."

"How so?" Evalyn raised an eyebrow.

"Let's call a turnip a turnip, shall we? You need a husband. Joy will never be accepted fully into this community without a pa, and we both know it. And I need a wife. Mrs. Grant just gave us the answer."

Evalyn gasped. "I'm not sure what you have in mind, but I am not that kind of girl. I can understand how you came to that impression with Joy and all, but I barely know you Mr. Smith."

"I never thought of you as that kind of girl. But I'm afraid others will." Robert shook his head. "We'll be husband and wife, just not in the Biblical sense." Robert blushed, then shook his head, determined to continue. "I need help on the homestead. You know, someone to do the cookin', cleanin', and such. You and Joy can have a room all to yourselves. Look, I can't explain it all now, too many people watchin' Just promise to think about it, and we'll talk in greater detail later."

"And if I say no, you'll make a liar out of both of us. How will that help Joy?" asked Evalyn.

"If you think about it with a clear head, you won't say no. Just think about the benefits, what it means for Joy."

Evalyn hugged Joy closer. "I don't know."

"Just think about it, okay? That's all I'm askin'."

"I can never repay you for your help at the café and for seeing us here safely, so I guess it's the least I could do," said Evalyn. "But I'm makin' no promises, Mr. Smith."

Robert nodded. "That's all I ask, oh, and one more thing."

"What?" Evalyn sighed.

"You should really call me Robert, *Mrs. Smith*," he said with a wink.

Chapter Three

"So let me get this straight." Evalyn's older brother, Bill, paced around the kitchen table, where the family had gathered to meet Joy and welcome Evalyn home. "You go to Hollywood to become an actress and end up married with a child instead?"

Evalyn slowly nodded. Dovie had been quick to tell Evalyn's older brother, Bill, everything before she could decide what to say about Robert. Bill had taken on the position of their caregiver since their parents had abandoned them during the Great Depression.

"And you ended up marrying a man from Knollwood while in California? How did that even happen?" asked Bill.

"I'd rather not talk about it now, Bill. I'm very tired," answered Evalyn. "It was such a long trip, and I didn't sleep well on the bus. Could we talk about this later?"

"You come home with a child and a husband and expect to take a nap before tellin' me what happened? Have you lost your mind, Evie?" asked Bill. "How could you spring this on all of us? Not a mention of Robert, a marriage, or a baby in any letters you sent. I'd say you owe us an explanation."

"Well," Evalyn fumbled for the words. "I was in the cafeteria on the movie lot with Harriet one afternoon eatin' lunch."

"Did you get to eat with them movie stars?" Evalyn's eleven year old sister, Alice asked.

Evalyn shook her head. "No, they didn't eat with us. They had their own café."

"Not that it matters, Alice," said Bill. "Y'all can talk about that nonsense later, I wanna hear about you and Mr. ... what was his name again?"

"Robert Smith. His parents have some land just southeast of ours," answered Dovie, excitedly. "Go on, Evalyn."

"Like I said, we were eatin' in the cafeteria, and he and a friend sat across from us. It was a very busy time, and they couldn't find any other seats. Of course, Harriet was instantly gabby with the fellas while I ate my lunch."

"Were you eating hamburgers?" asked Alice, twisting her blonde ponytail. "I love hamburgers. Miss Annette started serving them at her café, and they are so good Evie. My mouth's watering just thinking about it."

"No, it was just a sandwich. Harriet and I couldn't afford to buy lunch there, so we had to bring our own."

Bill cleared his throat.

"Shhh...," said Evalyn, "or you'll wake Joy and I won't be able to finish."

"Then there's no time to waste. Finish," demanded Bill.

"As I said, Harriet started chattin' with the fella next to Robert, so naturally Robert and I started talkin' and found out we were both from Knollwood. And now here we are." Evalyn stood up.

"Evie." Bill's voice was harsh.

"Look, Bill, I'm tired and I don't feel like explainin' myself to you. I'm not a child anymore."

"No, you're not a child anymore, but you're acting like a stubborn mule." Bill slammed his hand on the table, causing a wail to start upstairs.

"Now, look what you've done." Evalyn gestured up the stairs. "I thought you'd be happy to see us, but all I get is an inquisition. I guess we should've stayed in California."

Evalyn turned and marched up the stairs.

"Bill," Lou Anne put an arm around her husband, "I think you were a little hard on her."

"I know I was, but I just can't believe it." Bill pushed down a splinter on the old table. "I'm glad she's back. I always knew she'd return, but I never thought it would be with a husband and baby. She's only been there a year and a half. We can all do the math. She didn't know this Smith fella very long before they got married. I'm just worried about her."

"Of course, you are," said Elmer, causing Bill to jump. He had forgotten his little brother was in the room. Elm was always so quiet. "We're a family and families worry about each other, or at least they're supposed to."

Bill nodded in agreement as Elmer stood and continued, "Joy and Mr. Smith are also our family now, no matter how it happened. That's somethin' we all best keep in mind." And with that, Elmer grabbed his hat and walked out the door to tend to his chores.

Bill looked at Lou Anne. "How'd he get so smart?"

"Takes after his brother, I'm sure," said Lou Anne bending to peck Bill on the cheek.

Dovie got up from the table and grabbed a basket of potatoes. "Are y'all staying for supper? Robert Smith will be here."

"If that's all right," said Lou Anne, knowing full well it was expected that she and Bill stay for dinner just about every night. "I'm sure Bill would like to spend more time with his sister and meet his new brother-in-law."

"Never has there been a truer statement," said Bill.

"Well, you better be nice," said Alice, crossing her arms. "I don't want Evie to leave again because you're actin' like a wet cat. I wanna play with Joy. I can't believe I'm an aunt."

"We're not goin' anywhere," said Evalyn from the stairs, carrying the small baby. "Whether at Rockwood or Quail Crossings, we're not leavin' Knollwood."

"Yay," said Alice, clapping her hands. "Can I hold, Joy?"

"Sure," said Evie, "right after Bill."

Before Bill could protest, Evalyn placed the babe in his arms. "Say hello to your Uncle Bill, Joy." Evalyn looked at Bill. "Be a doll and watch her while I warm a bottle."

"Warm a bottle?" Dovie questioned. "I was sure you'd fed her upstairs?"

Evalyn bowed her head, hiding her red cheeks. "I've had to bottle feed her. I couldn't do the other."

"Well, why on earth not?" asked Dovie, a little louder than intended. "Wasn't there a midwife or nurse to help you in California? Did you have her at home or in the hospital?"

"I just couldn't," snapped Evalyn, and then lowered her voice back to a whisper. "It's personal; can we drop it?"

Dovie squeezed Evalyn's arm. "I didn't mean to pry. I know how hard it is. Just surprised you didn't have anyone to help you after she was born. I'll have Elm drive over to the Clark's and get some goat's milk. It's easier on a baby's tummy."

"Thanks," said Evalyn. "California was lonely. I didn't really have anyone to lean on other than Harriet, and, of course, she didn't know any more than me about actually havin' a baby."

"Couldn't you lean on, Robert?" asked Lou Anne, joining in the conversation. "We were in class together up until the 8th grade. He was a very nice boy and stayed in school longer than most boys before lookin' for work. I could tell he wanted to graduate, but his dad made him leave. So I'd think he'd understand. After all, he is your husband."

"Yes, he's very nice," said Evalyn, trying to hide the cringe at Lou Anne's mention of 'husband'. "But I didn't think he'd feel comfortable talkin' about such things. Just as I don't feel comfortable talkin' about it now. Could we please change the subject?"

"And what subject would that be?" asked a voice from the back door.

Evalyn looked up just in time to see James, Dovie's father, enter the kitchen. Evalyn ran to him. "James, it's so good to see you. Dovie was afraid you wouldn't be back from market until late."

"The cattle sold quickly, so George and I were able to make it home early. I'm so glad you're home, Evie. This is a blessed surprise."

"George Wheaton?" Evalyn willed her voice not to shake. "Harriet's father?"

James nodded and looked at Joy. "And who's this?"

"This," said Bill, handing the baby to James, "is Joy, Evie's daughter."

"It's my turn to hold her," whined Alice.

"Daughter?" James ignored Alice and took the baby from Bill, getting a big grin from Joy.

"Oh, yes," said Bill. "Our Evie has come back from California a married woman with a family."

27

"Dad, she married Robert Smith," said Dovie.

"You did?" James raised an eyebrow. "Guess the Lord works in mysterious ways. I know George will be glad to see Harriet. He's talked about driving out and getting you two a number of times. He's been very worried about y'all being on your own so far away from home."

"Harriet isn't here." Evalyn blushed and hurried an excuse. "She decided to stay in California as a seamstress there in Hollywood. It's a good job. I just couldn't keep it with Joy in the picture, and Robert was ready to come home to Rockwood."

"I wouldn't know anythin' about that since I've lived right here my entire life," said James. "I'm glad you're home with your new family. Where is Mr. Smith?"

"He's at Rockwood," said Evalyn, going back to the stove to check the milk. "He's been gone for so long, he wasn't sure what shape the homestead was in. He wants to get it ready before Joy and I move in. Is it okay for me to stay here?"

"Of course," said James, "you're family. Mr. Smith can sleep here too until Rockwood is ready."

"That's okay, we know there aren't enough beds," Evalyn said over her shoulder.

"Nonsense," said Lou Anne, "we have a whole house a mile from here. Remember, it was built with the thought of y'all living with us. Elm can sleep over there for a while, and Alice can sleep in Elm's room, givin' you and Robert the big bed to sleep in."

"No, that's okay." Evalyn shook her head. "We have a plan. Robert can stay at Rockwood. We've been on a bus together for days, so some time apart will be nice."

Evalyn took Joy and sat to feed her.

"Evie, you said I could hold her," Alice whined again.

"After she eats, Alice," said Evalyn. "I promise."

"Well, whether he stays here or not," said James, "everything's gonna be all right. In fact, everything's better than all right now that our family is back together."

Chapter Four

The sound of a firm knock came from the front door. Dovie wiped her hands on a dish towel.

"It must be Robert," she said, going to answer it. "Who else would use the front door?"

It took a tug, but Dovie pulled the large winter door open. There stood Robert, hat in his hands, his hair combed neatly. He looked more ready for church services, than an everyday evening dinner.

"Robert," she said beaming, "welcome, please come in."

Robert Smith crossed the threshold. "Thanks for havin' me over for dinner, Mrs. Grant. Food is pretty scarce at Rockwood."

"Nonsense," said Dovie, taking his hat. "You're welcome here anytime. In fact, I expect you here every night for dinner until you get Rockwood fixed up enough for Evie and Joy to move in to."

"Oh no, I couldn't ..."

"Best not to argue with her," said James extending his hand to Robert. "She won't take no for an answer. Welcome to the family, Mr. Smith. Small world, you meeting our Evie in California."

Robert raised an eyebrow at Evalyn. She rushed over to give him a quick hug. "An even smaller world that your rail company was doin' work for the same studio I worked at."

"Yes, we were laying some tracks for a western movie," said Robert, following Evalyn's lead.

"Robert, this is my brother, Bill, and his wife, Lou Anne, who I think you went to school with," introduced Evalyn, before Robert could say any more.

Robert shook Bill's hand. "I believe I owe you an apology."

Bill cocked his head. "How so?"

"I should've consulted you before askin' Evalyn to marry me. I didn't have a way of getting hold of you without Evalyn findin' out my plans. I hope you understand."

"I appreciate the thought," said Bill. "How 'bout you tell me about yourself, and I'll decide if I give this marriage my blessing?"

Evalyn playfully hit her brother. "Oh stop, Bill. You're gonna make him nervous."

"Not if he doesn't have any reason to be," muttered Bill, getting another playful slap on the arm but from his wife this time.

"Let's not crowd around the doorway," said Dovie, placing a hand on Robert's shoulder. "Have a seat in the parlor. You men can talk while we fix dinner. I'm runnin' a bit behind with all this excitement."

Evalyn bit her lip. There was no time to tell Robert everything she had already told Bill. She needed to stay in the parlor. "Dovie, do you mind if I feed Joy in the parlor? I hate to run out on helpin' with dinner, but I feel like I'm feeding Robert to the wolves."

"Go ahead," said Dovie, "Lou Anne, Alice, and I can handle it. We'll call you if we need you."

"Thanks." Evalyn grabbed Joy's bottle and made her way to Dovie's favorite blue chair.

"So, Mr. Smith," Bill said, "you were workin' on the set with Evalyn?"

"Bill, I already told you that we met in the cafeteria." Evalyn smiled at Robert. "How you and your friend, John, sat across from Harriet and me because all the other seats were taken."

Robert nodded. "Normally, I wouldn't have thought to sit with young ladies I hadn't met, but we really didn't have a choice. Then when John started talkin' with Harriet, I felt that if I didn't talk to Evalyn, she'd find me rude. Truth was, my tongue was so tied by her beauty, I'm surprised I could talk at all."

Evalyn blushed.

"So Mr. Smith," continued Bill, "It must've been quite a blessin' to have little Joy come along so quickly When's her birthday?"

"Bill, stop actin' so foolish," Evalyn snapped. "Quit grilling the poor man, 'bout his own daughter like he wouldn't know that she was born on October 3rd."

Robert gave Evalyn a thankful smile. "It was a beautiful day in October. In fact, I just about missed the entire thing. When Evalyn went into labor I was laying railroad tracks for a movie scene. No one could find me. Finally, someone got word to the director and he told me. Made it to the hospital just before Joy was born, but the nurse wouldn't let me in to see them."

James chuckled. "Probably best you didn't go in. When my Sylvia had Dovie, she became a different person. Said words that would make the good Lord blush."

"Well, that's enough about such subjects," said Evalyn. "It isn't proper to speak of the matter."

"And how do you plan on supporting Evie and Joy here in Knollwood, Mr. Smith?" asked Bill.

"Please, call me Robert. Mr. Smith sounds too much like my father." Robert cringed. "And to answer your question, pigs."

"Pigs?" Evalyn said, eyebrows raised.

"You didn't know this?" asked James.

"I'm afraid that's my fault," said Robert. "I just told her we would raise livestock, and I'm sure she assumed I meant cattle."

"I'm married to a pig farmer?" Evalyn said again, looking dazed.

"Pork is going up. I watched them ship in bacon to California diners every day. We don't have enough land to farm or have a decent cattle herd, so pigs will be our primary income."

"Pigs?" questioned Bill.

"Pork prices have gone up steadily over the past couple of years. Not as much as beef, but it'll make us a comfortable living," explained Robert. "In time we'll be able to afford more land and maybe turn to cattle."

"But pigs stink," said Evalyn, wrinkling her nose.

"As do most livestock," said James.

"And you don't think you'll have any issues supporting my sister and niece?" Bill said. "It seems pretty convenient that you should meet Evie in California."

"What are you saying?" asked Robert, eyes narrowed.

"Now, fellas," warned James.

"With all due respect, Mr. Murphy, it appears Mr. Brewer is trying to say something about my character," said Robert.

"I'll tell you plainly what I'm trying to say." Bill stood. "You married Evie with the hopes of getting a piece of Quail Crossings one day. That's why you didn't ask my permission to marry my sister. If you had respectful intentions, you would've found a way to get a hold of me."

"Bill!" Evie gasped. "Stop it."

"Your sister has the right to make her own choices, so I didn't need to ask you." Robert stood. "The thought of gaining a piece of this place never crossed my mind because that is not the kind of man I am. I earn my way," Robert walked over to Evalyn and Joy, giving them a light hug. "I'm sorry, Evalyn, but I'm going back to Rockwood. I've lost my appetite. Please thank Dovie for the offer. I'll be back tomorrow. Goodnight."

James shook his head. "You don't have to leave."

"I'm afraid I do," said Robert, looking at Bill. "I won't bring an argument to your table."

"What's goin' on in here?" asked Dovie, throwing a kitchen towel over her shoulder. "You're not leaving yet, are you, Robert? Dinner's on the table."

"Thank you, Mrs. Grant, for your hospitality," said Robert as he eyed Bill. "But I do believe I've worn out my welcome."

Dovie looked at James and Bill. "What did you two do?" Then she shook her head and raised her hands. "No, I don't wanna know. Robert, you and Evie take Joy into the kitchen, so we can eat."

She returned her attention to Bill and James. "And you two can behave yourselves and treat our guest proper or eat outside with Norman, you hear? I can't leave you two alone for a second."

James held up his hands. "It wasn't me."

"Did you stop it?" asked Dovie. James dropped his hands.

Evalyn stood and looked at the men. "Well y'all heard, Dovie. That's enough of this hard-headed nonsense. Come into the kitchen. I don't know about y'all, but I'm hungry."

She gave Dovie a thankful nod as she passed, but her heart still sunk. She was now married to a pig farmer. So much for a Hollywood lifestyle.

Chapter Five

"Alice, you can either stay here at Johnson's Drug or come with me to the Knollwood Market while Dad is speaking with Pastor Spaulding. What do you wanna do?" asked Dovie.

"Ummm." Alice tilted her head. "I'd really like to buy Joy something, but I don't know what yet."

Dovie smiled as Alice looked at the shelves of jarred candy. "Guess you'll be staying here then, silly goose. I'll be back in about half an hour, and we'll see if you've made up your mind by then. You know Joy is too little to eat candy, right?"

"Yeah," said Alice, "but I thought I could give her a lick of mine. I've never been an aunt before, so I just wanna make sure I do it right."

"Alice, I can already tell you're gonna be the best kind of aunt to Joy the kind that spoils her rotten. Dovie laughed. "Meet me at the market when you're done."

Alice tried to decide what to spend her five cents on. She wondered what Joy would like. There were the peppermint candies that she always got when she came to Johnson's Drug Store, but maybe Joy would enjoy the butterscotch candies more. She briefly thought about getting a chocolate coin to share but shook the thought away, realizing it would melt before they got home. Chocolate coins were best eaten right after purchase. Alice opened the jar to the peppermint sticks and inhaled deeply, letting the minty scent tickle her nose.

Unable to choose, Alice put the lid back on the peppermint jar and again stared at the rows of candy, begging one to answer her question on which to buy. Suddenly, a hard bump pushed her hard into the shelf. She quickly caught herself before swinging around to see who did it.

Alice couldn't help but gasp in shock as a black boy paused beside her. She hadn't seen a colored boy in Knollwood the entire time she had lived there. She had seen many in the shelters and food kitchen her family had frequented back when they were homeless during the Great Depression, but seeing one in her hometown was like seeing an elephant away from the circus.

"I'm sorry. I didn't mean to," the black boy said before hurrying out of the store.

Alice shrugged and turned back to the candy. Accidents happened and he had said he was sorry. All the colored people she had met before were nice enough, she was sure this boy was no different.

Before she could continue her candy debate, three more boys bumped into her as they quickly left the store. None of them, however, stopped to apologize.

"How rude," she whispered before her eyes grew wide. Those three boys were sure in a hurry, and she didn't think it was a coincidence that they bumped her right after the colored boy.

Her candy quest forgotten, she followed the boys out of the store and watched as they ran down the crowded Main Street as if looking for someone or something. Alice searched the street but saw nothing alarming. As she turned to go back inside, a flash of movement caught her eye. Across the street, between the meat market and the post office, the black boy hugged the wall as if trying to disappear.

Alice glanced down the street again at the boys, who were now making their way back towards Johnson's. She waited until the boys went behind Annette's Café before spurting across the street to the black boy. She didn't stop when she got to him but grabbed his hand and pulled him along with her.

The boy resisted.

"Come on," whispered Alice, "I know where you can hide."

With wide eyes, the boy quickly nodded and followed Alice. She pulled him through the alley and across two more streets before they came upon the old Bailey Tractor and Supply store. Once a thriving tractor repair and parts shop, it, like many other businesses, had gone bankrupt during the Depression and never reopened.

Alice ran around the back of the store and ducked under a piece of sheet metal that led to a hole in the wall of the store. Letting go of the boy's hand, she crawled into the store. He followed closely behind.

Placing one finger against her lips, she grabbed his hand again and led him into an interior office. There they sat on the dusty floor.

"You'll be safe here," Alice whispered.

"Are you sure?" asked the boy, taking in his surroundings.

Alice nodded. "No one comes in here. It's been boarded up for years. I found the hole while chasing stray kittens about a month ago. What did you do to those boys?"

The boy sighed. "I walked into the store."

Alice's forehead wrinkled. "It had to be more than that."

"In some towns that's all it takes," said the boy. "I ain't the right color to be shoppin' in there, I guess."

Alice bowed her head. "I'm sorry. I never thought anyone in Knollwood could be so mean."

"Why are you apologizin'? You saved me. What's your name anyway?" he asked.

"Alice Brewer, and yours?"

"Jacob Henry."

"Where ya from, Jacob?" asked Alice.

"Georgia," he answered.

"Georgia?" Alice raised an eyebrow. "Awful young to be walkin' here from Georgia aren't you?"

"Well, in some parts of the country sixteen is grown." He chuckled. "Look at you? I guess you ain't even in double digits yet, but I bet you just saved my life."

"I'm eleven," said Alice, chin up. "I don't think they would've hurt you. Those boys are in my brother's class. They're all talk."

"I wouldn't be so sure about that," said Jacob.

"I gotta go," said Alice, "Mama Dovie will be looking for me. Will you be okay?"

Jacob looked around the place. "I will be now. Think I'll hole up in here for a couple of days. Make 'em think I'm gone and then head out after the sun goes down."

"Do you have any food?" Alice asked.

Jacob rooted around in his bag. "I've got a couple of apples. I'll be fine."

"That ain't enough for chickens to live off of, more or less a sixteen year old boy. Trust me, I have two brothers, and I've seen them eat." Alice got up. "I'll bring you some food tomorrow."

Jacob shook his head. "Don't get in trouble for me, Miss. Alice. I'll be all right. Thank you for what you did. I mean it, I don't wanna think about what those boys would've done to me had they found me."

"Think nothin' of it," said Alice. "I've gotta go. See you tomorrow. Be safe, Jacob."

Alice turned and ran out of the building.

Dovie hurried down Main Street toward the Knollwood Market. It was unusually busy for a Tuesday, but Dovie was happy to see everyone. Even with all the Brewers in tow, living in the country could be a bit lonely. She guessed her loneliness had very little to do with living in the country and a lot more to do with having lost her husband, Simon, and only child, Helen, in a car accident roughly six years before. There were days it seemed like yesterday, but most of the time now she carried her grief lightly.

Three boys bumped into her as they ran down the street, knocking her to the ground.

"Frank Kelley, your father will hear about his," Dovie yelled. "What is happenin' to today's youngin's? They've got about as much respect as a rooster on your day off."

Dovie heard a low chuckle behind her as a hand reached forward to help her up. "A rooster on your day off, huh? I haven't heard that one before."

She took the man's hand to stand and then began to straighten her dress. "My mother used to say it all the time but followed it with 'as if anyone ever had a day off'."

Dovie looked up and smiled. "Thank you, Mr. ...." Her hand flew up to her face.

"Simon?" she whispered right before she fainted.

Chapter Six

James gave Pastor Spaulding's open office door a light knock. The pastor looked up and gave James a quick smile.

"James, please come in," he said, rising and meeting James to shake his hand. "I bet you're here to talk about the tractor pull next Saturday."

Pastor Spaulding motioned to the chair across from his desk, and James sat.

"I am," said James, "I've got a couple of hogs lined up for the hog wrestling. Bud Clark is a big ol' brute. I know I wouldn't wanna tangle with him. He'll be good for the young men who want a challenge. I can't wait to see them try to wrap their arms around that greased beast."

"That sounds good, James," the pastor said, nodding. "It sounds like everything's fallin' into place. It's gonna be a real good time."

James sat for a moment. He knew what he wanted to say but was afraid to say it. That was an emotion that was foreign to him. He had always been a man who said what he thought.

"Is there anything else you'd like to talk about, James?" Pastor Spaulding asked.

"There is something, but I'm not sure how to say it," said James, running his hands through his salt and pepper hair.

Pastor Spaulding got up and closed his office door. "You know anything you say in here stays between us."

James nodded. "I know."

The pastor sat back down. "You'll find no judgment here, James."

"Well, that's part of the problem I think," said James. "I believe I'm the one guilty of judgin'."

The pastor raised an eyebrow. "Why is that?"

"It's Robert Smith, Evalyn's husband. Somethin's not sitting right with me," explained James.

"Why do you think that is?" asked Pastor Spaulding.

"It just seems odd," said James. "We barely hear from Evie and then she shows up with a husband and a baby. It just doesn't make sense to me. Even if she didn't tell Dovie and me, I can't see her not tellin' Bill or Lou Anne. I'm getting the feelin' I'm being lied to."

"So you don't think their marriage is legal?" asked the pastor. "That's a pretty big accusation."

James shrugged. "That's not it."

"Then what?" asked Pastor Spaulding.

James shook his head. "I guess I'm just hurt that she didn't tell us, so I'm looking for something to be wrong."

Pastor Spaulding folded his fingers together. "I understand, James. It did happen awfully fast. I can see why you're concerned. Maybe she didn't know how to explain such a whirlwind romance. Could be she was afraid y'all would think less of her."

James stood.

"Did I say something wrong?" asked the pastor.

James fingered his hat. "No, I believe I have an apology to make. I didn't welcome that boy into the family as I should've, especially since he's lost all of his. Thanks for listenin'."

"James," said Pastor Spaulding, causing James to pause, "you're a good man and an even better man for knowin' when you're in the wrong. Robert will be quick to forgive, and I believe he'll make a good home for his wife and child."

James gave another nod of thanks and quietly left.

Dovie woke with a start. "Simon?"

"Mama Dovie, are you okay?" Alice asked, her eyes wet.

"It's okay, Alice. I'm all right," she said raising onto her elbows. "I'm not sure what happened."

Dovie looked around the room and tried to place where she was as the town people huddled around her. There were stacks of bagged coffee beans, and canned goods lined the shelves. She had to be in the back room of the Knollwood Market.

She tried to sit up.

"Whoa, be careful Miss," said a gentle voice from behind. "You took a mighty hard spill. I caught you the best I could, but I wasn't expecting you to fall off your feet so soon after getting up."

Dovie rubbed her head as the memory came back to her. "I'm so sorry. I thought I saw my ... well someone."

She turned to look at the man. He wore tan pants with a white button up shirt, and on his head sat a brown fedora, just like Simon's. Dovie sucked in a breath.

The man grabbed her arm and placed his other hand behind her back. "Whoa now, don't be fainting on me again. Never knew I could have such an effect on a woman." He grinned.

Dovie shook her head. "I'm okay. It's just that my husband had a hat like yours, and you reminded me of him."

Now that she really looked at the man, he bore only a slight resemblance to her late husband. This man's eyes were a dark chocolate brown, his hair matching their color. She remembered Simon's features well with his lighter brown hair and hazel eyes. Simon had a long face. This man's was squarer and, unlike Simon, he had a cleft chin. Dovie felt her cheeks go red as the group looked at her.

"I'm fine, y'all," she said to the townspeople. "I probably shouldn't have skipped breakfast this morning. Please, go about your business. Thanks for your concern."

Dovie looked at the man who continued to prop her up as if she was a china plate.

"Are you sure you're, okay, Mama Dovie?" asked Alice, as everyone started to exit the Knollwood Market storage room.

"I'm sorry," said Dovie, sitting up taller and freeing the man of his supporting position. "I guess I'm still dazed. Thank you so much for your help, Mr. … "

"My name is Gabriel Pearce," he said, taking off his hat, exposing the rest of his brown locks parted on the side and combed over, just like Cary Grant's from the picture show.

Dovie stood, smoothed out her dress, and shook the man's hand. "I'm Dovie Grant and this is Alice Brewer. Thanks again, Mr. Pearce."

"Please, call me Gabe. It's the least you can do after falling on me." He smiled.

Dovie couldn't help but return his smile. She had only intended to give him a polite nod but couldn't tear herself away from his handsome gaze. Alice giggled, reminding Dovie she was there.

Dovie quickly turned her attention to Alice. "I thought you were at Johnson's. How'd you know I was back here?"

"Well," Alice swallowed hard and look toward the ceiling, "um... I decided you were right about Joy being too little for candy and decided to meet you at the store to see if there was something better for her here. That's when I saw Mr. Pearce pick you up and carry you inside."

Just then James ran into the storage room, followed closely by the store manager. "Dovie, honey, what happened?"

"It was just a case of mistaken identity. I'm okay, Dad." Dovie saw Gabe release a breath as soon as she said "Dad".

James turned to Gabe. "Mr. Pearce, apparently you're the hero of the day."

"I wouldn't say that," Gabe said as he reached out to shake James's hand. "I was in the right place at the right time."

"You two know each other?" asked Dovie.

"Yes, Mr. Pearce here is a pilot. He has a client from Amarillo who's looking for some new farmland in the area," explained James. "We met the other day in Annette's Café."

Dovie didn't know why, but she was disappointed by the news that Gabe didn't live closer. "So this is just a temporary stay in our little town then?"

Gabe caught Dovie's gaze and held it. "Oh, I'll be around. There are a lot of business men looking for cheap property and buying up foreclosed land. I'm the only pilot that's brave enough to land without a landing strip."

"Isn't that dangerous?" asked Dovie.

"The U.S. government made sure I could land anywhere, any time," answered Gabe.

"A member of the Air Corps, huh?" said James.

"Former member," corrected Gabe, "I served eight years and then got discharged when my father took ill."

"Can I see your airplane?" Alice asked, breaking into the adult conversation.

Gabe smiled. "I would love for both you and Mrs. Grant to come and see it. The plane is over at Ernie Murphy's farm." He looked at Dovie. "I really hope to see you there, Dovie."

Butterflies invaded her stomach as she watched Gabe walk out of the storeroom.

Chapter Seven

Bill drove behind the house at Quail Crossings to park his truck and laughed at a familiar sight. A red-faced Robert sat in the back of his own truck, looking exhausted. Bill put his truck in park and slid off the bucket seat. Reaching into the bed of the pick-up, he grabbed a broom. As he approached Robert, Norman, the goose, ran out from under the rear tire, hissing and raising his wings at Bill.

Bill poked the hefty goose with his broom. "Up to your old tricks again, huh, Norman? Go on, git!"

After a couple of sweeps of the broom, Norman retreated toward the pond, honking in his usual laughing way.

"How long have you been trapped back here?" asked Bill.

"A while." Robert pointed in Norman's direction. "That bird is crazy. He attacked Evalyn when we first got here and now me."

"Norman is the best guard goose this side of the Mississippi. A few years ago he saved Alice from a rabid dog and a dust storm, if you can believe it." Bill chuckled. "He's an ornery ol' bird, I'll give you that, but he'll always have a home here. He'll get used to you and leave you alone, for the most part. He did the same thing to me the second day I worked here. I sat in the truck all day until James and Dovie got back. That bird took a chunk out of my arm." Bill lifted his arm so Robert could see the scar. "Where's Evie?"

Robert hopped out of the truck. "I have no idea. I hollered for her a couple of times but got no answer. Mr. Murphy and Mrs. Grant don't seem to be around either."

"They ran into town to pick up Alice from school and run some errands," said Bill. "Elmer's working after school at the meat market, so I guess it's just the two of us which is good 'cause I ain't finished talking to you."

"Well, that's gonna have to wait." Robert squinted off into the distance. "We're about to have company."

Bill looked over his shoulder and sure enough, Evalyn, Joy, and Lou Anne were walking to Quail Crossings from Bill's place.

"About last night, I'm not saying I acted right," Bill said "but you can understand my suspicions. Evalyn's my sister after all."

Robert narrowed his eyes. "Actually, I can't. You've never met me before but already have me pegged as some kind of land hound. So where I can understand your concern for Evalyn and Joy, I can't understand your opinion of me."

"It's just all too convenient for you," said Bill. "You wanna expand your farm, and Evalyn stands to inherit part of Quail Crossings one day. Everyone in town knows that Dovie and James are passing the land onto us when the time comes."

"First of all," Robert snapped, "I had no idea that Evalyn was to inherit any land at all when I met her. Secondly, when I talked about expanding, it was to Rockwood which doesn't share a property line with Quail Crossings, so your reasoning is just plain wrong."

"So in all that time with Evalyn, she never mentioned she lived at Quail Crossings and that James gave me land?" asked Bill, an eyebrow raised.

"Of course she told me that she lived here, just not that she was inheriting anything," said Robert. "You've got me all wrong, Bill. I only want what's best for Evalyn and Joy."

"I want what's best for Evie and Joy as well. I'll make you a deal," said Bill as the girls walked closer. "We don't have to like each other, but we can tolerate each other when they're around."

Robert thrust his hand out. "It's a deal."

Elmer weighed the last of Mrs. Pearl's ground beef and wrapped it in white paper. Tiny Clark walked in as Elmer was handing it to Mrs. Pearl.

"Elm, I'm surprised you're here," said Tiny. "I just knew you'd go home once you heard the news. It seems awful insensitive for you to be workin' right now."

Taking Mrs. Pearl's money, Elmer counted back change before looking at Tiny. "What are you talking about, Tiny?"

"Didn't you hear? Mrs. Grant fainted outside of the Knollwood Market. She bumped her head, and there was blood all over. Some stranger had to carry her to their store room. She was unconscious for hours; the doctor doesn't know if she'll make it," Tiny rambled. "You really must go, Elm. Jeepers, I can't believe no one told you. I'd be at Quail Crossings myself, but I've got to wait for my pa to give me a ride, unless you give me one."

Mrs. Pearl chuckled. "I believe someone has been stretching the truth, young Mary."

Tiny cringed at her given name, before responding. "Frank Kelley told me and he was there."

Mrs. Pearl nodded in agreement. "Yes, he was there, as was I. He knocked over Mrs. Grant as he and his friends ran through the streets like hoodlums. What Mr. Kelley failed to see as he was running away, was Mr. Pearce helping Mrs. Grant up. She must have gotten to her feet too quickly because she fainted. Thankfully, Mr. Pearce caught her before she bumped her head, but he did indeed carry her into the store-room of the market. Mrs. Grant regained consciousness shortly after and is fine." She placed her hand on Tiny's shoulder. "You mustn't believe everything you hear, young Miss Clark, and be careful of the company you keep."

Tiny watched Mrs. Pearl leave the store. "She is an odd duck, I'll tell you that. Did you see the way she touched my shoulder? Who is she to tell me who I can and can't hang out with? My mother does a fine job of doin' that. Jeepers." Tiny rolled her eyes.

"She's right, you know," said Elmer, wiping down the counter.

"Oh yeah, 'bout what?" Tiny placed her hands on her hips.

"Frank Kelley. He's bad news, Tiny," said Elmer.

Tiny smiled and changed the subject. "How 'bout you get out of here early and take me for a ride in your truck? It's been so long since you've driven me home, and it's been forever since we've hung out. I don't think anyone at school knows if we're a couple or buddies. Half the time, I don't know."

She looked at Elmer expectantly.

"Well?" She tapped her foot.

Elmer shook his head. "You know I can't leave early. This is my job and I'm glad to have it. I have to go help Mr. Brice in the back."

"Fine then, Elmer Brewer, I think I'll just get a ride home with Frank then."

"Suit yourself," said Elmer as he headed to the back. He hated fighting with Tiny, but he wasn't sure how to talk to her anymore. He had thought of Tiny as his girl for the past five years, but she seemed to want more. He supposed it had a lot to do with the other girls going on dates. In all fairness, he could ask her to go to Johnson's Drugstore for a milkshake after work.

Elmer hurried back into the store front and out the door to catch Tiny. He stopped dead in his tracks as he saw Frank Kelley helping Tiny into his pickup. Closing the door, Frank caught sight of Elmer and tipped his hat at him, following the action with a wicked smile. There was nothing friendly about either gesture.

Elmer headed back inside. He felt like he'd been hit in the gut. Tiny was usually all talk. Every time he thought about that sleazy Frank sitting next to his girl, he got nauseous. He shook his head. Frank Kelley may be taking Tiny home, but it would be the last time.

The truck was unusually quiet as James drove Dovie and Alice home. James was used to Alice talking his ear off any time they went anywhere. "Cat got your tongue, Alice?"

"Just thinkin'," she replied.

"'Bout what?" asked James.

"Whether or not I should tell y'all somethin' important. I think I should, but maybe I should just let it be," explained Alice.

Dovie bit her lip. "There are definitely times you should let it be, but there are also times when talkin' it out with people you trust will help you figure it out."

"Well," started Alice, "something happened today, and it makes me scared to think about it. A boy bumped into me," said Alice.

"Did he mean to?" asked Dovie.

Alice shook her head. "No, he was actually trying to get away from Frank Kelley and his friends. They were chasing him for no reason."

"Knowing boys, I'm sure there was a reason," said James. "They were probably just carrying on like boys do."

"I don't think so, Mr. James," said Alice. "That's why I hid Jacob, that's the boy's name, in the old tractor shop."

"Alice, I don't understand," said Dovie. "You hid the boy?"

Alice nodded. "Yes, I think Frank Kelley and his friends were chasing Jacob because he is colored. And since we don't get many colored folks in Knollwood, I thought it would be best for him to hide. To be honest, I was scared for him."

"You did the right thing, Alice." James shook his head. "I knew some folks felt that way. I just didn't realize any of them would act on it, especially kids."

"What should we do, Dad?" asked Dovie. "That boy is in trouble. Do we go get him?"

James shook his head in thought. "Well, we can't go back tonight. That would bring attention to us. Jacob sounds like a smart boy. As long as he stays put, he should be okay. Alice, do you think you can take him some supplies tomorrow mornin'?"

Dovie gasped. "Dad, she can't do that. It's not safe."

"She's the only one who can," said James. "If you or I are caught going into that old Bailey place, people will know something's up. Alice can say she's feedin' kittens or a stray dog."

"You mean lie?" Alice asked.

"Alice, usually I would never ask you to do that, but this is an exception. If Jacob gets caught, it could be very bad," said James.

"Then I'll do it," said Alice with a look of determination in her eyes.

James pulled into the drive of Quail Crossings and was thankful Robert was there. He had not forgotten his need to make an apology.

Chapter Eight

Lou Anne sat up and stretched her back. It had been a long time since she had milked a cow; Elmer very seldom missed a day. However, the men were already in town helping to set up for the Saturday market on Main Street, and she wanted to give Dovie and Alice some time alone with Evalyn and Joy.

The truth was that it was hard to be around Joy. She loved her new niece, but every time she looked at that little baby, she was reminded of what she so desperately wanted – a child of her own. She and Bill had been married for almost five years. Their marriage was a good one, full of romance, but she hadn't taken with child yet.

She touched her belly and wondered what was going on in there. Could it be that her insides were all messed up, and she couldn't carry a child? Her heart sank as she realized that was a very real possibility since she hadn't conceived yet. As hard as the truth was to admit, she and Bill might never have a baby.

She sighed as she went back to her milking. Little Joy would not pay the price because she didn't have a child of her own. Her mother had told her there were ways to help the process of conception, and Lou Anne debated if she should start trying some of those remedies. She really wanted things to work out naturally, but since it didn't look like that would happen, maybe it was time to seek some help from others.

Dovie would know about such things, but so far Lou Anne hadn't had the nerve to ask her. It was such a private issue, and Bill was like a son to Dovie. But Lou Anne had begun to think of Dovie like a mother as well. Since her own family had moved away, the Quail Crossings clan had become very dear to her.

Mrs. Pearl would also know the remedies Lou Anne was thinking about. If she talked to her instead of Dovie, she could avoid some of the awkwardness with Bill, but Mrs. Pearl wasn't as easy to talk to as Dovie. Lou Anne wondered if she'd have the courage to talk to either of them.

She pictured Evalyn holding Joy and then smiled to herself as she thought about cradling her big belly as Bill's child grew inside. She would find a way to talk to Dovie or Mrs. Pearl soon. There had to be something that would help.

Lost in thought, she didn't see Norman enter the barn. The goose stalked his prey, toddling ever so quietly. Norman flew up, and landed on Lou Anne's back, flapping his wings and honking. Poppy, the milk cow, let out a loud "moo" as she tried to break free of her halter to escape the wild foul.

Lou Anne jerked up trying to get the crazed goose off her back and, in the process, kicked over the milk bucket, spilling every drop.

Norman flew to the loft and hissed at Lou Anne as he glared at her.

Lou Anne stomped her foot. "Norman! Look what you've done!" She pointed to the overturned milk bucket. "You are a good for nothing ol' thistle. Mark my words, Norman. You'll pay for this."

Lou Anne unhooked Poppy, grabbed the empty buck, and stormed out of the barn to the tune of Norman's trademark honking laugh.

Alice looked at little Joy in front of her and wrinkled her nose.

"Go ahead, Alice," encouraged Evalyn. "You wanted to change Joy's diaper, so here's your chance. You've been beggin' me for days to do it."

"How did somethin' so small, make somethin' so gross?" Alice grabbed the cleaning cloth and dabbed at the mess.

"Oh, for cryin' out loud, we'll be here all day if you go about it like that. Just clean her up as you'd clean yourself," said Evalyn, trying to mask her smile.

"But, Evie, I don't make near this mess when I go." Alice held up her hands in defeat. "I don't know what to do."

Evalyn playfully scooted her sister out of the way with a bump of her hip. "If you're going to babysit for me, you're going to have to learn how to do this." And in no time at all Joy was in a fresh diaper.

"That was fast," said Alice, eyes wide in amazement.

"Trust me," said Evalyn picking up Joy. "You don't wanna wait too long, or she might just go on you."

Alice took a step back. "You mean she's wet ..." She wrinkled her nose instead of saying the words "on you?"

Evalyn nodded when Alice couldn't finish her sentence. "More than once, and you'd be surprised at how much a little one can wet."

"Babies are nasty," said Alice, eyeing her little niece. "I'm not sure I wanna babysit anymore."

"No," said Evalyn as she stroked little Joy's cheek, "they just don't know any better. And you better get over it because I will need your help from time to time. It's no different than cleaning the chicken coop."

Alice raised her eyebrows. "I'd say it's a lot different. I never have to touch the chicken poop with my hands."

"Alice, are you ready?" Dovie called from downstairs. "We better get movin'."

"Be right down," said Alice.

"Where are y'all going?" asked Evalyn. "The Saturday market doesn't start until noon."

Alice lowered her voice to a whisper. "We're on a secret mission."

Evalyn laughed. "Well, okay then, be safe."

"You wanna come?" asked Alice.

Evalyn shook her head. "Robert is gonna take Joy, Lou Anne, and me into town later. Right now, I'm going to put Joy down for a nap and maybe take one myself. I can't wait to sleep through the night again."

"Maybe when you get to Robert's house, she'll sleep better," said Alice before hopping down the stairs.

Evalyn tried not to cringe, but Alice was right. Soon she would be moving in with Mr. Smith. She hated all the lying, but as she looked at Joy, she knew she'd sacrifice everything to give her a good life.

Alice tried to act normally as she walked down the streets of Knollwood carrying her bundle of goods for Jacob. Her mission was simple. Once she got to Johnson's, she was supposed to act like she was following a kitten and take the alleys.

"Kitty, kitty, kitty," she called as she turned between the meat market and post office, retracing her steps from the day before. As she rounded the corner, with the Bailey place in sight, the little hairs on the back of her neck stood up. Something wasn't right. She fought the instinct to run and get Dovie right then. She knew that she had to check on Jacob first because if people saw her running back and forth, they'd know something was up.

Alice cautiously approached the secret entrance to the shop.

"Miss Alice," came a strained voice.

She swung around at the sound of her name, making eye contact with Jacob. She swallowed a scream as she ran to him and knelt beside him. He sat propped up by a tree. He had a large gash on his forehead and both eyes were swollen shut. His lips had been busted open so many times it was hard to tell where they stopped and his skin began. His shoulder looked funny, and Alice could see many bruises covering his arms.

"Who did this to you?" she cried as she used her hanky to dab a cut on Jacob's forehead, trying to keep the blood from dripping into his eye.

"I need to get out of town before they come back." His voice cracked with pain. "I have till nightfall or they'll kill me. You have to go. If they see you, they'll hurt you too."

Alice shook her head. "I won't let that happen. Be strong, Jacob, and don't move. I have to go get help."

She turned to leave and he grabbed her hand. "Be careful," he said before passing out.

Chapter Nine

Tears stinging her eyes, Alice ran until she reached Dovie just outside the Post Office.

"You have to come," Alice cried in a hushed whisper. "It's Jacob; he's hurt."

"Where is he?" asked Dovie.

But Alice, sobbing, couldn't answer.

Dovie narrowed her eyes. "Alice Brewer, get yourself together. Tell me where Jacob is and then run and get Dad. He's at the feed store."

Alice took a deep breath. "He's in that little wooded area behind Bailey's. They beat him up real bad, Mama Dovie. You've got to help him."

Dovie gave Alice a quick hug. "You did good by coming to get me. Now go get Dad. I'll take care of your friend."

Dovie watched Alice run toward the feed store. Her heart raced, but she willed herself to walk at a normal pace with a pleasant look on her face. With every familiar face that passed, with every "hello" and "good morning" she heard, all she saw were possible monsters. Who could have done this to a child? In a town the size of Knollwood, it had to be someone she knew.

Cautiously, she made her way to Jacob. It wasn't easy trying to look nonchalant while going toward an empty building. Looking both ways to see if anyone was watching, she hurried behind the building and toward the woods.

She stopped short when she saw the boy. Alice hadn't exaggerated. They had severely beaten him.

"Jacob?" she said quietly as she slowly approached him. "My name is Mrs. Grant. Alice came and got me for help. I'll need to examine you, if that's okay."

He didn't respond and as she got closer, she realized it was because he was out cold. She looked to the sky. "Dear God, please help me save this boy."

Kneeling in front of Jacob, she tenderly laid a hand on his chest while putting her ear close to his mouth.

"I wouldn't do that if I were you. You might catch something," came a wicked voice from behind her.

Ignoring the voice, she waited until she could hear Jacob's shallow breath. "You're going to be okay," she whispered, giving him a reassuring pat before rising to face the assailant.

Turning, she swallowed her gasp as she encountered five young boys, no older than Elmer. As she suspected, she knew each and every one of the boys, as well as their parents.

"Did you do this, Frank Kelley?" she demanded more than asked.

Frank sneered. "Of course I did. The likes of him have no place in this town."

"You ought to be ashamed of yourselves." She looked at the boys. "All of you."

"There ain't nothing to be ashamed of," said Frank. "His kind were meant to be slaves and beaten on a daily basis. I'm just showing him his place in this world."

"How dare you," Dovie hissed. "The sheriff will hear about this, as well as your parents."

"Who do you think told them to do it?" came a voice from the woods as Frank Kelley's father walked out, surrounded by the fathers of the other boys. All the men carried clubs, while Mr. Kelley twirled a rope that had been fashioned into a noose.

Every part of Dovie's body was screaming at her to run. But she knew if she did, Jacob was dead.

"Mr. Kelley." Dovie squared her shoulders and planted her feet. "You will answer to the law about this."

"This is no place for a woman. You could get hurt," said Mr. Kelley, a toothpick dangling between his lips. "Mrs. Grant, if you know what's good for you, you'll run along and forget you ever saw this boy,"

"I will do no such thing," said Dovie, moving closer to Jacob, her knees shaking so violently she was afraid they'd buckle under her.

"Don't say we didn't warn you." Mr. Kelley and his men moved toward Dovie as their sons did the same.

"You know better than to touch me, Mr. Kelley," said Dovie. "You'll go to jail."

"Oh, I'm not worried about that," said Mr. Kelley. "We just want the boy." He looked over her shoulder at his son and then rest of his men. "Keep her out of the way and grab the boy."

A gunshot rang through the air, causing the men to freeze.

"Step away from the lady."

Dovie let out a sigh of relief when she saw Gabe Pearce, his pistol trained on Mr. Kelley, with her father, Bill, and Elmer spread out behind him, their rifles raised.

"You don't know what you're doing, stranger," said Mr. Kelley as he raised his hands in a peaceful gesture. "She's trying to protect this nig ... "

Bill cocked his rifle before Mr. Kelley could finish. "Y'all are done here. No one else has to get hurt," he said.

Mr. Kelley smiled. "Y'all are outnumbered ..."

"And y'all only have sticks," countered Gabe.

Mr. Kelley produced a wicked grin. "All right fellas, it seems this here boy found himself some guardian angels." He focused on Dovie. "You can't save them all, Mrs. Grant. Next time this boy won't be so lucky and neither will you. It ain't right for them to live among us. The Lord tells us we are the guardians of all, and it's my job to make sure fellas like him stay in their rightful place."

Chills raced through Dovie's body as Mr. Kelley's smile told her this wasn't the first person of color to run into Mr. Kelley's wrath.

Kelley's men waited for their sons to join them before they retreated into the woods. Frank glared at Elmer. "Your girl, Tiny, really enjoyed the ride I gave her yesterday, in more ways than one."

Elmer started toward Frank. James pulled him back, shaking his head. "He's not worth the trouble, Elm."

As soon as Kelley's men had retreated far enough into the woods, Dovie knelt in front of Jacob once again to make sure he was still breathing.

"I'm so glad y'all came when you did," she said, looking at the men after ensuring Jacob was still alive. "Of course, I wasn't expecting so many of you. Where's Alice?"

"When Alice told me what was going on," started James, "I knew there might be trouble. Thankfully, Bill and Mr. Pearce, here, were both at the feed store when she came in upset. We picked up Elm on the way."

"We made Alice wait with Mrs. Pearl at Johnson's Drug," said Bill. "She wasn't too thrilled about it, but when Mrs. Pearl told her to stay, I think she was too intimidated to not do as she was told."

"I'm so very thankful. I'd hate to think of what would've happened ..." Dovie stopped and hugged herself. "Dad, can you get the truck? We need to get him out of here."

James nodded and started back toward Main Street. "Elm, you'd better come with me. Butcher Davis said he'd give us ten minutes before he'd round up the cavalry. The last thing we need is this town pulled in two."

Dovie pulled some cloth napkins out of the picnic basket she was taking to the Saturday market and started tending to Jacob's wounds.

"How bad is it?" asked Gabe, kneeling beside her.

"They did a number on him, that's for sure. If he doesn't have bleeding in his belly, then I think he'll pull through. If he does, we'll have to take him to Tuckett to the doctor, and I'm not sure he'll survive the trip. Hate to think of what would've happened to this poor boy had Alice not found him yesterday and checked on him today," said Dovie.

"I'd hate to think of what would have happened to you, had Alice not found us," said Gabe. "You do have a knack for trouble, Dovie."

Dovie glared at him. "This is not the time to be making jokes, Mr. Pearce."

Gabe held up his hands. "You're right; I always make jokes during awkward situations. It's my way of trying to ease the trouble."

A few moments later, James drove his truck up and with Dovie's careful instructions, James, Bill and Gabe lifted Jacob's beaten body into the bed of the truck.

Bill hopped out of the truck bed. "I'm going to go get Alice. We'll meet y'all back at Quail Crossings."

"Bill," said Dovie, covering Jacob's body with a wool blanket, "give us a head start, will ya? I'd like to have him cleaned up a bit before Alice gets there. She's already seen him once in this mess. I'd hate for her to see him like this again."

Nodding, Bill left to stall Alice as Gabe settled himself in the bed of the truck next to Jacob. Dovie placed her hands on her hips. "Mr. Pearce, I really do appreciate your help, but we've got it from here."

Gabe raised an eyebrow. "Do you? What if those men know you're on your way home with the boy? I'm here to help, just in case. Plus, with Bill keeping Alice busy and Elmer back at work, you'll need help in getting Jacob inside."

Dovie nodded. Gabe was right. She guessed they'd all be going back to Quail Crossings.

Chapter Ten

Evalyn squinted her eyes as she watched James's pickup truck approach. She looked at Robert and Lou Anne, "I wonder what they forgot. They weren't supposed to come back home until after dinner time."

As they got closer, she saw Dovie in the bed of the truck with a stranger and knew something was wrong. Lou Anne's quick intake of breath told Evalyn that she wasn't the only one concerned. Placing Joy on her hip, Evalyn raced to the truck with Robert and Lou Anne on her heels.

"What is it? What's wrong?" she asked, as Robert pulled down the tailgate.

"This boy is hurt. We need y'all's help," said Dovie, jumping out of the truck. "Robert, will you help Mr. Pearce get him inside? Lou Anne, please show them to my room. We'll tend to him there."

Evalyn watched as Dovie stood for a moment to catch her breath.

"Dovie, what happened to that boy?" Evalyn asked.

"Some kids beat him up after their fathers told them to," Dovie bluntly answered.

Evalyn wrinkled her forehead. "Where's Alice? Please tell me this isn't part of the secret mission she was talking about his morning."

Dovie nodded. "Alice is fine, but unfortunately, she is the one who found him like this."

"Did you know about Alice's plan and this boy?" asked Evalyn. "Who is that man who came here with y'all? Tell me where Alice is. Is she okay?"

"I did know about the boy. Our plan was to bring him out here today and then get him out of town. As you can tell, someone found him first." Dovie started toward the house. "That man is Mr. Pearce, who thankfully came to my aid today, and Alice is still in town with Bill. Both are doing a lot better than that boy there."

"So you let her go see him?" Evalyn screeched, causing Joy to start crying. "Do you know how dangerous that was?" Evalyn hadn't intended to raise her voice to Dovie but couldn't help herself.

Dovie stopped and glared at Evalyn. "I knew exactly how dangerous it was, and it went against my gut to send her to check on him this morning. But it was the only way, and I'm glad she went because if she hadn't, if I'd listened to my gut, that boy would be dead." Dovie sighed. "We can talk about this later. Now I need your help. Calm Joy down and fetch me the kit."

Evalyn stared at Dovie for a moment watching her walk back toward the house. This conversation wasn't over, but for now it could wait. Evalyn bounced Joy on her hip and made soft "shhing" noises. She couldn't deny that Dovie was right about one thing, the boy needed tended to, and Evalyn knew how Dovie worked. Evalyn was the perfect person to help Dovie and get the boy on the mend. The sooner he was healed, the sooner he could get out of town and away from Quail Crossings.

Entering the house, Evalyn placed the now calm Joy on a quilt in the living room and handed her some toys. She looked at Robert who had just left Dovie's room. "Can you watch her? I need to help Dovie."

She saw a flash of panic before he nodded. She mumbled a quick thanks before fetching the kit that contained clean bandages, gauze, salve and an assortment of other medical items Dovie might need.

She entered Dovie's room, followed closely behind by Lou Anne who carried a basin of water. The three ladies quickly went to work examining Jacob.

"He's got a dislocated shoulder," said Dovie as her hands then moved to feel his legs. "No broken bones here. Let's pull these boots off."

As the ladies worked to get his laced up boots off, Jacob awoke and started screaming, jerking his feet away from the girls. "Get off! Get off me!"

He rose to get away, and then screamed in agony as he fell back onto the bed. Dovie raced to his head.

"Jacob, it's okay. Remember, I'm a friend of Alice's. We're here to help. You are safe. Do you understand?"

Tears fell down his face as he slowly nodded, looking directly at Dovie through his swollen eyes as she gently rubbed his forehead with her thumb. "Good. I need to look you over to make sure you don't need a doctor. The girls are going to remove your boots, and I'm going to unbutton your shirt, so I can examine your chest and stomach. Can you tell me where it hurts?"

"Everywhere," he whispered.

Evalyn fought back her own tears as she unlaced Jacob's boot.

"Okay," said Dovie, "we'll get you fixed up. You just try to stay calm."

Jacob nodded again, closed his eyes and leaned his head back, causing a few more tears to fall along his dark purple cheekbones.

Evalyn removed Jacob's shoe and sock as Lou Anne removed the other one and held it up. Evalyn could see a quarter-sized hole right where the pad of his foot would come down. How long had he been walking in those shoes, she wondered.

The girls stood on the opposite side of the bed while Dovie examined Jacob's stomach.

"Good, Jacob," Dovie said softly, "I don't see any signs of bleeding inside your belly. That's really good. I'm going to examine your ribs now. I suspect you have a few broken ones. This will hurt. Do you want a wooden spoon or something to bite down on?"

Jacob shook his head slightly but held up his hand. Evalyn immediately grabbed it, feeling her motherly instincts kick in. "You squeeze as hard as you need to, Jacob."

As Dovie began to feel around Jacob's ribs, he bit his lip and squeezed Evalyn's hand, not tightly, but just enough for Evalyn to know he was glad to have a caring hand to hold.

"He's got two broken ribs on his right side and three on his left," said Dovie before laying her ear against his chest. Evalyn held her breath as she watched Jacob's chest slowly go up and down. Dovie stood tall and pulled Jacob's shirt together, covering his chest. "I don't hear anything that leads me to believe that the ribs have punctured a lung. That's another good sign."

As Dovie continued her examination, she found two broken toes, a broken thumb, and more bruises and cuts than she cared to count. Evalyn kneeled close to Jacob as Dovie left the room.

"You'll be right as rain in no time, Jacob." Evalyn smiled down at him. "I'm Evalyn, by the way." She pointed to Lou Anne. "And that's Lou Anne."

"Thank you," Jacob whispered.

Evalyn glanced up at Lou Anne as Dovie re-entered the room with Robert and Gabe, James stood in the doorway holding Joy. "Don't thank us yet, Jacob."

"Jacob," said Dovie, "we have to reset your shoulder. I've brought Robert and Mr. Pearce in here to help me. They are going to hold you down, so we get it right the first time. Okay?"

Jacob nodded.

"Mr. Pearce, you hold his legs and, Robert, you hold his other shoulder. I need him not to move, but mind, he has other injuries, and we don't wanna worsen any of those. Hold him firmly, but not too tightly. Understand?"

The men nodded.

Dovie looked back at Jacob as the men took their places. "I'm gonna do this on the count of three." Dove grabbed Jacob's hand and wrist with both hands and placed her foot on the bed. "One. Two." Dovie pulled. Jacob screamed out in pain before becoming unconscious.

Alice ran into the room, followed closely by Bill who was trying to keep her back.

"What happened, Mama Dovie?" Alice cried. "Is he dead?"

Dovie grabbed a towel and wiped her hands. "No, Alice, Jacob will be fine. I had to reset his shoulder. I know it was painful, but he'll feel a lot better now that it's done." She looked Alice in the eyes. "He's alive because of you, Alice. What you did for this boy was above and beyond what most adults would've done. I'm proud of you."

"But why, Mama Dovie?" asked Alice, tears flooding her cheeks. "Why would anyone do this to another person? Is it just because he's colored?"

"I wish I had an easy answer to that question, Alice, but I don't. This kind of hatred goes back a long time and, unfortunately, some family members pass their hatred down the line. That is what has happened here." Dovie gently took Alice by the shoulders. "But as long as we have more and more people like you, this kind of hatred won't happen as often."

Alice hugged Dovie. "Oh, Mama Dovie, it was so scary."

Dovie patted Alice on the back. "Yes, it was child. Yes, it was."

Chapter Eleven

Dovie, Evalyn, and Lou Anne sat in the parlor exhausted. They had spent the last hour cleaning Jacob's wounds and finding him fresh clothes. It hadn't been easy. Not only did they have to tend his injuries, but it was clear that Jacob had been on the road a long time.

They did their best to bathe him and wash his hair as he rested. Lou Anne found some clothes of Elmer's she thought might fit the boy, and, although they were a little short in the legs, they worked out well.

"I'll make him some pants tonight," said Evalyn. "And a few shirts."

"There's some fabric in the upstairs closet," said Dovie. "But don't worry about it tonight. Get some rest and tend to your baby. He ain't goin' anywhere soon."

Evalyn shot up. She hadn't even thought of Joy. "Where's Joy?"

"I'm sure with her father," said Dovie casually.

"Her father?" Evalyn spun around glaring at Dovie before remembering their lie. "I'm gonna go check."

She started toward the door, trying not to run. Robert knew nothing about taking care of babies. She was sure Joy was scared and crying, or hungry, or dirty.

Barreling out the back door, she scanned the farm. There by the corrals stood Robert, Joy cradled in one large arm next to James's horse, Tex. As Joy reached up and touched the tip of Tex's nose, she giggled.

Evalyn stomped over to Robert. "That horse could bite her hand off."

"I bet this horse wouldn't hurt a fly," said Robert, rubbing Tex's neck.

"How would you know?" snapped Evalyn, grabbing Joy from Robert causing the baby to cry out. "Look what you've done."

"What I've done?" Robert took a step back. "We were just fine until you came out here snapping like a turtle." He took a deep breath and lowered his voice. "I get it. She's been your child, and only your child, for a long time. But now she's *our* child. It will look funny if I never hold her or take care of her." He touched Joy's cheek, making them both smile. "I would never let anything happen to Joy."

Evalyn sighed. "I know you're right. It's just hard to let go, and this whole business of lying doesn't sit right with me. What if people find out we're not married? Joy's life will be ruined. I don't know why I agreed to this."

Robert placed his hands gently on her arms. Evalyn fought the urge to jerk away. "You agreed to this, so Joy would have a good life. So she wouldn't be ruined before she even got started. You are doing this *for* her." Evalyn felt her body relax as Robert continued. "No one is gonna find out that we aren't married unless one of us slips up. I'm not planning on doing that. Are you?"

"Of course not," said Evalyn, tucking a stray baby hair behind Joy's ear and sighing. "I didn't mean to snap. I was just scared. I think dealing with that boy has put me on edge. Something like this happened back when I was about ten. We still lived with my ma and pa then. A rumor started that the colored boy was carrying on with a white girl. Most of us knew it was a lie, but it didn't seem to stop the mob. The pastor tried to save that poor colored fella, but the men of the town came for him and beat the pastor senseless. I'm afraid the colored man didn't fare so well. When we walked to school the next day, he was hanging from a tree, and the pastor spent the next week in bed getting over his injuries. What if the men who did this come after James or Dovie? What if they come after Alice who found him help before they could finish the job?"

"I don't really think they will," said Robert, rubbing his chin. "Mr. Murphy is a pretty respected man in Knollwood. Besides it's been just about ten years since that incident happened."

Evalyn kissed Joy's forehead. "I hope you're right. I'd hate to think that Joy would be in any danger staying here at Quail Crossings. This has always been the place I've felt safest."

"Then come home with me," said Robert.

"Oh, I couldn't," Evalyn stammered.

"Why not? You're my wife, remember."

"Didn't you say the place wasn't fit for a child?" asked Evalyn.

"I've spent the last few days working on it. There's still work to be done, but the homestead held up pretty good while I was gone. This has to happen sooner or later, so why not now, just in case?" He laid a reassuring hand on her shoulder. "Remember, you two have your own room."

Evalyn glanced up at Robert and then back at Joy. She remembered the stories circulating at school the day after the lynching took place and shivered. "Okay."

Robert's eyes widened. "You're really gonna come?"

"I said okay, no reason to make a ruckus about it." She handed Joy to Robert. "You're right. If we're gonna make this work, it has to look like a real marriage which means we have to live together. I'll go gather our things."

Evalyn turned to leave, and Robert grabbed her hand. "I want you to think about somethin' else while you're gathering your stuff."

"What's that?" asked Evalyn, trying not to sigh. She appreciated Robert and all he was doing, but she felt as mentally tired as she did physically.

"I think we should get married for real," said Robert.

Evalyn wrinkled her forehead. "We've already told everyone we're married. We can't exactly go to Pastor Spaulding and ask him to wed us."

"You're right; we can't do that," said Robert. "But we can go over to the next county and get married in front of the Justice of the Peace. That way it'll be legal and we won't have lie anymore."

"I don't know," said Evalyn.

"We're already in this for the long haul," said Robert. "If Joy's to have a good life, and no one's to know be the wiser, we should do this. That way it won't really be a lie."

Evalyn nodded. "I guess you're right. When do we go?"

Robert smiled. "As soon as possible."

Dovie and Lou Anne continued to sit on the couch after Evalyn left to find Joy.

"I can't believe anyone in Knollwood would do this," said Lou Anne. "I thought this was the perfect place to raise a family."

"Oh, it is," said Dovie. "More of the town thinks like us than the Kelleys, I'm sure, and when you have your own little one, you'll teach him right from wrong."

Lou Anne looked at her flat belly. "I'm not sure that will ever happen."

Dovie looked at her and patted her hand. "In good time, it'll happen."

"Will it?" asked Lou Anne, tears welling up in the corners of her eyes. "We've been trying for five years, Dovie." She bit her lip. "I think I'm barren."

Dovie wrapped her up in a hug. "Oh, honey, I'm sure that's not the case. Lots of women don't expect a child right off."

"Name one," said Lou Anne defiantly.

Dovie remained silent.

"See," said Lou Anne, "it should've happened by now."

The two sat in silence for a few minutes before Lou Anne got up the courage to speak again. "Dovie, I know there are home remedies that are said to work."

"Lou Anne, there is only one thing that works and that's time," said Dovie.

"You know what I'm talking about," said Lou Anne.

Dovie nodded. "I do."

"Will you help me?" Lou Anne asked. "You must know some of the remedies since you know so much about healing people."

"My mother told me a few, but Lou Anne, she also told me they were nothing but silly tricks used to make the woman confident enough to relax and let things happen. Please, don't go doing anything foolish. Just give it some more time." Dovie heard Alice enter the back door talking to Mr. Pearce.

"Dovie, I'm tired of waiting," said Lou Anne. "Something's wrong inside of me. I just know it."

"If you aren't expecting in the next year, I'll take you to see a special doctor in Amarillo," Dovie whispered quickly. "Until then, just give it time."

Lou Anne thought about what Dovie had said, but a year just seemed so long. There were other ladies in the community who knew the remedies. She would ask them.

"How's Jacob?" Alice asked, sitting between Dovie and Lou Anne.

"Resting," said Dovie.

Alice looked at Lou Anne. "Are you okay, Lou Anne? It looks like you've been crying."

"I'm just tired, Alice, but thank you for asking. Mr. Pearce, I'm so glad you were here to help," Lou Anne said, trying to get Alice's attention on someone else.

"And this isn't the first time he's helped," Alice piped in.

"What do you mean?" asked Lou Anne.

"Alice, you hold your tongue," said Dovie, pointing a finger at her.

"Why?" asked Alice. "Is it a secret that you fainted outside the Knollwood Market the other day and Mr. Pearce had to carry you inside?"

"Well, if it was, it isn't now." Mr. Pearce chuckled.

"So, it's true." Lou Anne clasped her hands together. "Tell me more, Alice."

"Alice Brewer, that's enough," Dovie warned.

Alice shrugged. "I don't really know any more anyway. By the time I got to the market, she was out cold and Mr. Pearce was tending to her."

Lou Anne looked at Mr. Pearce as Evalyn entered the room. "Why don't you tell us what happened, Mr. Pearce?"

"What did I miss?" asked Evalyn.

Lou Anne turned and looked at Evalyn over her shoulder. "Well, it appears this is the second time Mr. Pearce has come to Dovie's rescue. She fainted in town the other day and he caught her."

"Y'all are making way too much out of this," said Dovie, standing. "Mr. Pearce, we should probably get you back into town. I'm sure you have things to tend too." She ushered him toward the back door. "I'm sure Dad can drive you."

"You'd think after rescuing her twice, she'd call me Gabe." Gabe winked at the girls as he allowed Dovie to push him toward the back door.

"Well, that was interesting," said Evalyn.

"She sure was in a hurry to get him out of here," said Alice.

"You know," said Lou Anne, tilting her head, "he looks an awful lot like Simon."

"Dovie's dead husband?" Evalyn gasped.

Lou Anne nodded.

"I think we need to find out more about this Mr. Pearce," said Evalyn, with Alice and Lou Anne nodding in agreement.

Robert leaned against his truck and waited for Evalyn to bring out the rest of hers and Joy's bags.

"So I hear Evie's headed to Rockwood," said Bill as he wiped his hands on a bandana.

"Mrs. Grant has enough going on around here, so we thought it would be best to get Joy out from under foot," said Robert.

"Did it occur to you that Dovie might need Evie's help with Jacob?" Bill narrowed his eyes. "Or is it just my wife that's expected to help out? Maybe you don't want Evie around a colored boy."

Robert took a deep breath to steady himself. "You know, you've got a real knack for makin' assumptions about me."

"Well, if the shoe fits," said Bill.

Robert stood tall. "You know nothing about me, and I can tell you exactly where to put that shoe."

"What's going on out here?" asked Evalyn as she exited the back door.

"Nothing," said Robert, hurrying to grab her bags. "Your brother just isn't ready for you to go home with me."

Robert glanced at Bill who plastered on a smile for the sake of Evalyn.

"He's right," said Bill. "I'm not, and I don't think I'll ever be ready to see you go home with him."

Chapter Twelve

Evalyn stood outside Rockwood with Joy in her arms and looked over her new home. She didn't expect it to be like Quail Crossings, but the rickety old cabin looked to be on its last legs. Calling it a cabin was actually an exaggeration. It looked more like a shack, with its worn, splintered wood and broken shutters.

"Are you sure it's safe?" Evalyn asked Robert, eyeing the odd angle of the roof which made the house seem more like a lopsided triangle than a square.

"Of course, or I wouldn't have brought you here," said Robert, holding the two bags Evalyn had packed for herself and Joy. "Rockwood is older than Quail Crossings. It was actually my grandpa who built it. The slanted roof was to keep the snow from settling. Pa's family came from Minnesota where snow was a problem, and that's all my grandpa knew how to build. So he did what he knew."

"So it's not about to fall in?" Evalyn was still skeptical; she had never seen such an oddly shaped house.

Robert chuckled. "No, that old house is as sturdy as a rock. Would you like to see inside?"

"Might as well," answered Evalyn. "There's no going back to Quail Crossings now, not without making Bill question your intentions again."

"He's very protective," said Robert.

"You can thank my parents for that," said Evalyn, squeezing Joy a little tighter, silently promising Joy she would never feel the ache of parental rejection. "They left without a word, and Bill had to look after us. He did it alone for a long time. The best thing he did for all of us was to take the job at Quail Crossings. We've never really felt hungry or cold since then, but Lord knows I didn't make it easy for him to keep his job. If only I knew then what I know now."

Evalyn let the words hang in the air as she thought of all the trouble she had gotten into when trying to get Bill fired from Quail Crossings. Looking at Joy, she understood Bill's sense of responsibility even more. She sighed. "Let's go in. Joy will wanna eat soon."

"That reminds me," said Robert with a smile. "I bought a goat from the Clarks, that way Joy can have fresh milk all the time. She's around back and her name is Applecrisp. Apparently, the Clarks name all their animals after their favorite foods. Tiny was telling me about a dog named Jelly she used to have, and that was how she and Elmer became such good friends."

"Oh yes," said Evalyn walking toward the house, trying to shake the shiver that came with her last memory of Jelly the dog. "We had to put Jelly down because she was rabid and almost bit Alice, so Elm took her one of Button's pups after he trained it."

"So that's what Bill was talking about," said Robert. "Norman saved Alice from Jelly."

"Yep," said Evalyn, stepping onto the long front porch that housed two rocking chairs. "That crazy ol' bird does have his good side."

"I honestly just thought they felt sorry for the poor fella." Robert sat the bags down and opened the front door. "Well, here it is, your new home."

Evalyn took a deep breath before entering the house, afraid of what she might see. When she stepped inside, it was just as she thought it would be. Piles of dirty laundry sat in a corner just outside the kitchen area which led into the sitting room they were currently standing in. Old newspapers and farm reports were stacked high on the sitting room table, with more covering the small dining table. There were dishes in the sink, but not as many as Evalyn had expected, probably because Robert had been eating at Quail Crossings instead of cooking for himself. A thick layer of dust covered everything except for the sofa and the farm reports Robert had apparently been reading.

"Well, I can see why you said you needed me to help out around here," said Evalyn, sneezing as the dust tickled her nose.

Robert blushed and rubbed his neck. "I wasn't expecting y'all today, or I would've picked up." He hurried to the dining table and began stacking the farm reports. "I had some studying to do. It's been a long time since I worked on a farm, and now I own one."

"It's okay," said Evalyn. "Will you please show me where we'll be staying?"

Robert hustled over, picked up Evalyn's bags just outside the door, and then walked to the opposite side of the sitting room. He opened a small door. "Y'all will be in here. It used to be my parents' room. My pa built Ma a fireplace when she was so sick, so y'all will be able to stay nice and warm during the winter."

Evalyn noticed a crib sitting in the corner by the fireplace. "Was that your crib?"

Robert set her bags on the floor and walked over to the crib. Evalyn followed and realized the crib looked far too new to have been Robert's.

"No," he said, I made it for Joy."

Evalyn traced her fingers around the hearts etched on the end pieces and felt the smooth boards that made up the bars. Inside the crib on wire mesh, sat a mattress that looked slightly used but in good condition.

"I bought the mattress from the Clarks when I bought the goat. Little Ruthie outgrew it a few years ago and now sleeps with Tiny, so they weren't using it."

"Robert this is …" Evalyn couldn't find the words as tears threatened. Little Joy had never had a real bed. Ever since she was born, they had shared one. She placed Joy in her new crib.

"So you like it?" Robert asked.

Evalyn threw her arms around him in a surprise hug. "It is wonderful, thank you."

Elmer and Tiny sat under the only cottonwood tree on the school grounds eating their lunches and enjoying the spring breeze.

"Elm," said Tiny, "I was really mad at you the other day when you wouldn't take me on a real date. I talked to my mom about it when I got home. Jeepers, she wasn't too keen on the idea of Frank Kelley driving me home."

"Neither was I," mumbled Elmer.

Tiny ignored him and continued. "She said that you're a nice boy who works hard, and I shouldn't hold that against you. So I'm sorry for leaving you like that. It's just sometimes I don't know what we are, but I know what I'd like for us to be. When that doesn't happen, I get mad and then act without thinking."

Frank Kelley walked up and kicked the bottom of Elmer's boot with his own. "I heard you got yourself a visitor out at Quail Crossings."

Elmer stood to meet Frank's glaze. "What happens out there is no concern of yours."

"Well, I think it does concern me since your Mrs. Grant got in the way of my business," retorted Frank.

"Elm, what in the world is going on?" asked Tiny, standing.

"Maybe you should ask Frank," answered Elmer. "Ask him how he treats others that aren't like him."

Frank held up his hands and took a step back. "It was just a misunderstanding, but let Mrs. Grant know that I always finish what I start. It's the type of man my father taught me to be." He looked over at Tiny and winked. "Lookin' good, Tiny. See ya later."

Elmer fought the urge to punch Frank. He knew it was the wrong thing to do, but one solid punch into Frank's jaw would make him feel a lot better. He steadied himself and grabbed Tiny's hand as Frank walked away.

"What was that all about?" asked Tiny.

Elmer paced to calm his nerves. "Frank Kelley and some other boys beat a colored boy named Jacob half to death the other day. He's got broken ribs, a swollen face, and more cuts and bruises than I care to count. Dovie found him in the nick of time and wouldn't let them finish the job."

"Jeepers," Tiny whispered. "I can't see Frank doing that. He's always been a gentleman around me. Are you sure it isn't just a misunderstanding like Frank said?"

"I was there, Tiny. He's no gentleman."

"I don't know," said Tiny. "I just don't see it."

Elmer let go of her hand. "Have you ever known me to lie?"

Tiny shook her head. "No, Elm, it's not that. It's just such an awful thing to do, I can't imagine anyone I know being capable of doing such a thing. I'm not saying it was the right thing to do, but I wouldn't get all riled up over a colored boy. Now that he's out of town, I'm sure that's the last we'll hear of it. Honestly, it's better that he left."

Elmer cocked his head at Tiny. "He didn't leave, Tiny. He couldn't even if he wanted to. That's how badly they beat him." He looked for Tiny to recognize the seriousness of what Frank and the other boys had done to Jacob. When she didn't, he just shook his head and walked away.

"Elm, wait!" Tiny called out.

Elmer turned. "If you don't think it's that big of a deal, then come over for dinner sometime this week, and I'll show how big of a deal it is. Until then, I don't think I can be around you."

Tiny called out again, but Elmer just kept walking.

Chapter Thirteen

Evalyn looked at herself in the full-length mirror that hung on the wall in the courthouse bathroom. She hadn't had time to sew an entire new dress for her wedding day, so she had altered the emerald green one she had worn to Bill and Lou Anne's wedding five years before. Never had she thought she'd be wearing a bridesmaid dress as her wedding dress. She had always pictured something white and full of lace at a grand wedding surrounded by family and friends.

She took a deep breath. "I guess it's now or never."

She exited the bathroom and joined Robert in the waiting area outside the courtroom. Robert's mouth dropped open at the sight of her.

"Thanks for letting me change," said Evalyn. "I couldn't let everyone at Quail Crossings see me in this dress when we dropped off Joy, or they would've known somethin' was up."

"You look lovely," he said.

Evalyn fingered the hem of her dress. "Thank you."

The judge peeked his head out the courtroom door. "Y'all ready?"

"You good?" asked Robert, and Evalyn gave her head a sturdy nod. There was no backing out now. She was doing this for Joy, to protect her.

The judge held the door open, letting Robert and Evalyn into the room. "Do y'all have any witnesses?"

Robert shook his head no. "Do we need some?"

"You do," said the judge. "But don't worry. I can have my secretary and the county clerk serve as witnesses. Do you have your license?"

Robert handed over the single sheet of paper. The judge looked at him and then nodded. "Let me gather the witnesses. I'll be just a moment."

"You can still back out," Robert said after the judge left.

"Do you want me to?" asked Evalyn, wondering if he was the one wanting to back out.

"No," said Robert. "I really believe this is best for Joy, and for you."

"For me?" Evalyn cocked her head.

"I don't want your life to be any harder than it has to be," said Robert. "If we're married, your reputation will never be questioned. Our lie will never be found out."

The judge walked back in, followed by a man and a woman. Everyone followed the judge up to the front of the courtroom and then the clerk and secretary sat in the first row while Evalyn and Robert continued to stand in front of the judge.

"We are gathered here in the presence of God and these witnesses for the joining of this man and this woman in the unity of marriage. There are no vows more solemn than those you are about to make. There is no human institution more sacred than that of the home you are about to form. Do you understand this?"

Both Robert and Evalyn muttered. "Yes."

As the judge continued, Evalyn thought about his words. She was vowing to stay with Robert for the rest of her life, and she barely knew him. For all she knew he could be a wife beater or an animal abuser. She had to bite back her gasp as she thought about the possibility of Robert hitting Joy.

She looked around the room, panic about to consume her. Could she still say no? The ceremony wasn't over yet. She could still get out of this and just go home and tell the truth. It wasn't too late.

A flash of Robert holding Joy as they petted Tex entered her mind. The way he looked at her little girl spoke volumes. He would never hurt her. In fact, Evalyn was sure he'd never hurt either of them.

Robert nudged Evalyn out of her daydream. She looked at him and then at the judge. He smiled politely. "Do you, Evalyn Brewer, take this man, Robert Smith, as your lawful husband?"

Evalyn blushed as she realized that the judge had to repeat the question. "Yes… I mean, I do."

The judge looked at Robert. "Do you, Robert Smith, take this woman, Evalyn Brewer, as your lawful wife?"

"I do," said Robert without hesitation.

"By the power invested in me by the great state of Texas, I now pronounce you man and wife. You may kiss your bride."

Evalyn's heart raced. She had never kissed a boy before, and now here she was married to one. She was about to share her first kiss with a man who was practically a stranger in front of a bunch of other strangers.

Robert gave her a pitiful look that let her know he wasn't sure how to proceed. She could feel the eyes of everyone on them. She had to do something, or the judge would know it was all a show. She quickly jerked forward and pecked Robert on the lips before turning and walking out of the courtroom, leaving Robert behind to collect the signed paperwork.

Evalyn paced the waiting room. That was it. That was her first kiss with her husband. It was more like a kiss she'd share with Elmer than with a husband. She squared her shoulders and straightened her dress as she reminded herself this was a marriage of convenience. Romance was best saved for the Hollywood screen, and she didn't have anything to do with that now.

Robert exited the courtroom, followed by the secretary and clerk, who both mumbled a quick congratulations before returning to their jobs.

"The judge was willing to back date the marriage license," said Robert. "I explained to him that we had a child. Now no one will be the wiser."

"You told him about Joy?" Evalyn felt heat rise to her cheeks. Lord only knew what the judge thought of her now.

Robert shrugged. "He was very kind about it and said it happens more often than we would think. He agreed back dating the license was the best thing for Joy."

"Until someone realizes we didn't live here during the date that's on the license." Evalyn crossed her arms. "I guess it doesn't matter now. It's done. Let's go back to Rockwood. Just make sure you hide that thing where no one will see it."

Evalyn walked into the bathroom to change back into her everyday dress. As she locked the door, tears flooded her face. She was never one to have romantic notions, but the loss of the possibility of courting and a real wedding in the church hit her hard.

She washed her face in the sink and looked in the mirror.

"Robert is a good man," she reminded herself. "You may not have romance or a big wedding, but you have done what's best for Joy, and that is what matters."

She changed her clothes and then picked up the emerald dress. All she could see when looked at it was broken dreams of love. Wadding the dress into a ball, she threw it in the trashcan. She didn't need any reminders of what she was giving up hanging in her closet.

Evalyn felt exhausted as she slouched on the sofa next to Robert after finally getting Joy down for the night. She leaned her back and closed her eyes.

"You really did look lovely today," said Robert.

"Thank you," Evalyn said with a sigh.

"You've been awfully quiet since the ceremony," said Robert.

Evalyn opened her eyes to see him looking at her over his paper. "I'm just tired."

Robert laid down his farm report. "I know today probably wasn't your ideal wedding day. I wish I could have given you what you wanted."

"It is what it is," said Evalyn, shutting her eyes again. She really didn't want to talk about it. She had left all those thoughts, along with the wedding dress, in the courthouse bathroom.

"I bet we could get Dovie to plan us a reception, since they couldn't be involved," Robert suggested.

"I think it's best we don't bring attention to ourselves," said Evalyn, rising off the sofa. "I'm going to bed."

"So soon?" Robert frowned.

Evalyn sighed. "I'm exhausted, and Lord knows Joy will be up in a few hours, hungry or wet. I'll see you in the morning."

"Okay," said Robert, "I understand. I was just hoping we could celebrate our wedding night somehow."

Evalyn raised an eyebrow at Robert. "I'm not sure what you were thinking but don't forget this is a marriage of convenience only."

Robert raised his hands. "I wasn't thinking about that, honestly. I was thinking of maybe playing some cards and listening to some music on the radio, just spending time together."

Evalyn pursed her lips together. "It seems I just vowed in front of a judge to spend time with you for the rest of my life."

She hated how awful she sounded towards him. He hadn't done anything to merit her wrath. Evalyn sighed and went into the bedroom, tears threatening to fall again. She guessed she hadn't left everything in that courthouse bathroom.

Chapter Fourteen

Dovie timidly knocked on the door of Evalyn's new home. She wasn't sure Evalyn would accept her help, but she wanted to show her support nonetheless. It had been a week since Evalyn had moved to Rockwood, and they had barely seen her or Joy. Dovie had to make sure everything was okay before Bill brought in the cavalry.

Evalyn answered the door with a bandana wrapped around her hair and smudges of dirt on her cheeks.

"Dovie?" Evalyn tried to compose herself. "What are you doing here?"

"Now is that any way to greet a visitor?" Dovie pushed her way past Evalyn and into the house.

"Dovie, it's not…" Evalyn tried to explain as she closed the door.

"It's exactly what I thought it would be," said Dovie. "I was here often enough when Robert's ma was ill to know it would be in bad shape now, no matter how hard Robert tried. I'm here to help. Put me to work."

Dovie pulled her apron out of her bag. "I also brought some cleaning supplies since I wasn't sure if Robert had any on hand." Evalyn's eyes grew as Dovie began pulling bleach, steel wool, and an assortment of other cleaning products out of her bag.

"Did you leave anything at Quail Crossings?" Evalyn asked, wiping her brow. "I appreciate the help, but you really don't need to. You have Jacob to look after as well as Quail Crossings, and I can't possibly pay you back for these supplies."

"Nonsense, Lou Anne is tending to Jacob, and you and I both know Quail Crossings will keep for a few days." Bag unloaded, Dovie looked around the room. "Where's that sweet baby?"

"She's napping. Come look." Evalyn led Dovie to the bedroom where Joy slept soundly in her new crib. Dovie let out a small sigh as she took in the sight of the baby sleeping in the beautiful handmade crib. As she tiptoed out of the room, she wondered where Evalyn had gotten it.

"Oh, what a beautiful bed," Dovie whispered as Evalyn shut the door. "Did Robert make that for her?"

Evalyn nodded. "It was a total and wonderful surprise."

"Poor Helen never had anything so fancy. She slept with Simon and me until she was old enough to move into her own bed. There were times when I swear that girl slept diagonally across the bed, her head in my ribs and her feet poking Simon's legs. We were so worn out from sleeping with a restless toddler that the first night she slept in her own bed, Simon and I slept for twelve straight hours." Dovie grew silent as she thought about her long-deceased husband and child. Most days she felt pretty normal, but then out of the blue, grief would smack her in the face again.

She shook herself out of it. "What can I do?"

Evalyn wiped her forehead. "I don't even know where to have you start. Most of the laundry is done and hangin' on the line. I'm working on the kitchen now."

"All right," said Dovie, tying on her apron. "I'll start in here. Does Robert need all these old farm reports and newspapers?"

"I honestly can't tell you what he's read and what he hasn't," said Evalyn.

"Fine then," said Dovie, grabbing a broom that was propped against the wall. "I'll sweep that corner by the fireplace and then stack them there. If he doesn't need them, they'll make good kindling."

Evalyn sighed and Dovie realized the poor girl was completely overwhelmed by the task at hand.

Dovie patted her on the back. "Don't worry, Evie, we'll have this place sparklin' like a millionaire's diamond in no time."

"Thank you for dinner, Mrs. Grant," said Tiny. "Don't tell my ma, but you make the best roast in Knollwood."

"I can't take any of the credit this time, Tiny," said Dovie gathering the dinner dishes. "Lou Anne did the majority of the work while I was helping Evie get Rockwood in order."

"Has Jacob eaten?" asked Elmer.

Dovie cocked her head and glanced at Tiny. They had all agreed to keep Jacob's whereabouts within the family until he recovered. "No, he was asleep when I checked on him. I saved him a plate."

"We'll take it him," said Elmer. "Tiny and I."

"I'm not sure that is a good idea," said Dovie.

"I wouldn't offer if it wasn't needed," said Elmer.

Dovie raised an eyebrow at Elmer's vague reply. "Then do what you need to do. I'll go with you. I should check his ribs anyhow."

Elmer grabbed Jacob's plate in one hand and Tiny's hand with his other and followed Dovie to Jacob's door.

"I ain't gonna lie to you, Tiny, he ain't pretty. They did a number on his face, and it's still really swollen. Try not to stare and, for Pete's sake, don't say 'Jeepers'," said Elmer.

"I swear, Elm, you treat me like such a child sometimes." Tiny pushed past Elmer and entered the room right after Dovie.

Elmer followed Tiny inside and watched as her jaw dropped. She quickly turned and faced the door.

"What are you doing?" whispered Elmer.

"You told me not to stare, and this was the first thing I thought to do so I wouldn't stare," answered Tiny.

"It's okay," said Jacob. "I know it looks bad, but don't worry, Miss, my face wasn't too pretty to begin with."

Elmer chuckled at Jacob's joke as he approached the bed. "I see you're feeling better. I brought you some food."

Jacob nodded. "Yeah, the pain in my shoulder is almost gone. Wish I could say the same for my ribs."

"It's gonna take a while, Jacob," said Dovie. "But you're getting stronger every day."

"Tiny," said Elmer, "you can turn around now."

Tiny slowly turned only to have her jaw drop open again. She snapped it shut and approached the bed. "I never thought anyone could be so cruel."

"Not just anyone," said Elmer, "Frank Kelley and his friends."

Tiny shook her head. "I just can't believe it."

"Believe it," said Elmer.

Tears formed in Tiny's eyes as she whispered. "Jeepers."

"Stop the truck here," said Frank to his buddy Paul. "I'm just gonna look around a bit. Pa is sure they've got that colored boy here at Quail Crossings. As soon as I know where he is for sure, we'll show that boy what he gets for coming to our town and teach Mr. Murphy and Mrs. Grant what happens to colored lovers."

"Frank, are you sure?" said Paul. "Mr. Murphy is a good man, and Mrs. Grant brought us some eggs and milk a few years ago, you know during the bad days. I think we would've starved to death, had it not been for their kindness. I don't know about all this; it ain't sitting right."

"Just shut up and stay here," said Frank before sliding out of the vehicle. "Your pa would tan your hide for takin' the Murphy's side, eggs or no eggs."

Frank made a wide circle to the orchard and crouched down. Everyone was inside, and from the silhouettes he could see, they had just finished dinner. Having never been to Quail Crossings before, Frank had to guess which room the boy would be staying in. One wrong window and he'd be caught for sure.

He just needed a glimpse of the colored boy to make his father proud. Pa had been looking for a reason to knock James Murphy off his pedestal and this was the reason. But Pa was smart enough not to go after Mr. Murphy until he had proof they were harboring the boy.

Frank snuck up to the house and started to look in the first set of windows. All the windows had heavy blue curtains. It was nearly impossible to see through them, but if he could get at just the right angle, he might be able to see through the crack where the curtains met on each side.

As he leaned to the right, he heard a low hiss behind him.

"Paul, I told you to stay in the truck."

Frank turned around and came face to face with a large grey and white goose. "Go away, you stupid bird."

Norman hissed again, this time louder.

"I said git," Frank said in a loud whisper.

Norman hissed even louder and raised his wings.

Frank picked up a rock and hurled it at Norman, hitting the goose in the chest.

Norman launched himself at the intruder knocking Frank to the ground, hissing and honking in-between bites to Frank's face.

"Get off!" yelled Frank. "Get off!"

But Norman just bit harder.

"What's going on out here?"

Frank could see light from a lantern headed his way.

"Norman, get off that boy!" yelled James.

Norman dropped and stood by James, wings still raised. James lifted the lantern. "What in the world are you doing out here, son?"

"I was out for a walk," lied Frank as he got to his feet.

"Way out here?" James narrowed his eyes. "You're that Kelley boy, aren't you?"

"So what if I am?" snapped Frank.

"Now you listen here, I don't know if your pa put you up to this or not, but you're not welcome here. You ought to be ashamed of yourself, beating up that boy like that. Just who do you think you are?" James grabbed Frank by the collar. "I ought to call the law on you for trespassing and for what you did to that boy." James released Frank's collar, pushing him back. "But I won't because you're young and stupid, and it ain't your fault your pa taught you a bunch of nonsense. Now git, and I don't wanna see you around here again, or I'll let Norman finish the job he started."

Norman raised his wings and hissed as Frank ran as fast as he could back to Paul's truck.

"Did you see the boy?" asked Paul, before doing a double take. "And what happened to your face?"

"Just drive," said Frank, "and mark my words, by the time I'm done James Murphy and Elmer Brewer will wish they never heard the name Frank Kelley."

Chapter Fifteen

"I don't feel right about leaving Jacob out here by himself," said Dovie. "Y'all just go to the tractor pull without me."

"You know that will look suspicious," said James. "We all need to go."

"I can stay here," volunteered Elmer.

James shook his head. "We all need to go."

"Or we could all just stay here," said Dovie.

"And not go to the tractor pull?" Alice's eyes fell.

"In order to keep Jacob safe?" said Dovie. "Yes."

James sighed. "We are all going. Look, Dovie, you've volunteered to help judge the pie eating contest. I volunteered to help with the hog wrestling, Bill with the tractor race, and Elmer with the mutton bustin'. Lou Anne and Alice are to sell ticket for the church raffle. Like it or not, our family is involved in this tractor pull, and if we don't show up, people will start asking questions."

"Just tell them I have one of my headaches. Then Evie and Lou Anne can judge the pie eating contest," countered Dovie.

"Sounds to me," Evalyn interjected, "that there is only one real answer."

"What is that?" asked James.

"Robert and I should stay here with Jacob." Evalyn crossed her arms. "Dovie's right, Jacob can't stay out here alone."

Dovie let out a smug grunt.

"But James is right too," Evalyn continued wiping the smug look off Dovie's face. "If y'all don't do what you volunteered to do, then that will raise questions. Joy's been fussy all morning, and I'm sure Robert won't mind missing the tractor pull." She looked to her husband who nodded his approval. "It's settled then."

Dovie twisted her apron. "Okay, as long as Robert stays with you. I don't like it, but I guess y'all are right. We better get a move on."

Less than an hour later, leaving Evalyn, Joy and Robert behind, Dovie and her family entered the parking lot for the tractor pull. A big crowd started to file in as the activities were slated to begin soon.

"I'm so glad we're here, Momma Dovie," said Alice. "I want Jacob to be safe, but I also didn't want to miss the tractor pull."

Dovie bent down and gave Alice a serious look. "Not a word to anyone about Jacob, you here? Don't even say his name. Got it?"

Alice nodded.

"Good," said Dovie. "No one can know he's here."

She grabbed Alice's hand, and they made their way to the hog wrestling which was about to begin.

Dovie and Alice took their seats in the bleachers overlooking a large corral as James and Bud Clark greased down a large boar hog.

Alice wrinkled her nose. "I don't know why anyone would want to wrestle a greased hog."

"Me either," said Dovie. "But it looks like Elm's gonna give it a try."

Elmer shook out his arms and legs, trying to keep himself loose. All he had to do was be the first of the boys to wrestle the pig to the ground and hold him there for three seconds in order to win the twenty-five dollar grand prize. It was the largest prize being given away that day, and Elmer needed the money to put in his savings. One day he'd have his own place and his own dog training business. Every dollar now would be needed then.

He thought about the kennels he could afford to build and how he would build them. He wasn't surprised to see that his vision included Tiny. In fact, if he won, he'd take Tiny out on a real date and buy her all the milkshakes she wanted.

"So you tore yourself away from your colored boy long enough to come to town, huh?" said Frank Kelley as he walked up behind Elmer.

"What happened to your face?" asked Elmer, trying to hide his smile.

"Nothin' that I can't handle," sneered Frank.

"Oh, I know exactly how you handled it," said Elmer. "You ran away like a chicken."

Frank balled up his fist and stepped toward Elmer as Elmer stepped up to meet him.

"Hey, boys," Bud Clark yelled at Frank and Elmer. "Save it for the hog. Anyone who throws any punches at another wrestler is disqualified."

Elmer took a step back. Frank wanted them to brawl in public, and Elmer shook his head in disgust at himself for taking the bait.

"All right, fellas," Bud yelled again, "when the bell rings, that hog is gonna run for his life. I guarantee he's gonna kick and bite like the dickin's. The first of you fellas to pin the hog to the ground for three seconds wins. Ready?"

Before the boys could answer, Bud rang the bell, and James opened the gate to let the huge hog out. Bud hadn't been exaggerating, and the pig took off in a sprint. The boys hesitated for a moment at the size of the brute before someone let out a war cry, and they all ran toward it.

The hog squealed and ran faster. Frank jumped and caught the pig's tail end, only to slide right off, face first, in the mud. Elmer stayed with the pack of boys circling the pig, watching as boy after boy tried to tackle the hog as Frank had done, only to slide off. But he realized with each boy's try, the pig became less greasy as the grease was being transferred onto the boys' clothes.

Frank tried again, getting a grip closer to the hog's head. The pig turned and bit Frank's arm, causing Frank to let go and fall in the mud again.

Elmer knew that if he was going to win the money, he needed to act fast. Frank was determined, and Elmer couldn't let Frank win.

Letting out a warrior yell, Elmer ran through the boys and leapt onto the back of the boar. He instantly locked his arms and legs around the brute, careful to grab just under the chin of the hog, so he wouldn't get bitten. As Elm had hoped, the pig dropped to the ground in an attempt to roll Elmer off.

Elmer kept his legs and arms locked around the pig as it rolled. He could hear a collective gasp from the crowd as the pig rolled on top of him. He ducked his head and used his strength to help the pig roll all the way over before pinning him to the ground.

"One Mississippi."

Elmer heard Bud start to count.

"Two Mississippi."

The hog squirmed and kicked, trying to dislodge Elmer.

"Three Mississippi! We have a winner- Elmer Brewer!!"

Elmer took a deep breath before letting go of the pig and rolling in the opposite direction. The boar was angry and headed right for the group of boys who still stood in the corral. They scattered in all directions, but not before the boar took Frank's legs out from under him, giving him yet another mud bath.

"Come on, Momma Dovie." Alice pulled Dovie along as they followed Gabe to where his plane sat. He had taken it out and put it on display for everyone to see at the tractor pull. "This is so exciting."

"It's just a plane," said Dovie, but she couldn't help but feel a tingle of excitement at being able to get an up-close look at a real-life plane. She had seen pictures of planes in the newspaper and once in a copy of Life magazine at Johnson's Drug, but she never in her life thought she would be able to touch one.

"Oh this is more than just a plane," said Gabe, smiling from ear to ear as they walked up to the shiny aircraft. "It's a bi-plane and I call her Bumblebee."

"Because you've painted it black and yellow?" asked Alice.

"That, and she'll sting you if you make her mad," said Gabe. "She's a testy ol' bird, but I love her."

He patted the nose of the plane like it was a horse.

"It really is amazing," said Dovie, "and bigger than I thought."

"You must be rich," said Alice.

"Alice, don't be rude," Dovie reprimanded.

Gabe laughed. "No, I'm not rich. I bought her cheap from a fella in Canada who won her in a poker match. He had no idea or inclination to fly a plane, so I got a good deal."

"I understand where he came from," said Dovie. "I can't imagine not having my feet firmly planted on the ground. If we were meant to fly, God would've given us wings."

"Oh, but Dovie, He did," said Gabe. "When He gave us the know-how on how to build a plane."

Dovie laughed at his enthusiasm. "So what's it like, flying in the sky with the birds?"

Gabe gave her a big smile. "It's a lot like being in a whirlwind romance, lots of ups and downs and your stomach is twisted in all kinds of good knots. And every time you're away from flyin', you just can't wait to do it again."

"That doesn't sound like anything I would enjoy at all," said Dovie, fanning herself.

"Guess I'll just have to change your mind," Gabe said with a wink.

Chapter Sixteen

April 1940

Evalyn was surprised to see a truck pull into the drive at Rockwood as she kneeled outside washing diapers. It was a beautiful April day, and Joy was enjoying lying on her back and playing with her toes on a big quilt in the grass.

Shielding her eyes, Evalyn tried to make out who was coming and felt her heart leap into her throat as the figure of Kathleen Wheaton marched toward her. She glanced at Joy and then back to Kathleen before setting her laundry basket directly in front of the baby, blocking Kathleen's view.

Tucking her hair behind her ear and smoothing out her dress as best she could, she walked toward Kathleen. "Mrs. Wheaton, this is quite a surprise."

"Is it?" Kathleen cocked her head.

Evalyn hugged herself and tried to rub a fresh set of goose bumps away. "I don't know what you mean."

"Oh, Evalyn, you had to know I'd come and … "

Evalyn held her breath.

"… and talk to you about Harriet," finished Kathleen. "I've been so worried about her, well the two of you, since you left for California. It was against my better judgment and Harriet knew that, but I also knew I couldn't stop her if her mind was made up. And now that you're back, and she's there all alone, well I'm really worried. Evalyn, how could you leave Harriet?"

"Leave Harriet?" Evalyn shook her head in confusion.

Kathleen took a deep breath and smiled. "Let's start again, shall we?"

Evalyn still confused, nodded.

"I've been in Oklahoma tending to my ma and just got back to town. I ran into Mrs. Spaulding, and she told me you had returned. Now I'm really concerned about Harriet being in California alone. I haven't heard from her in weeks, and the last letter we received didn't give us any clues she was over there alone. Did you and Harriet have a fight? Is she okay?"

Evalyn cleared her throat. "Yes, Mrs. Wheaton, I'm afraid that Harriet and I did have a falling out, but it was about needing to come home. I didn't wanna leave her there alone, but I had to. I begged her to come and she refused. I'm sorry, Mrs. Wheaton, but I did try."

"Have you heard from her?" asked Kathleen, a twinge of hope in her voice.

Evalyn shook her head. "I'm afraid I haven't, and I'm certain she won't write me."

Joy gave a low cry, telling Evalyn she had noticed her mommy's absence. Kathleen's hand flew to her face. "Is that a baby? Mrs. Spaulding didn't say you had a child."

Before Evalyn could stop her, Kathleen rushed over and picked up Joy, giving her a little bounce while making a "shushing" noise and smiling all the while. . "She is gorgeous."

Joy giggled and then let out a high-pitched hiccup. Kathleen's smile faded. "Harriet used to giggle and hiccup just like that as a baby." Kathleen traced Joy's face, her blue eyes filled with memories. "You know she looks a lot like Harriet did as well …" Her voice trailed off as a tear fell on her cheek. She handed Joy to Evalyn. "You must excuse me, just remembering the old days, putting your baby in place of my own, now-grown children. Make sure to cherish every moment, Evalyn. They grow up so fast." She touched Joy's check. "She is beautiful."

Evalyn grabbed Kathleen's hand and gave it a gentle squeeze. "I'm sure Harriet is fine. She took to California like a cat to cream. I'm sure she'll write soon."

Kathleen patted Evalyn's hand. "I'm sure you're right, but if she gets in touch with you, will you let me know?"

"Of course," said Evalyn before watching Kathleen slowly walk back to her truck.

Evalyn put Joy back on the quilt and kneeled over the baby. "She's such a nice lady. Too bad I can't be honest with her about her own daughter. I guess I didn't totally lie. Harriet and I did have a falling out, but you and I both know it wasn't about me leavin', was it?" Evalyn pecked Joy on the nose and went back to washing diapers.

A few minutes later, Robert pulled into the farm followed by a large Alkire Bros. livestock truck. The stench of pigs cooped up for three days on a truck from Missouri assaulted her nose. Evalyn sighed, it was official; she was married to a pig farmer.

Hanging the last of the diapers on the line, she watched as Robert directed the driver of the large truck to the pigpen. The driver took off down the makeshift road, sending dirt flying onto Evalyn's freshly watched diapers.

Evalyn frantically grabbed at the wet diapers, trying to get them all down before she had to rewash, but it was too late. The wet diapers were soiled almost immediately. Evalyn threw them into the basket and huffed. An entire morning's work gone.

She picked up Joy and took her in the house for a bottle and nap while Robert got the pigs unloaded. There was no reason they should stand outside and inhale the foul odor, and she couldn't rewash the diapers until the truck left.

Joy had decided it was a good day to sip her bottle instead of guzzle it, so it was a good half hour before Evalyn went back outside to see how much longer the truck would be there. The Alkire Bros truck was just leaving, and a trail of dust still hung in the air behind it. Evalyn waited for it leave before making her way to the pig barns.

Robert had built them about one hundred feet from the house. That would help with the stink, but Evalyn couldn't help but wonder how the winter would be with Robert having to travel all that distance in the cold when it came time to tend to the pigs. Evalyn shrugged her shoulders. It was his own fault for wanting pigs in the first place. If he'd have to walk a few extra feet come winter, so be it.

She found Robert at the opposite end of a large pigpen, spraying the dirt and some pigs down with water. She flinched at all the water on the ground but then remembered the dusty days of the dirty 30's were behind them for the most part. She grimaced at the sight of the mud, already being rolled in by the newly freed and somewhat washed pigs. There had to be at least twenty boars and sows in the pen.

"Robert," she hollered. "I need to talk to you."

"What?" asked Robert.

"That truck ruined my clean laundry," she complained.

"What? Come on over, I can barely hear you over the pigs." He continued to wash the pigs. "Oh, can you bring in that bucket of slop?"

Evalyn looked to her left and wrinkled her nose at the sight of half rotted vegetables and other food waste swarming with flies. "This bucket?"

"That's the one," he yelled.

Evalyn fought the urge to vomit as she picked up the bucket. She sat it back down quickly. "Oh, you know, I don't wanna get my shoes all muddy since I just cleaned the house. You should just come and get it. It'll be far faster than me going to the house to get my mud boots."

"Nonsense," said Robert, "I brought down an extra set of mud boots for that very reason. They're just inside the barn. Slip those on." He turned as if the conversation was over and hosed down another pig.

Evalyn huffed and stomped toward the barn door. She was not a pig farmer. He was the pig farmer. She wanted nothing to do with the foul creatures, unless it was frying them up for breakfast. She would let him know right now that this work was on him. She would milk the goat, feed the fowl, and do all the housework, but she was not working in the pig barn.

Finding the boots, she pulled them on over her shoes since they were twice the size of her own feet. Even with her regular boots on, the mud boots were cumbersome.

"This is it," she mumbled to herself as she shuffled her feet back to the slop bucket. "This is the first and last time I do this."

Grabbing the bucket, she let herself in through the gate. The pigs swarmed around her, begging for her bucket.

"Quick, pour it in the trough before they knock you over," hollered Richard.

Evalyn shot daggers at Richard as she shuffled to the trough. Going along the long feeder, she poured the slop and the pigs followed. Once the bucket was empty, the pigs didn't pay her any attention. Instead, they all were fighting for a bite of food. She hung the bucket on a pen post.

"Thanks," said Richard, turning off the hose.

"Now listen here, Mr. Smith." Evalyn stomped her foot. "You are the pig farmer, not me. If you wanna wallow around in this filth with the pigs, fine, but don't expect me to do it, 'cause I won't. Pigs are nasty creatures, and I'll have nothing to do with them, and that truck ruined my clean laundry, so now I have to do it all over again. I'm here to take care of Joy and the house. That's it; that was the deal."

As she turned to leave, a couple of pigs vying for a prime trough spot bumped her hard. She tried to maintain her balance, but between her being in the process of turning and the big boots, it was impossible. She threw her hands in front of her to try to catch herself as she fell face first into the mud.

Evalyn lay still for a moment.

"Evalyn, are you okay?" she heard Robert say as he hoisted her up and onto her feet. "Let me help you."

"I'm fine," she growled, throwing off his hands. "I'd be even better if these god-forsaken pigs weren't here! This was a foolish decision."

Robert's face turned from concerned to annoyance. "This *foolish* decision is our livelihood, so you best get used to it." He stormed to the gate.

"Where are you going?" asked Evalyn.

"Inside to check on Joy, while you wash off in the stock tank."

"In the stock tank?" Evalyn shivered at the idea. It was spring but still definitely not warm enough to go for a swim.

"Yes," stated Robert, "I don't want you to stink up our clean house.

Evalyn let out another scream of disgust as Robert continued to walk away.

Chapter Seventeen

Alice tapped on Jacob's door and then looked around to see if anyone was watching. She knew she shouldn't visit Jacob without Dovie on account of his injuries, but she had a gift for him, and she couldn't wait for Dovie to get back from town.

"Come in," came Jacob's voice from behind the door.

Alice peeked her head in. "Hi."

"Miss Alice, my guardian angel." Jacob's face filled with a smile. "Please, come in; don't be shy. I owe you my life."

Alice blushed and waved him off as she entered the room. "Nah, Mama Dovie is the one who is makin' you better. How are you feelin'?"

"I'm feelin' all right," said Jacob. "I'll be right as rain in no time."

"I brought you something," said Alice.

"Oh yeah?" Jacob cocked his head.

Alice held up her worn copy of *Peter Pan*. "Do you remember that huge dust storm we had about five years ago, the one they called Black Sunday?"

Jacob nodded.

Alice sat near Jacob's feet, careful not to jostle the bed and hurt his ribs. "Well, me and Mr. Norman were caught up in that storm."

"Mr. Norman? Is he your father?" asked Jacob.

Alice shook her head and giggled. "No, Mr. Norman is our goose and my bestest friend. I'll introduce you to him when you feel better. Mama Dovie won't let him in the house even though he's a good goose."

"I bet he is," said Jacob. "He'd have to be in order to be your bestest friend."

"Anyway, after the storm I got dust pneumonia and had to stay cooped up in this house for weeks. It just 'bout drove me crazy not being able to go outside. So Mama Dovie gave me this book and helped me learn to read it. I thought you might like to read it since you can't go outside right now."

"That's mighty nice of you, Miss Alice, but you keep your book. Thanks all the same," said Jacob.

Alice's head fell as she felt her lip start to tremble. "Oh, okay then."

Jacob frowned. "Miss Alice, it ain't like that. I appreciate your gift. I really do. It's just that I won't have much use for it."

"It's a book," said Alice, wrinkling her forehead. "You don't use it for anything other than reading the story."

"That's just it," said Jacob in a soft voice. "I can't read."

Alice's eyes brightened as she inched further up the bed. "Would you like to learn? I could teach you just like Mama Dovie taught me when I was sick."

Jacob smiled widened. "You'd do that for me, Miss Alice?"

"Of course," said Alice. She grabbed the chair at the side of the bed and pulled it to where Jacob could see the book. "We can start right now."

Dovie sat in Annette's Café and sipped her coffee as she waited for Lou Anne to finish her errands. The bell above the door jingled, and Dovie turned to see who had entered the café, hoping it was one of her lady friends. Drinking coffee was nice, drinking coffee with friends was even better. Seeing Gabe Pearce, she quickly turned around and tried to shrink down in her seat.

"Why, hello there, Dovie. Thought I was gonna have to drink my joe alone," said Gabe, taking off his hat and sitting across from her before signaling to Annette. "I'd love a cup of coffee, Miss Annette and please, get Dovie here a refill on me."

"Refills are free, Mr. Pearce," said Dovie.

Gabe smiled as Annette filled a mug in front of him and topped off Dovie's coffee. "Well, then please bring us both a slice of apple pie, on me."

Annette nodded and then raised her eyebrows at Dovie.

"Mr. Pearce, that really isn't necessary," said Dovie, ignoring Annette's teasing look.

"When are you gonna start calling me Gabe?" he asked.

"I'm not accustomed to calling strangers by their first names," said Dovie, sipping her coffee.

"Now, I'm insulted." Gabe sat back in his chair looking defeated. "After all we've been through, you're still calling me a stranger."

Annette set the pie in front of them, and this time gave Dovie a 'just what have you and Gabe been up to, you sly dog' look. Dovie shooed her away.

"Fine, Mr. Pearce, I will admit you don't fit the definition of a stranger."

"Good, then call me Gabe."

"I'm not sure I can do that," said Dovie.

"I don't know why not."

Dovie sighed. "Let's just say you remind me of someone I knew long ago and being around you reminds me of how much I miss him."

Gabe nodded. "Can I tell you a story?"

"I don't know, Mr. Pearce. I really must be going." Dovie stood and Gabe grabbed her hand.

"Just listen until you finish your pie, then I'll leave you alone. Promise."

Dovie sighed and sat back down. "Very well."

"Back a dozen years or so ago, I was in love. Her name was Barbara, and she had hair the color of night and eyes as blue as the day sky. Oh, and her laugh was prettier than birds singing."

"She sounds lovely," said Dovie.

"Oh, she was, until she got in a car with a man from New York and broke my heart," said Gabe.

Dovie blushed at Gabe's confession. "I'm sorry to hear that."

"Don't be," said Gabe, shaking his head. "It was for the best. My point is I understand some injuries that are unseen."

Dovie cocked her head at Gabe. "Truer words have never been spoken."

"I would just like us to be friends. I'm not trying to take the place of whoever I remind you of, Dovie."

"My husband," Dovie blurted and then blushed at her sudden confession. "You look like my late husband, Simon."

Gabe shook his head, placed Annette's money on the table and stood. "Say no more, I understand."

Dovie stood with him. "No, you don't, 'cause I'm not sure I understand it myself. Sometimes I feel more confused than a bee in a jar. It's been almost six years since Simon passed, and I'm acting like a child by not accepting your friendship. Please forgive me, Gabe, I've been pig-headed."

"Well," said Gabe smiling, "now that you've said my name, all is forgiven."

With a wink, he grabbed his hat and walked out the door.

Lou Anne walked slowly toward the small house where Mrs. Pearl lived. Dovie's words about waiting and relaxing in order to get pregnant echoed through her head. Lou Anne stopped and turned back toward the street. Dovie was right, and she should just give it more time. Although five years felt like an awfully long time. She turned back toward the house.

"Mrs. Brewer are you gonna dance on my walk all morning?" came Mrs. Pearl's no-nonsense voice from the porch. "Come on up here and say what you need to say."

Lou Anne had to stifle her startled scream. She hadn't seen Mrs. Pearl on the porch sitting in a rocking chair just to the left of a large wild rose vine. Mrs. Pearl sat with her hands folded onto a worn Bible as she slowly rocked back and forth. Lou Anne took a deep breath. There was no going back now.

As she stepped onto the porch, she smiled at Mrs. Pearl. "I hate to bother you, Mrs. Pearl, but I was hoping you could help me."

"Help you with what, Mrs. Brewer?" Mrs. Pearl motioned to the chair next to her. "Please sit down."

Lou Anne sat and looked at her hands. "It's a bit of a delicate situation."

"Mrs. Brewer, if you're gonna ask for my help, the least you can do is look at me."

Lou Anne blushed and looked up. "Sorry, please excuse my lack of manners."

"That's better," said Mrs. Pearl. "I know your mother brought you up right. Speaking of mothers, when are you and Mr. Brewer gonna start a family? It seems far past the date to start."

Lou Anne wondered if her face would ever regain its natural shade as she blushed again. "That's what I've come to talk to you about, Mrs. Pearl. We have been trying, but nothing's come of it yet."

Mrs. Pearl nodded her head. "Why come to me? Seems like a matter between you and Mr. Brewer."

"I was hoping you knew of some ways to help me get with child," said Lou Anne. "Do you know of any?"

"Of course," said Mrs. Pearl, "I suspect you would prefer a boy, Mrs. Brewer."

"I think Bill would prefer a boy, but at this point it doesn't really matter to me," answered Lou Anne.

"Eat lots of red meat, the rarer the better, to ensure you have a boy," Mrs. Pearl started. "As for conception, drink two raw eggs every morning, eat a hot pepper in the late afternoon, the hotter the better, and then after you and Mr. Brewer have had relations, stand on your head."

Lou Anne had nodded at every item on the list until the last one. "Stand on my head?"

"It helps everything get to where it needs to go faster," said Mrs. Pearl without hesitation.

"Anything else?" asked Lou Anne.

"Yes, sit on a chair directly after a woman who is expecting." Mrs. Pearl paused. "And I'm afraid someone might have to pass before you conceive."

Lou Anne's hand flew to her mouth. That was more ludicrous than standing on her head. "Someone has to pass, as in die?"

Mrs. Pearl nodded. "In some cases, yes. One soul has to leave the world for another one to enter. But hopefully it doesn't come down to that, Mrs. Brewer."

"Yes, let's hope," said Lou Anne rising. "Thank you very much for your time, Mrs. Pearl. I must go meet Dovie now."

"Mrs. Brewer, do as I say and you'll have youngin's in no time," hollered Mrs. Pearl as Lou Anne hurried down the walk.

Chapter Eighteen

Dovie watched Evalyn feed Joy and wondered if she should broach the subject that weighed heavily on her mind. It was a touchy one, and there was no way to know how Evalyn would react. It wasn't long before everyone would be in for Sunday dinner at Quail Crossings, so if she was going to do it, it had to be now.

Dovie sighed. There was no one else. Lou Anne was barely older than Evalyn, and Evalyn's mother hadn't been seen in a coon's age. There were things Evalyn needed to know, and Dovie felt it was her duty to make sure she knew it.

"Evie, how are things with Robert?" Dovie asked casually while plucking a chicken for dinner.

"Fine," said Evalyn, but Dovie could hear a catch in her voice. Evalyn may not have been her daughter by blood, but Dovie knew that catch meant that everything was not fine.

"Are you settling in okay at Rockwood? You and Robert getting into a routine?" Dovie pried.

"Guess you could say that," said Evalyn, this time without a catch.

"And Joy? How's she liking her new home?" asked Dovie.

"She's doing just fine, like the rest of us." This time Dovie could hear the annoyance in Evalyn's voice.

"Having a baby changes things among married couples," said Dovie, diving right into the conversation she had debated having at all.

"I haven't noticed any changes," said Evalyn.

Dovie raised an eyebrow and glanced over her shoulder. Evalyn was wiping a bit of oatmeal off Joy's chin.

"That's good. It was hard for Simon and me, the adjusting I mean," said Dovie. "It was just the two of us for so long and then poof, this baby was taking up all my time. Oh, and the time I was expectin' also put a wrench in the works."

"Why would being with a child do that?" asked Evalyn.

"Oh, just the normal things that go along with expecting. You know what I'm talking about. You've been there." Dovie glanced over her shoulder. The look on Evalyn's face spoke volumes. Evalyn had no idea what Dovie was talking about.

"Dovie, we're fine. I promise," said Evalyn quickly, almost begging to not have to have the conversation.

"I'm sure you think everything is fine." Dovie plucked the chicken harder. "But after the first knowledge of the little one, there's very little relations going on. I know when I was expecting, my back and ankles hurt all the time, and I threw up more than a dog eating grass. Oh, I was so exhausted. It was all I could do to get my chores done before crawling into bed. I had absolutely no interest in doing anything with Simon after the lights went out."

Dovie glanced over her shoulder. Evalyn was staring at her, mouth wide open.

Dovie continued, might as well get it all out now. "Then right after Helen came, I wouldn't let Simon touch me with a ten foot pole. I hurt so badly afterwards and was afraid relations would be painful as well. My own mom was gone by the time I had Helen, so I didn't have anyone to talk to, and it's not like she told me all these things before she passed. Anyway, Simon started to get really, really grumpy, but it didn't occur to me what the reasoning was until one day in town. We were at the butcher and our order was mixed up with another families. I thought Simon was gonna blow a gasket."

Dovie giggled remembering the day. "Oh my, he stormed out of the store and started pacing. Then he came back in and apologized. Mrs. Pearl saw the whole thing, and I was probably redder than a radish. I didn't think it could get any worse until Mrs. Pearl looked right at me and said, 'Mrs. Grant, a man has needs. You better tend to yours.' It hit me like a ton of bricks, but the next day, Simon wasn't so grumpy, and I was relieved to know it didn't hurt."

"Dovie, please stop." Now Evalyn was begging. "I understand what you're saying. Please, don't say any more. I'm gonna take Joy up for a nap, and I think I'll lie down as well. This conversation has made me dizzy."

Dovie watched Evalyn walk up the stairs and went back to her chicken. As she plucked, she couldn't shake the look on Evalyn's face when she talked about not having any pregnancy symptoms. Evalyn was a private girl. Dovie knew that, but something wasn't right, and Dovie was going to find a way to help Evalyn no matter how uncomfortable it got.

Robert opened and closed the door on the chicken coop making sure it was level.

"Don't you have your own farm to work on?" asked Bill, walking up behind Robert.

"I could ask you the same question, but I'd hate to seem rude to someone who's just tryin' to help out," answered Robert.

"There was nothin' wrong with the chicken coop," Bill huffed.

"Actually," said Robert, "there was a gap under the door that was large enough for a couple of chicks to escape. James asked if I minded fixing it when I got here with Evalyn. He said you'd been really busy with the livestock. I said I was happy to help. It sure beats sitting in the parlor and twiddling my thumbs."

"So I guess y'all are staying for dinner again," said Bill.

"Mrs. Grant has made it clear, we're welcome any time. Regardless of how you feel about the situation, I'm not gonna keep Evalyn away from Quail Crossings, and I'm not going to avoid comin' just because you've got it in your mind that I'm bad for your sister." Robert latched the gate and turned to face Bill. "Are you ever gonna just let me be?"

Bill flicked his hat before turning back to the barn. "Probably not."

Jacob looked at the sky and absorbed the sun. He felt like he had been in that room for a lifetime and was thankful Bill and Elmer had helped him to sit by the pond. He was even more thankful Mrs. Grant had allowed it. He could tell it was against her better judgment. But since his ribs were feeling better, Mr. Murphy had convinced her it would be good for everyone.

Jacob was fairly certain part of her hesitation had to do with him being out in the open where those men and boys could find him again. Jacob had no delusions about how much his being at Quail Crossings put all of them in danger.

But the pond had good tree cover thanks to the orchard, and the only thing he really wanted to do was enjoy the sunshine and work on his reading. Alice had praised him the day before, saying he was a quick study, but he knew he had a ways to go before being able to read on his own. He hoped he'd be around long enough to get the basics, so he could practice after he left Knollwood, Texas, for friendlier pastures.

Jacob pulled out Alice's copy of *Peter Pan* and flipped it to the middle. Using his finger as a guide just like Alice had taught him, he started to say each letter sound out loud, trying to remember everything he had learned the night before.

After a few pages, he set the book on his leg and closed his eyes. He smiled as visions of Wendy and her brothers flying through the sky with Peter Pan on their way to Neverland, entered his mind. A rustle caused his eyes to pop open. As safe as he felt at Quail Crossings, he never felt completely secure.

A sigh of relief escaped as a goose hopped through the bushes. Jacob chuckled to himself. "You must be Miss Alice's Mr. Norman," he said to the goose. "She says you are her bestest friend ever, so nice to meet ya."

Mr. Norman studied Jacob, tilting his head from one side to the other before his gaze dropped to the book that sat on Jacob's lap.

Jacob picked up the book and smiled. "Miss Alice is teaching me to read. I thought I'd come down here and practice."

Mr. Norman narrowed his eyes at the book and hissed.

"It's all right, Mr. Norman. Miss Alice knows I have it," Jacob explained. "She's letting me borrow it."

Mr. Norman waddled toward him, and Jacob had to fight the urge to run. He was propped up against a tree, and there was no place to go even if his ribs would've let him scramble away. Mr. Norman let out a loud hiss before grabbing the book with his beak and waddling away as fast as a goose could waddle with a book. Even as cumbersome as Mr. Norman was, all Jacob could do was watch him go for fear of hurting his ribs.

"Oh, okay, Mr. Norman, I see how things are gonna be," Jacob yelled at the bird. "That book better get back to Miss Alice."

Chapter Nineteen

The yellow yolks of the two raw eggs stared at Lou Anne as if they were just as surprised as she was that she was about to drink them. She swirled them around, trying to dislodge their bulging stare from her memory.

"Come on, Lou Anne," she said to herself. "If you wanna have a baby, you've got to try everything. You eat eggs every morning. This is no different. Just like sunny side up, but a bit sunnier."

With a nod to herself and a pinch of her nose, she tilted the glass up and let the eggs slide into her mouth. The raw eggs sat on her tongue before her stomach revolted, causing Lou Anne to run to the sink and lose the raw eggs along with her dinner from the night before.

Before she knew it, Bill was behind her, his gentle hands on her shoulders as she finished the purge.

"Are you all right, honey?" he asked.

Lou Anne nodded as she grabbed a dishtowel to cover her mouth. "Yes, I'm· fine, Bill. You can see to your chores."

"Are you sure? You don't seem fine. Maybe you should lie down." Bill's brows wrinkled with concern.

"Honestly, Bill, I'm okay," Lou Anne reassured.

"I think I should go get Dovie," said Bill, heading to the door.

"No!" Lou Anne called out. "Bill, don't get Dovie. I don't think I could face her."

Bill rubbed his forehead. "Why exactly?"

Lou Anne sat down and buried her head in her arms. "Because she'd just laugh at me."

"Laugh at you?" Bill sat by his wife. "Lou Anne you're gonna have to help me here. I don't know why Dovie would laugh at your being sick."

She looked at her husband. "Because I made myself sick by drinking raw eggs."

Bill grimaced and then his lips twitched, and Lou Anne could tell he was biting back his own laugh. "See, you're laughing at me."

Bill shook his head. "No, honey, I'm not. But why were you drinking raw eggs?"

"To help me get pregnant." Lou Anne looked at her hands. "It's been five years, Bill. I feel as if I've let you down. I should've had at least two of your children by now."

Bill wrapped his arms around her. "Lou Anne, you haven't let me down at all. We could grow old and grey without a single child and I would still love you just as much, if not more, than I love you today."

"Don't you want children, Bill?" she asked.

"Of course I do," said Bill. "But if it's not meant to be, then I'm okay with that as well. Here's the thing Lou Anne, I think it is in our future. It's just not the right time yet. Trust me, I know better than anyone that God can be kind of pokey about answering prayers, but He always gives us what we need. And what I need is you, no matter what. I'm blessed because He gave me you."

Lou Anne smiled as her heart swelled with love for her husband.

Bill rose. "I would kiss you right now, but ..."

Lou Anne blushed as she raised the towel to her mouth again and shooed him out the door, more determined than ever to have Bill's baby. She cracked two more eggs into the glass and swallowed them in one gulp without a second thought.

"You did what?" Dovie had to sit down. Her head was spinning at the news she had just received from her father.

"I hired Gabe to help Bill and me add onto the barn," said James.

"But why?" Dovie stammered. "And why would he accept? I mean, he has his flight business to tend to."

"His airplane needs a part, and it has to come from south Texas. It'll be almost a month getting here. Until then he needs employment, and I need the help. Besides I like the thought of having him around while Jacob is here," explained James.

"Dad, it is not your job to give every soul work and having Gabe here just might bring more attention to Jacob," said Dovie. "You keep doing this to me. First it was Bill ..."

"Which has brought us nothing but blessings," interrupted James. "Who's to say that hiring Gabe won't be a blessing as well?"

Dovie narrowed her eyes. "Dad, I have only ever loved one man. I made vows to Simon that I'll never forget. I have no intentions of loving another man ever."

"Dovie, honey, I wasn't talking about that," said James. "I was talking about getting the barn up before the summer heat sets in."

Dovie felt color rush to her cheeks as she shot out of her chair and grabbed a broom. "It's not like I can stop you anyway. Do what you want."

"And for the record," said James as he grabbed his hat, "Simon would want you to be happy and find love again. We both know that. You are as stubborn as a mule sometimes, Dovie."

"Well, I come by it honestly," said Dovie as James walked out the back door.

Alice entered the kitchen and set her arithmetic book down. "Mama Dovie, I was wondering if you could help me with my multiplication tables."

Dovie felt her cheeks flush again. She had forgotten Alice was doing her homework in the parlor. She wondered how much Alice had heard. "Of course, Alice, just let me finish up this floor."

Alice fiddled with the edges of her book. "Mama Dovie?"

"Yes," said Dovie, concentrating on her sweeping.

"Are you happy?" asked Alice.

Dovie stopped and looked at the little girl. "Now why on earth would you ask such a question?"

"Well, 'cause your husband is gone, and you won't ever be in love again," Alice said very matter-of-factly. "You just said that to Mr. James."

Dovie swept her dust pile into a corner and then placed the broom over it before sitting across from Alice. "I have you and your siblings. Y'all fill my heart with so much love, that I don't need another husband to make me happy."

"Okay, but we're family now. You have to love us, and I don't think it's the same. Don't you wanna get married again? I've watched Bill and Lou Anne, and that is as mushy as it gets. I know Bill's happier than he's ever been, even though he's had us his entire life. I just want you to be that happy."

Dovie felt her heart drop. She had been lonely since Simon's death, but that was just the life of a young widow. She grabbed Alice's book and changed the subject. "Let's learn these tables shall we?"

Lou Anne carefully placed the two hot peppers she had purchased at the Knollwood Market the day before on a plate. The grocer had insured her they were the hottest he had. She had never cared much for hot peppers, but she was desperate to conceive and would do anything to help the process.

She debated between taking little bites or just taking two large bites of each pepper. Mrs. Pearl had said she only needed to eat one, but Lou Anne wanted to increase her odds by eating two. She swiped up a pepper and took a huge bite, chewing quickly and swallowing fast. She did the same with the second pepper.

"Well, that wasn't so bad," Lou Anne said, but she quickly changed her mind as the fire started in her throat and quickly raced up to her mouth and lips.

Lou Anne started fanning her mouth, but it wasn't helping. She bolted up, causing her chair to fall over, and dashed to the icebox. She grabbed the milk and drank directly out of the glass bottle. She dashed to the sink and poured it over her lips.

"Thirsty?" asked Bill.

Lou Anne let out a groan. The man had horrible timing.

"I was trying a new pepper from the market," said Lou Anne. "I was thinking about canning some peppers in with the stewed tomatoes this year."

"Guess you won't be doing that." Bill raised an eyebrow as Lou Anne wiped off her mouth, lips still tingling from the heat.

"Guess not," she said, as the flames reignited in her mouth. She mentally begged for Bill to leave.

"I guess I'll let you get back to your day." Bill looked at the plate holding two pepper stems and then back to his wife. He headed toward the back door. "You might find a chunk of cheese will help."

"I'm fine," yelled Lou Anne. As soon as she heard the back door slam, she raced back to the icebox and grabbed the cheese.

Chapter Twenty

Tiny licked her ice cream as she walked down the street with Elmer. He had been given a short break from the butcher shop and had offered to buy her a cone to make up for the last time he had passed on buying her a milkshake. It was a bit chilly for April, but Tiny didn't care. In her mind it could never be too cold for ice cream.

She placed her arm through Elmer's, hoping some of his warmth would rub off on her. As they passed the Knollwood Market, the door shot open, ramming into Tiny's elbow and causing her to drop her ice cream.

"Ouch," yelled Tiny.

"You okay?" asked Elmer.

Tiny nodded as Elmer turned to see who had hit Tiny with the door. A boy and a girl just a few years older than Elmer and Tiny ran down the street hand-in-hand and giggling.

"Sorry 'bout that," yelled the boy as they rounded the corner.

Elmer kicked the dirt. "If he were really sorry then he'd buy you another ice cream."

"It's okay, Elm. I was just about done anyway. Besides everyone knows Johnny and Sally are in love, and they don't see no one but themselves," said Tiny, brushing her dress to make sure it was free of ice cream.

"Love is no excuse for being rude," said Elmer, grabbing Tiny's hand. "I don't have enough money for another ice cream, but I could buy you some penny candy if you want."

Tiny shook her head. "No thanks."

Elmer placed Tiny's arm back through his. Tiny bolts of electricity shot through her skin at his touch. She bit her lip. "You know love does funny things to people."

"I reckon," said Elmer as he steered them to the city park swing where they had shared their very first kiss almost six years before.

"Like with Johnny and the door. He's a nice boy and had Sally not been there, he wouldn't have hit me and if he had, he would've apologized immediately," Tiny rationalized.

"More than likely." Elmer agreed as he led Tiny to a swing and then sat on the one next to her.

"I think love is the greatest emotion in the world," said Tiny as she twisted the chains on the swing and then let go so she could twirl back around.

"Some would say it makes a person stupid," said Elmer.

Tiny planted her feet to steady her swing. "How so?"

"Well, take Johnny for example. That was a right awful thing he did with the door. He should've stopped to see if you were okay."

"Don't you think you'll be so wrapped up in love one day that you'll do something stupid?" asked Tiny.

"I sure hope not," said Elmer, digging the toe of his shoe in the dirt.

"What about me?" asked Tiny.

"What about you?" Elmer raised an eyebrow.

"You don't think you'll be so in love with me that one day that you won't see anyone else?"

Elmer shrugged. "Why can't I see you and everyone else?"

Tiny kicked the dirt and let out a growl. "Because, Elmer Brewer, if you love me than I'm supposed to be your whole world!"

"Well that's just silly," said Elmer.

Tiny stood and stomped her foot. "It is not silly. Jeepers, Elm, don't you know anything?"

"I just think it's nonsense to let your whole world revolve around someone else," muttered Elmer.

"Well, I think it's nonsense that I continue to be the girlfriend of a boy who has no idea how to be a boyfriend or what being in love is all about." Tiny popped her hands on her hips.

"I'm sorry you feel that way." Elmer stood. "I've got to get back to work. I'll pick you up for the Spring Dance Saturday at seven."

Tiny crossed her arms. "Well, I ain't going with you anymore. I think I'll just go by myself, I'd have a lot more fun that way than with a person who thinks love is nonsense."

Elmer grimaced. "Well, if that's what you want."

As he started to walk away, Tiny said the one thing she knew would get him to stop. "Or maybe I'll just go with Frank Kelley. I bet he knows all about love."

Elmer did stop, and Tiny flinched when she saw his shoulders slump. It was as if she'd hit him with a cane one too many times, and his spirit just broke.

He glanced over his shoulder. Tiny opened her mouth to apologize, but Elmer spoke first. "I guess if that's what you wanna do, then I can't stop you."

Tiny bit back tears as she watched Elmer walk back toward Main Street. She wanted desperately to tell him she was sorry, but her mouth failed to find the words. She realized what she wanted even more than for him to take her to the dance, was for him to fight for her.

Evalyn dried the last dish and placed it in the cabinet. As she wiped the counters down, she hummed along to the music playing on the radio. She smiled as she heard Robert singing along. He had a very nice voice. In fact, Evalyn loved to sit next to him at church and listen to him sing during the hymns. Very seldom did she sing along now but instead enjoyed listening to Robert's baritone in perfect harmony with the choir.

She had tried to convince him to join the church choir on a number of occasions, but he had always blushed and said they didn't need an old rooster like him messing up the music with his crowing. She wished there was a way for him to hear himself as she and others heard him.

Turning, she expected to see Robert sitting in his chair in the parlor as he read yet another farm report or western novel. He had recently discovered Zane Grey novels and couldn't get enough of them. It seemed like every time she turned around, he had checked out another Grey novel from the town's school library that was also open to the public To Evalyn's surprise he wasn't in his chair.

She followed his voice to her room. As she peeked in, she saw Robert sitting on the bed with Joy on his lap and facing away from her. He was bouncing Joy on his knee as he sang along with Gene Autry's *Back in the Saddle Again*.

Evalyn listened until the song ended and then tiptoed back to the kitchen. She wanted Robert to have his moment with Joy. Even more than that, she wanted Joy to have her moment with her daddy. He really was the best kind of father, and Joy wasn't the only lucky one to have him around.

Lou Anne pulled the covers over her body. "Bill, I think I hear something outside."

Bill lay on the bed, eyes closed, barely conscious after their marital relations. "I'm sure it's just a raccoon."

"Go outside and check," she said. "Now."

Bill opened one eye at her. "Do I look like I'm going anywhere?"

"Please, Bill," she whined, it could be one of those boys looking for Jacob. They might set the house on fire."

Bill sighed. "Fine. I'll go check."

As soon as he was out the door, Lou Anne hurried to the wall, and put her head and hands down before throwing her legs up and standing on her head.

"Lou Anne Brewer!"

Lou Anne let out a small scream before her knees crashed to the ground. Bill hurried and picked her up.

"Did you see anything outside?" she asked, hoping to change the subject.

"You and I both know there was nothing out there." They got up and sat on the edge of the bed. "Now tell me what's going on with you. Just today I've seen you drink raw eggs, eat hot peppers, and that steak you had for dinner was so rare it was mooing at me. We have a great night together in bed and then you force me to go look for imaginary intruders. I come back in to find you standing on your head."

Lou Anne burst into tears. "You wouldn't understand."

Bill wrapped his arms around her. "Try me."

"Everything I have done today has been to help me get with child," confessed Lou Anne. "It's all stuff Mrs. Pearl told me to do."

"Lou Anne, sweetie, I appreciate all you're trying to do to help, but there is only one way to get with child."

He kissed her gently on the lips before moving down to her neck. Lou Anne scooted back on the bed as he followed, covering her in sweet kisses. As she surrendered to his embraces, Lou Anne couldn't help but smile. This was the best thing she had tried all day.

Chapter Twenty-one

The morning had been hard on Robert. A bunch of hogs got in a tussle and broke part of the fence, causing him to have to chase pigs all over the yard, and then a sow refused to let her runt suckle. Farm sense told him to put the runt down since the little pig would hardly be worth anything at the market come next spring, but he couldn't force himself to do it.

He had put down animals before, but they had all been sick or too injured to mend and it had been in the animal's best interest. He had also sent animals to market, but that was putting food in hard working people's bellies. He could not think of one good reason to put the little piglet down other than the time it was going to take to bottle feed it.

As lunchtime approached, he hoped he had his speech ready enough to convince Evalyn to help hand-feed the little piglet. It wasn't going to be an easy sell as she had made it very clear where she stood on helping out with the pigs.

His stomach growled and his mouth watered at the thought of the leftover meatloaf sandwiches Evalyn would have ready for him on the table. He didn't know much about his wife, but he did know she could cook.

Entering the back door, he stopped. The house felt eerily quiet and the dining table stood empty. Robert wondered if Evalyn had laid Joy down for an early nap. Even if that was the case, where was Evalyn?

His heart began to race as he feared the worse. Evalyn had never fallen down on her duties, so chances were good that she was hurt somewhere and that little Joy could be with her.

"Ev ...," Robert rounded the corner and swallowed the rest of her name as Evalyn lay sound asleep on the sofa. She had been working night and day making Rockwood back into the home it once was. She'd done everything from scrubbing the floors to making new curtains, and with Joy in the mix, Evalyn, without a doubt, put in more hours of work in the house than he did on the farm.

He stared at his wife. She looked so young, yet had the radiance that came from being a mother. There was no denying that she was beautiful. He had thought so on the bus as well, when he first saw her, but something was different now. He was learning that her beauty wasn't just in her looks.

A squeak came from the bedroom, and Robert knew Joy was awake and probably ready for lunch as well. His first instinct was to wake up Evalyn and let her take care of Joy, but he stopped himself. He was Joy's father now, in every way that mattered, which made her his responsibility as well.

Leaving Evalyn to her nap, he quietly walked into the room. Joy sat on her little mattress and giggled at him as he entered. His heart instantly jumped with delight. Joy giggled again, this time a little louder.

"Shhh, little Joy, we don't wanna wake up your momma." He picked the baby up, and she instantly grabbed both his cheeks and went in for a big sloppy baby kiss. Robert propped her on his hip and gave her a little kiss back on the nose. "Aren't you just the sweetest?"

He tried to make his face serious but found it hard with Joy's toothless grin beaming up at him. "Your momma is asleep in the parlor, so I'm gonna make us some leftover meatloaf. Sound good?"

Joy giggled.

Robert gave her a nod. "I'm taking that as a yes. Now, be quiet so we can let her sleep, she's worked really hard."

Robert took Joy out of the room and stopped just long enough in the kitchen to grab the leftover meatloaf from the icebox and a fork, before taking Joy out back. His meatloaf almost slid off the plate as he tried to shut the door softly while juggling their lunch and Joy.

"I don't know how your momma does it," he said, sitting on the back step and propping Joy on his lap.

He mashed part of the meatloaf into a mush before feeding it to Joy, and then took a big bite of the unmashed portion. It didn't take long for their bellies to fill and the plate to be empty.

"Robert," came Evalyn's voice from the screen door, "please tell me Joy is with you."

"She's right here," said Robert, glancing over his shoulder.

Evalyn came out and sat beside Robert. "I only meant to lie down for a minute. You two must be starving."

Robert pointed to the empty plate that sat between his feet. "Nah, I took care of it."

Evalyn reached for Joy who gladly reached back at the sight of her momma. "Well, let's get this little one fed then."

"That's taken care of as well," said Robert.

"What did you feed her?" asked Evalyn, looking for a bottle.

Robert again pointed to the plate at his feet. "Meatloaf."

Evalyn gasped. "You fed her meatloaf?"

Robert shrugged. "She seemed to like it. I made sure to smash it down really good before giving it to her."

"Well," Evalyn's mouth dropped open. "I … uh …" She blushed. "Thanks."

"Don't thank me yet," said Robert. "I need your help."

"Oh no," said Evalyn. "I already told you that I want nothing to do with the swine."

"What if I told you the swine was a little piglet runt whose mother won't feed her, so we need to either bottle feed her or put her down? And right now I don't have time to bottle feed her."

"I'd say you aren't playing fair," Evalyn teased, then sighed. "Fine, I'll feed the runt. But that's it. I have enough to do around here to keep me busy for a hundred years."

Robert stood and smiled at her. "Well, it's nice to know you'll be around that long."

Lou Anne lingered just outside the soda shop in the back of Johnson's Drug and watched the woman formally known as Charlotte Wheaton as she devoured a banana split while her ever-patient husband, Peter Williams, looked on.

Lou Anne lightly laughed when she thought about all the trouble Charlotte had put her through when Bill first moved to town. Charlotte had it in her mind that Bill was going to marry her and not Lou Anne. But Lou Anne and Bill's connection and love had been instant and even the beautiful Charlotte Wheaton couldn't beat that.

Lou Anne glanced over the rows of nail polish and took in her former rival. Poor Charlotte already had three children and now was carrying Peter's fourth without so much as a whisper between them. The pregnancies had not been kind to Charlotte, and she now held an additional seventy pounds on her once slender frame.

As Charlotte finished her banana split, Lou Anne inched forward. She would gladly gain a hundred pounds if it meant having a baby. If what Mrs. Pearl said was right, all Lou Anne needed to do was sit down on the very spot where Charlotte now sat. It was going to be tricky getting into the booth without Charlotte noticing her, but Lou Anne was willing to take the risk. Besides it had to beat drinking down raw eggs. Lou Anne gagged a little at the thought.

As Charlotte and Peter exited toward the cash register, Lou Anne slipped into the soda shop from the other side of the store and slid into their former booth. She wondered if it mattered that her dress lay between the seat and herself.

"Here, just let me clean that off for ya," said a voice, making Lou Anne jump. "What can I get you?" asked Mark, the man who ran the shop.

"I think I'll just have a root beer today, Mark," said Lou Anne.

Mark gave her a quick nod, but as he left to get her root beer, Charlotte appeared out of nowhere and loomed over Lou Anne.

"Oh, hi, Charlotte," said Lou Anne, hating the way her voice made it sound like she was doing something wrong.

"Well, Lou Anne, I haven't seen you in ages," said Charlotte, her voice dripping with sweet sarcasm. "What are you doing in here all by your little lonesome? Bill too busy for you? It must be nice to be able to enjoy an afternoon alone. I bet you can do just about anything you want, being that you don't have any children."

The words punched Lou Anne in the gut like a prize fighter. She fought the urge to bow her head, instead rising to meet Charlotte. "Oh, do sit down, Charlotte, your legs must get awfully tired carrying all that weight." She paused, letting Charlotte absorb her true meaning before adding. "You know the weight of taking care of all those children, with another on the way."

Lou Anne instantly hated herself for stooping that low, but Charlotte had hit a nerve that caused Lou Anne to forget all being nice.

"I told Bill he'd regret marrying you," snapped Charlotte.

"I assure you I do not," said Bill as he came up behind the ladies. Lou Anne felt her heart soar.

Bill walked over and gave Lou Anne a peck on the cheek. Peter also joined the ladies.

"Bill, I didn't know you were in town," said Lou Anne as he wrapped his arm around her.

"Dovie, told me you had come in to mail a package and were staying to pick up Alice from school," explained Bill. "I rode in with James in the hope that I could catch you and take you to lunch. Have you ordered?" He pointed to the soda bar.

"Just root beer," said Lou Anne.

"Let's see if Mark will get us a couple of bowls of ham and beans," said Bill. "I could smell it down the block, and it smells so good."

"I think we'll join you," said Charlotte.

"Charlotte, we just had lunch and you followed it with a banana split. You can't possibly be hungry again," said Peter. "Besides, we've got to pick up the kids from my ma's house. I'm sure the boys are driving her crazy by now." Peter smiled with pride. "My boys sure do have some energy. I swear they'd give a roadrunner a run for his money."

Charlotte sighed. "Fine, I guess we'll do it some other time."

"Do take care, Charlotte," said Lou Anne sweetly. "Have fun with all those boys."

Lou Anne felt guilty again as Charlotte's face went from smug to sad before she walked out with Peter.

"That girl will never change," said Bill, sitting down.

Lou Anne sank into the booth across from him. "I shouldn't have said what I said."

"About what?" asked Bill, grabbing his wife's hand.

"She was just being herself, and I fell for it and then acted as ugly as she does," confessed Lou Anne. "I used to not let her get to me."

"Does this have anything to do with what we talked about the other night?" asked Bill.

"Kind of," said Lou Anne. "She, in her own Charlotte way, was rubbing it in that we don't have kids yet, and she has given Peter three boys. I guess it got to me because I've been so upset about us not having children yet."

Bill laughed. "Charlotte has three boys that she has absolutely no control over. They run her ragged, and if she has another boy, the fourth one will probably do the same. I'd bet the farm that she's jealous of you."

"Of me?" Lou Anne waved Bill away. "Doubtful."

"Of course she is." Bill winked and gave her an ornery grin. "If for no other reason than that you've got me."

"Well, that does make me the lucky one." Lou Anne smiled, squeezing Bill's hand. "Let's order, shall we. I'm starving."

Chapter Twenty-two

Robert walked through Johnson's Drug Store hoping to find the sequel to Zane Grey's *Knights on the Range*, *Twin Sombreros*. It was too new to be at the library yet, and Robert just had to see what was going to happen next. He had to stop himself from jumping in delight when he found the store had one copy of *Twin Sombreros*.

He leaned against the half wall that separated the merchandise section from the food section of the drug store.

"Can you believe that Evalyn Brewer is back in town?"

The sound of his wife's name caught his attention, and he couldn't help but listen to the two girls, roughly Evalyn's age, who sat in a booth directly behind him.

"I thought she was going to be a Hollywood actress," said the other girl. "Instead she comes home with a husband and baby, so much for being a film star."

"You know, it serves her right to come back here no more famous than the rest of us. She always acted like she was above everyone in our class. She and Harriett Wheaton were the biggest snobs."

"Well, we both know she'll never amount to anything now. I feel so sorry for the kid. Can you imagine having a mother like that?" The girls giggled.

Robert walked around and faced the girls. "I'll have you know my wife is the most generous, kind, and loving mother around. You two ought to consider growing up a spell before talking about things you know nothing about."

Robert felt a hand on his shoulder and turned to see Bill standing there.

"I was just coming over here to say that exact same thing," said Bill. "I'm sorry about the way I've been treating you. It seems you're just the kind of man Evalyn needs and deserves."

Bill thrust out his hand. Robert shook it immediately. "I promise to always try to be."

Dovie squinted from all the dust in the air as she cleaned the cobwebs out of the corners of the well-house with a broom. She knew more spiders would come and start spinning their webs, but she hoped that by destroying their hard work, they would soon find other places to dwell. She wasn't one to get all riled up about bugs, but spiders were a different story. She hated the eight-legged critters more than snakes, bees, and scorpions combined.

Setting the broom down, she surveyed her work, checking each corner. In the final corner, she spotted it. The one creature that made her body shiver with terror: the poisonous black widow spider. Even in the dim light of the damp well house, she could see the famous red hourglass on the black spider's abdomen.

Dovie's body froze in fright, her eyes reluctant to blink, in case she lost sight of the vile creature. Sweat beaded along her forehead as her breath quickened. She stepped back slowly, only to hear a loud hiss behind her.

"Not now, Norman," she said softly, as if not to spook the black widow. "I need to get out of here."

Norman hissed louder and cast a shadow has he raised his wings, making the spider hard to see. Panic raced through Dovie's veins as she refused to take her eyes off the spot where she had seen the black widow. She continued to back up slowly. "Norman, please don't do this. Get out of my way."

Dovie caught a shadow of movement before full flight mode kicked in.

"I've got to get out of here!" she screamed as she barreled right over Norman and fell directly into Gabe's arms.

"Are you okay?" he asked, helping her to her feet as Norman hissed at them both before waddling toward the pond. "Did that goose hurt you?"

"Norman's nothing but a barking dog with no teeth." Dovie shook her head as her cheeks glowed red. "There's a black widow in the well house. I was trying to run away from it when Norman got in my way."

Gabe nodded and tried to swallow his smile. "I think you're safe now."

Dovie covered her face with her hand. "Oh, I must sound more ridiculous than a rooster crowing at the moon."

Gabe smiled. "Not at all, it's nice to see the fearless Dovie Grant has a chink in her armor."

"It's so silly to be afraid of a little spider," said Dovie, now hiding her own smile behind her hand.

"You wanna know a secret?" asked Gabe. "I hate lizards. They give me the creeps."

Dovie laughed. "Lizards? Really?"

"Anything that can run that fast isn't natural," he said, "and they're bigger than spiders." He gave her a wink, causing her face to feel hot again.

"Being that spiders are little is part of the problem," said Dovie, trying to take her mind off the wink. "They're fast, and you never know where those little boogers are hiding. Plus, most lizards won't kill you with a single bite." A sly smile crossed her face. "Speaking of which, do you think you can take care of the black widow in there?"

Gabe faked a look of shock. "You mean you want me to risk my life to defend your well house from the vicious spider?" The shock turned to a grin as he grabbed her hand and planted a soft kiss on the back of it. "For you, my lady, anything."

With that he entered the well house, leaving Dovie tingling all over.

Alice laid down the primary reader and looked at Jacob as they sat at the kitchen table. "Your reading is getting really good, Jacob."

"Thanks to you, Miss Alice," said Jacob. "I never thought I'd be able to read. In most places it's against the law to teach us colored folk."

"Jacob," said Alice, while fingering the end of the primer, "can I ask you 'bout your life before you came here? I mean, you've been on your own for a long time."

Jacob nodded. "Yeah, I've got lots of brothers and sisters, and it was time I made a life of my own, so my ma wouldn't have so many mouths to feed. She didn't like that I was leaving, but I know she was having a hard time making ends meet. I send her money when I can, but I guess I don't make enough to share most of the time."

"Where did you go first?" asked Alice. "You know when you first left home."

"I went to Atlanta, trying to find work. I made a few dollars here and there, but there's not a lot of work for a colored boy. So I decided I'd start walking west until I found a farm that would hire me."

Alice bowed her head. "Have you ever run into problems like here in Knollwood?"

Jacob sighed. "Yeah, Knollwood ain't any different than a lot of small southern towns. My friend, Red, and I were in a small town in Louisiana. We thought if we could make it to New Orleans, we could find some work. Wouldn't yam know it? We ran right into a group of white men who were looking for trouble. They sent hound dogs after us." Jacob bared his teeth. "They were the meanest dang dogs I'd ever saw. Red and I, we ran for our lives, ended up jumping in the swamp and then climbing some trees so they'd lose our scent. That was a scary night. But Red and I had a good laugh about it a couple of days later."

"What happened to Red?" asked Alice. "Why isn't he with you now?"

Jacob frowned. "Poor Red wasn't so lucky when we ran into a group of the same type over in Oklahoma a few months ago."

"Dogs got him?" Alice gasped.

Jacob shook his head and looked in the corner. "It was far worse than that, Miss Alice, but I'd rather not speak of such things."

Chapter Twenty-three

Dovie watched Elmer out of the corner of her eye as he sat on the sofa. There was no doubt about it, the boy was brooding. Normally, the thought of Elmer brooding wouldn't have crossed her mind. He wasn't the brooding type, but she was certain Elmer had something on his mind and that he didn't like it.

The family had gathered around the table at Quail Crossings for dinner. Even with Evalyn, Robert, and Joy not joining them, it was a tight fit. Soon they'd have to get a bigger table. Everyone was knocking elbows as it was.

"Elm, you coming?" asked Dovie, scooting her chair to the side to give him some room to sit.

Elmer picked himself up like he weighed a thousand pounds and ambled to the dinner table. Everyone sat and James said a quick prayer before the plates started being filled.

"You doing okay, Elm?" asked Dovie, passing the potatoes.

Elmer nodded.

"I thought you were going to the dance tonight with Tiny," said Bill. "I was surprised to still see you here after we brought the cattle in."

"Tiny decided she didn't wanna go with me," Elm said, stabbing a slice of roast beef a little harder than necessary.

Dovie raised an eyebrow. "Why on Earth would she do that? You two have been tied by the toes for years."

Elmer's face turned red as he shook his head and shrugged.

Dovie gave Bill a little kick to his ankle.

"Ow, what did I do?" asked Bill, eyes wide.

Dovie glared at Bill and then jerked her head in Elmer's direction. Bill took a hard swallow of his potatoes as he realized what Dovie wanted him to do.

"You could just go alone," said Bill, receiving a second kick under the table, this time from Lou Anne. "Ow, I mean you could meet Tiny there. Maybe she's changed her mind."

Bill looked from Dovie and then to his wife, waiting to see if he was going to get kicked again.

"Nah," said Elmer. "I don't understand what she wants from me. I'll probably just end up making her madder."

"So she's mad at you?" asked Dovie, trying to sound nonchalant.

Elmer nodded. "Guess so, said she'd rather go to the dance with Frank Kelley."

The entire table halted their dinners. Then they all spoke at once.

"Well, we can't have that," said James, putting his fork down, supper forgotten.

"Why would she want to go with Frank Kelley instead of you? That's like trading a steak for a piece of liver," said Dovie.

"That Frank Kelley doesn't deserve Tiny," said Alice. "Elm, you gotta go get her. She's being dumb."

"She made herself clear," said Elmer, bringing everyone to silence.

"Then we'll just have to change her mind," said Bill, standing. "Go upstairs and get on your Sunday clothes. You're going to that dance."

"No, I ain't," said Elmer. "I'm not gonna watch my girl dance with Frank Kelley all night."

"You're right; you're not," said Bill. "You're gonna get Tiny back."

The family all looked up at Bill, mouths open. He cleared his throat. "Remember that hoedown when I had to watch Lou Anne dance with all the other boys because Charlotte was goading her? That was sheer torture. I waited too long before letting Lou Anne know that she was the girl for me and wasted too much time trying to do what I thought was the right thing." He shook his head. "No, you're not gonna repeat my mistakes. I'm taking you to that dance, so you can tell Tiny how you feel. If she still doesn't want you to be there, then we'll leave and none of us will say another word about it. But Elm, you've gotta try."

Bill looked down at Lou Anne and smiled. "I wish I would've tried sooner."

Elmer pulled his napkin off his neck. "Okay, let's do this."

Less than an hour later, Bill and Elmer sat in front of the school.

"Now listen," said Bill. "You just go in there and tell her how you feel. Don't worry about Frank Kelley or what anyone else might say about it. I'll be right in the doorway. If it goes south, we'll leave. If Frank Kelley gives you any grief, I'll hang him by his collar on a coat hook in the hallway. Lord knows, that's less than he deserves."

"I don't know about this," said Elmer, eyeing the school. "I don't know what to say. She could laugh right in my face."

"This is Tiny we're talking about," said Bill. "Don't let some jerk like Frank Kelley stand in the way of what y'all have had for the past five years."

Elmer didn't move.

"Do you wanna do this?" asked Bill softly.

Elmer shrugged. "I like Tiny, but why should I fight for her when she's the one who said she was gonna go with Frank Kelley? She knows how I feel about him."

"Love makes people do stupid things," said Bill. "Sometimes it makes things come out of our mouths that we really don't mean. Do you know for sure she was going with Frank Kelley?"

Elmer shook his head and then rested it on the pickup window. "I guess I don't. She was mad at me when she said it."

"So go in and see what's going on," said Bill. "You'll always regret it if you don't."

Sitting up, Elmer nodded. "You're right. She might not even be in there with him."

Elmer opened the door, and Bill reached for his own handle.

"It's okay, Bill," said Elmer. "I'll go in alone. Just wait here, will ya?"

Bill nodded and removed his hand from the door. "I'm not going anywhere."

Elmer closed the pickup door and walked slowly to the school. The spring air was still crisp so the dance was being held in the gymnasium instead of the outside dance square. As he entered the school, Elmer straightened his shirt and ran his hands through his hair. He had known Tiny since they had moved to Knollwood, and never in all that time had he been so nervous to see her.

Making his way through the gym doors, he slid past a few wallflowers and scanned the dance floor. His mouth ran dry and his lungs lost air as he saw Tiny dancing with Frank Kelley to a slow country waltz.

Her eyes met his and her mouth dropped open in surprise. Elmer shook his head as he turned and left the dance. He had just reached the outside doors when he heard her running up behind him.

"Wait, Elm, it's not what you think," said Tiny. "I was only dancing with him because …"

Elmer held up his hand. "It's okay, Tiny. I had my chance, and I blew it."

With that he leaned on the door and slid out into the dark night, ignoring Tiny's calls to come back.

Bill started the truck without a word as Elmer slid in beside him. Just as Bill was about to back out of his parking spot, Tiny hit the hood of the truck with her hands.

"Now, Elmer Brewer, you come out here and let me finish what I was saying," said Tiny, glaring through the windshield and daring Bill to keep driving.

Bill immediately turned off the truck and looked at his brother. "I'll go for a walk. I think you had better hear her out."

Bill hopped out of the truck, letting Tiny slide into the driver's seat.

"You don't need to explain," said Elmer. "It's ain't your fault. I already said I messed up."

"You're darn right you did," said Tiny, before sighing. "Jeepers, Elm, I didn't think you were gonna come tonight, especially after our disagreement the other day."

"That doesn't mean you had to come to the dance with Frank Kelley." Elmer folded his arms.

Tiny's face softened. "I shouldn't have said what I said about going to the dance with Frank. I only said it because I knew it would make you upset. I never meant it." She bit her lip. "I didn't come to the dance with him and I was only dancing with him because of Jacob."

Elmer cocked his head at Tiny, and she held up her hands. "Elm, please just let me explain."

With a nod from Elm, Tiny continued, "Suzie got dumped by Barry this morning at school. Then Daisy, Suzie's cousin, told Suzie that I had been dumped by you. I didn't tell Daisy that. My sister Ruthie did when Daisy came over to buy some of my ma's goat soap. But you know how Suzie is, she came barreling over and said we were going to the dance with each other 'cause boys were stupid. She didn't want to stay home and mope around over Barry, and I didn't want to stay home and mope about you. Not that she would've let me anyway."

"I don't see what this has to do with dancing with Frank," said Elmer, crossing his arms.

"I'm getting there," said Tiny. "So we came to the dance. I wasn't gonna come, honestly, Elm. I felt awful about our fight. But Suzie had a point. Anyway we got here, and I overheard Frank's buddy Paul talkin' about Jacob. They know he's still in town somewhere and they're planning something real bad, Elm. Frank is convinced that Jacob is at Quail Crossings, and I was afraid that all of you were in danger, so I decided to dance with Frank and try to convince him that Jacob was gone."

"Did it work?" asked Elmer, sitting a little taller. "Does he think Jacob's gone?"

Tiny shook her head. "I never got that far. I saw you come in and then when you rushed out after seeing me dancing with him, so I rushed out after you." Tiny inched closer. "You do believe me, don't you, Elm?"

Elmer nodded.

"Are we okay?" asked Tiny. "I mean as friends?"

"No," said Elmer.

Tiny's face fell, and Elmer could see her bottom lip start to quiver. He pulled her close, wrapping her up in a hug. "We are better than okay and much more than friends."

She looked up at him, cheeks wet from stray tears. Elmer wiped the wetness from her face. "I'm sorry I ever made you cry or not feel special, Mary. I promise to do my best to never be the reason for your tears again."

She lifted her chin, enjoying the way her given name sounded in Elmer's voice, and smiled right before he placed a gentle kiss on her lips.

Chapter Twenty-four

"Lou Anne," said Dovie, sliding out of the truck at Bill's house. "Why didn't we just walk over? I'm not an old woman yet. You didn't need to drive me a mile to look at fabric samples."

Lou Anne shrugged. "I'd hoped you'd help me with some patterns, and I wasn't sure how long that would take, so this way I can get you home safe if it's after dark."

Dovie placed her hands on her hips. "I've been walking this property longer than you've been alive. I can walk it blindfolded if I have to. What's going on?"

"Nothing," said Lou Anne, "like I said, I just need help picking out fabric for some new bedding."

"And it has nothing to do with the fact that Bill and Gabe are walking over here right now?" asked Dovie, tapping her foot. "You're up to something, Lou Anne Brewer."

Lou Anne hurried over to Dovie. "It wasn't my idea but please just go with it, or you'll really hurt Alice's feelings."

"Go with what?" asked Dovie, but Lou Anne didn't have time to answer as Bill and Gabe walked up.

Bill looked at Lou Anne. "I've done my part." He then turned to Gabe before starting back toward Quail Crossings. "I hope you understand I had no choice. The wife said I had to."

"Wait," said Gabe, "you mean we aren't fixing a jammed door?"

"Nope," Bill hollered back without turning around.

Gabe looked at Dovie. "What's going on?"

"Never mind him," said Lou Anne before Dovie could speak. "Let's go in the house."

Gabe and Dovie followed Lou Anne inside her house and were instantly greeted by Alice. "Welcome to Alice's Fancy Restaurant, may I take your hat sir?"

Gabe shrugged and handed his hat to Alice, who promptly placed it on the coat rack that stood next to Gabe.

"I have your table ready, right this way," said Alice.

"Our table?" Dovie grabbed Alice's hand. "What's going on here, young lady?"

"Mama Dovie, you're ruining the mood," Alice whispered.

"I'm gonna ruin your behind if you don't start talkin'," said Dovie.

Alice sighed. "I wanted to do somethin' nice for you and Mr. Pearce, so I had Evie and Lou Anne make you dinner, and I'm gonna wait on you."

Gabe leaned in close to Dovie. "I think we're on a date."

Alice's smile confirmed his suspicions.

Dovie dropped Alice's hand. "Well, I never ... Alice Brewer, you know better than to meddle in other people's affairs."

"So what's on the menu, madam?" asked Gabe without a trace of sarcasm.

Alice made her face very serious. "Tonight, sir, we have a lovely selection of fried catfish pulled fresh from the pond just today by our resident fisherman, Jacob Henry. We've put that with a mix of wild greens, hushpuppies, and pickled beets."

"Pickled beets, you say?" asked Gabe.

"They're my favorite." Alice nodded, dropping out of character.

Gabe turned to Dovie and offered his arm. "Shall we?"

Dovie glanced around the room. Gabe was being such a good sport, and she could see Alice's face grow sadder with each passing moment. The smell of fried catfish wafted into the room, and Dovie's mind was made up. She could never turn down fried catfish, much less hushpuppies.

She placed her arm on Gabe's. "Well I don't see any harm in it, I guess."

Evalyn and Lou Anne had moved the small kitchen table into the parlor. The drapes had been closed and lighted candles littered the room. Dovie had to give them credit. The room felt as if it had dropped straight out of one of the dime romance novels she secretly bought at Johnson's Drug. Her mood instantly warmed with the ambiance.

Gabe walked her to a chair as Alice pulled it out for her.

"Alice, where did you learn to be a fancy restaurant worker?" asked Dovie.

"Evie told me," answered Alice. "She and Harriet had dinner at one once in California." Alice pulled the cloth napkin off the table and laid it gently in Dovie's lap as Lou Anne came in with two goblets of red wine.

"Lou Anne, is this your sand plum wine?" asked Dovie before looking at Gabe. "It is the best in the county. Every time I have a glass, my tongue gets looser than a singing canary."

Lou Anne winked at Dovie. "That is the point."

Evalyn soon followed with two plates overflowing with the described special of the night. She placed them in front of Dovie and Gabe before scooting Alice and Lou Anne out of the room. Dovie had no doubt they would be watching from the doorway, but she didn't care.

She leaned over her plate of food, closed her eyes, and inhaled the rich aroma. Thinking how silly she must look, she opened her eyes in time to see Gabe doing the very same thing.

"This smells better than anything I've ever eaten in a fancy restaurant," said Gabe.

Dovie picked up her fork. "I don't get to make fried catfish often. My dad doesn't care for it or the way it makes the house smell. This is indeed a treat."

"As is the company," said Gabe, taking a big bite.

Dovie shooed him away. "It's okay, Gabe, you don't have keep playin' along."

Gabe raised an eyebrow. "Who says I'm playing? I do enjoy your company, Dovie, very much."

Dovie felt her cheeks flush and hurried to change the subject. "I can't imagine flying in an airplane, just bein' able to go anywhere. Where's the furthest you've flown to?"

"I had to fly to Mexico once," said Gabe. "An oil man was looking for new locations to drill, but all he found was tumbleweeds and dust."

"You could've said the same about Quail Crossings a few years back," said Dovie.

"I was thankful to be in the Air Corps during the Depression," said Gabe. "Lots of men my age weren't lucky enough to have a job, much less be able to do something they loved to do. The Corps gave me food and lodging and by the end of it all, I had enough saved up to buy my own plane."

"As far as the Great Depression goes, we had it mild compared to most," said Dovie. "At least our bank never closed. We lost a lot of livestock but got by. I was able to put food on the table every night. Most couldn't even do that. We helped where we could, and I am glad we were able to do that."

"Including taking in four hungry kids," said Gabe. "You and your dad are saints."

Dovie shrugged. "I'm no saint. I was downright angry with Dad when he brought those kids into our home."

She looked up and smiled at Alice who was peeking around the corner. She remembered the skinny six year old who had stood on her back stoop with a bouquet of flowers straight out of her own flowerbed in her tiny hand. She was nothing but skin and bones, her flour sack dress hanging like it was three sizes too big.

Even if Alice hadn't resembled Helen so much, there was no way Dovie could have turned them away. She wondered if Helen would look like Alice did now, or if her hair would have darkened to be more the color of Dovie's. She thought about what Helen's life would be like if she had lived. Would she still love reading under the big cottonwood tree by the pond or climbing the apple trees in the orchard?

Dovie cleared her throat to chase away the thoughts and quickly added. "But I'm really glad he did and that we could help them. I can't imagine my life without them."

"Your mind went some place just now," said Gabe. "Do you mind if I ask where?"

"I was thinking of my daughter, Helen, and how she'd be today if she were …," Dovie answered honestly before shaking her head. "I'm sorry; I'm not trying to burden you. Sometimes she just shows up in my mind, but we should talk about happier things."

"Talking about your daughter doesn't burden me." Gabe reached over and held Dovie's hand. "And even if it does, I've got some pretty strong shoulders."

"I don't see why they couldn't have sent over some catfish for us," said Bill, shuffling cards around in his gin rummy hand, as they sat around the kitchen table at Quail Crossings. "I mean, there ain't nothing wrong with leftover roast, but it's not catfish."

"Because catfish smells up the house and tastes just as bad," said James, discarding a card. "They taste like mud."

"Then you haven't tried Evalyn's catfish," said Robert, picking up James' discarded card. "Nothing that girl cooks tastes like mud."

"That we can both agree on," said Bill.

Robert glanced over at Joy who lay napping in a makeshift crib in the parlor. "Speaking of Evalyn, just what is it they're doing over there?"

"Playing matchmaker," said Bill, "Trust me. It's best to stay out of it."

"Elm, would you turn up the radio," hollered James. "The nightly news is fixin' to come on."

"So what do you think's gonna happen in Europe?" asked Bill.

Robert shook his head. "It doesn't sound good. The Nazis are invading all over the place. I can't believe they invaded France."

Bill nodded. "Some fellas at the feed store don't think Holland is gonna last too long. Something has to be done. The Germans have to be stopped."

"Not much we can do about it way over here," said Robert. "We're still fixing our own messes after the Depression."

"That's just it," said Bill, "I think we should get involved. It's obvious the British need our help and our men still need jobs."

"I think Mr. Churchill will sort it all out," said Robert. "No need for us to get in the middle of it. It's not our fight, and President Roosevelt has plenty of programs in place to help men find jobs."

"So you're telling me," Bill pointed his cards at Robert, "if you're walkin' down the street, minding your business, and you see a bunch a fellas beating up on a guy, you're just gonna keep walkin'?"

"Of course not," said Robert, running his hand through his hair, "but if the U.S. goes to war, that means you and I go to war. That means leaving behind our families with a big possibility that we'll never come I just found my family, and I ain't interested in leaving them any time soon."

Bill's mouth dropped open. "It's about doing what's right. Of course, it won't be easy to leave our families. I don't wanna leave Lou Anne, but it's our duty as Americans to help out."

"Sometimes those little guys will surprise you," said Robert.

"Well, if the U.S. joins this war, I'll be the first in line to sign up for the Army," said Bill. "It'll be hard, but we can't let Hitler win this one. Besides, who's to say he'll stop once he gets done with Europe. Next thing we know he'll be on U.S. soil."

"Let's hope it never comes down to that," said James, finally interrupting the younger men's debate. "The horrors of war are something that men can't forget. I was lucky to make it out of World War I, not only alive, but without injury. Most of my friends weren't so lucky. Many died in my arms, handing me bloody letters to send back to their families."

James' eyes glossed over as he remembered. "When I enlisted I thought I'd be brave because of my faith. If I died, I had no doubt that Heaven awaited me. But, you better believe, I prayed every moment of every day until I got home that I would see my family again. That's the thing about being in battle, we were all prayin', but many of those prayers went unanswered. I'm very thankful mine were answered."

Chapter Twenty-five

Evalyn fussed with the ribbon, trying to get it to stay on Joy's head, but the soft baby hairs had other ideas for Easter Sunday. They would blow wild and free, and no ribbon would be able to stay put in their silky strands without a good helping of glue. Evalyn had considered using a dab of glue on Joy's head to keep the bow in place and quickly dismissed the thought as she pictured Joy pulling out the bow, glue and all, along with a good portion of her fine brown hair.

"Y'all about ready," Robert called out. "We better leave soon, or we won't have a place to sit. You know how crowded Easter Sunday gets."

"Just about," Evalyn hollered back. She knew Robert was right. There were two types of Christians in Knollwood, those who went to church every Sunday like Robert and her and those who only came on Christmas and Easter.

She buttoned the last button on the Easter gown she had made for Joy, just in time for Joy to spit up all over both of their Easter dresses.

"Oh no," whined Evalyn.

Robert hurried into the room. "What's wrong?"

"Joy just spit up all over our new clothes." Evalyn stood, displaying the spit up down the front of her dress.

Robert grabbed Joy. "She doesn't look too bad. I'll get her cleaned up while you change."

"Now I don't have anything to wear," said Evalyn rushing to the sink, trying to get the spit up off her new clothes.

"Why don't you wear the dress you wore to our wedding?" Robert asked, following her to the sink with Joy.

"You don't wear a wedding dress to Easter Sunday and even if I wanted to, I couldn't because I threw it away," Evalyn confessed.

Robert stopped dabbing at Joy's dress and cocked his head at Evalyn. "You threw it away?"

Evalyn nodded. "Yes, it reminded me of things I didn't want to remember."

Robert still looked confused, but went back to cleaning up Joy. "You mean our wedding day?"

Evalyn's face fell as she thought about how she sounded to him. She put a gentle hand on his arm. "Robert, I'm sorry, that wasn't what I meant at all."

Robert shook his head, his face sad. "It doesn't matter. Go get changed. We'll wait for you here."

As much as Evalyn wanted to explain further she knew they had to leave. With a promise to herself to clear the air with Robert after services, she rushed to change.

The boys had moved Dovie's kitchen table into the backyard for Easter dinner. It was a beautiful day, and they were going to take full advantage of the lovely spring weather. They all clapped as Dovie brought out a large ham, followed by Evalyn, Lou Anne and Alice with the sides of mashed potatoes, green beans, and deviled eggs.

Everyone took his or her place around the table and joined hands as James bowed his head. "Dear Lord, Thank you for this beautiful day, not only for the weather but for the resurrection of our Lord and Savior, Jesus Christ. Help us to remember this is a day to celebrate life and to realize that we are truly blessed to have a loving God whom would give his only son for our sins. Help us to remember His sacrifice when making our own and living our lives, each and every day. Please bless every soul surrounding this table, and bless this food to the nourishment of our bodies. In your name we pray on this holiest of days, amen."

James carved the ham as everyone sat and started filling their plates full of the glorious meal.

"It's a good thing we don't eat like this every day," said Lou Anne, spooning some gravy over her mashed potatoes. "Or you'd have to roll me around the farm."

Everyone laughed, and only a few more words were spoken while everyone devoured the meal. After clean up, Evalyn tried to convince Robert to go on a walk with her.

"I told Bill I'd help him round up the cattle," said Robert.

As if on cue, Bill popped his head out of the barn with a big smile. "Robert, we don't need you. Gabe is gonna ride with us, that is, if he can remember how to stay on a horse. Y'all might want to watch; this could get very funny."

"See," said Evalyn. "You can come with me. Please Robert."

Robert agreed and she led him to the orchard.

"I feel I need to clarify what I meant this morning about the dress," said Evalyn, sitting on an old bench James had made for his wife Sylvia years before.

Robert sat on the edge of the bench beside her and looked at the ground. "I believe you were quite clear."

"No," Evalyn grabbed Robert's hand, "I wasn't. I didn't throw the dress away because it would remind me that I married you. I threw the dress away because it reminded me of what I would never have. Stuff I didn't really need anyway."

"Like what?" Robert asked, turning toward her. "I'll give you anything you want."

"I believe you mean that, Robert," Evalyn said gently. "But you will never be able to give me the courtship that comes with finding a boy, falling in love, and then getting married in a big church wedding with our friends and family. We made our choices and now we live with them. It doesn't mean those choices are bad, but it did mean giving up that idea of romance. That is what I threw away with the dress."

"I meant what I said. I will gi …," said Robert, but stopped as he realized that Dovie and Gabe were in earshot.

Dovie felt her face turn red when she saw Evalyn and Robert. She hadn't meant to intrude on their conversation.

Evalyn shot to her feet. "Dovie, how long have you been listening?"

Dovie waved Evalyn off.

"Don't worry, Evie, I didn't hear y'all. I'm just surprised to see y'all out here by Momma's bench. I was about to show Gabe …" Dovie trailed off knowing her longer explanation was making thing more awkward.

"Well," said Evalyn, grabbing Robert's hand, "we should probably head back to Rockwood and get Joy into bed. I bet she's getting cranky."

"No need to rush off," said Dovie as Evalyn gave her a hug.

"We're not," said Evalyn. "We'll see y'all in a day or so."

Robert gave Dovie a hug. "Thank you for the wonderful Easter dinner. I haven't had such a grand meal on Easter for a long time."

Gabe shook Robert's hand as they said goodbye and then Evalyn and Robert hurried away.

"They seemed to be in a rush," said Gabe, taking a seat on the bench.

Dovie sat next to him. "We probably caught them whispering sweet nothings to each other. You know how young married couples are."

"Actually, I don't," said Gabe "being that I've never been married."

Dovie bowed her head. "I figured that girl broke your heart so bad it left a bad taste in your mouth about marriage and love."

Gabe chuckled. "I would hate to think that she had that much of an effect on my life, but maybe she did and I didn't realize it."

"Do you think about getting married and having kids one day?" asked Dovie. "You know you're not gettin' any younger," she smiled. Gabe grabbed Dovie's hand. "Well, I think it's gonna take the right kind of girl."

Dovie smiled at him. "And what kind of girl would that be?"

Gabe tucked a curl behind Dovie's ear, and goose bumps spread over her flesh at his tender touch.

He looked directly at her, and she felt as if she'd melt under his gaze. "The kind of girl like you."

Chapter Twenty-six

May 1940

Elmer scratched his head. He had taken his two best dogs out to hunt turkey as the sun came up that morning, but they kept leading him in a circle. He'd searched every acre of the ground the dogs kept going to, but there wasn't so much as a turkey feather. His dogs were usually very good at tracking, but he guessed everyone, including hunting dogs, were allowed an off day. They had been in the same area for over an hour, and he was ready to call it a hunt. Soon he'd have to leave for school. Elmer turned to head back home when Freckles went on point.

Elmer squinted to see into the distance as he tried to see what the dog was pointing at. Something rustled the bushes and he raised his gun. Maybe the morning wouldn't be a loss after all.

Taking a deep breath, Elmer steadied himself. A few years ago he couldn't shoot the broad side of a barn because he would close his eyes. However, he had practiced a lot since his first hunting trip, and even Bill had finally admitted that he was the best shot in the family.

The rustling sound grew louder, and Elmer took another deep breath and held it, placing his finger on the trigger. Freckles let out a low growl causing Elmer to look down. Before he knew it, Norman landed on his head, causing him to lose his balance. The gun went off, and the kick popped Elmer right in the collar bone. Elmer cried out in pain as Norman flew a few yards away and started waddling toward the house.

"Norman, you're lucky you didn't get yourself killed," yelled Elmer as he saw Jacob walking up the trail. "Give that goose a good kick on your way past, Jacob."

Jacob smiled and slowed before shaking his head as he approached Elmer. "No can do. That there is Miss Alice's friend, and I think it's best if I stay on his good side."

"He ain't got a good side," said Elmer, rubbing his shoulder. "Well, I best get back to the house for breakfast. School starts soon."

"I was just stretching my legs. I'll walk back with you," said Jacob.

"How ya feeling?" asked Elmer.

"Like I've got ants in my pants," said Jacob. "I like it here at Quail Crossings, and it's peaceful, but Miss Dovie won't let me do many chores, and I'm about to go crazy with nothing to do. I'm just glad that Miss Alice is teaching me to read. I'd like to get into town and buy her a new book or somethin' for all her help, but I don't see that happenin' any time soon."

Elmer shrugged. "I don't know. The town's been pretty quiet. I think most folks think you've left. Maybe if you went to the store while we were all at school, it'd be okay."

Jacob's eyes lit up. "You really think so?"

"You aren't our prisoner, Jacob," said Elmer. "We want you to be safe. Just ask James, he'll know what's best."

As if on cue, James came out of the barn as they approached.

"No turkeys?" he asked.

"Thanks to Norman," said Elmer. "He kept leading the dogs in circles. Gonna have a nice bruise on my shoulder because of that goose."

"Mr. James," said Jacob, "I was hoping I could go with you into town today and run into Johnson's Drug Store. I'd like to buy Miss Alice something for helping me learn to read, and Mr. Pearce gave me a bit of money for helping with the barn yesterday, handing him tools and such, while he was up on the ladder."

James rubbed his neck. "I don't know, Jacob. We've just about got you mended up. I'd hate for something to happen."

Elmer spoke before Jacob had a chance. "I understand where you're coming from, but as I just told him, he ain't our prisoner. Don't you think if he goes while Frank Kelley and his gang are at school and all the men are at work, he'll be okay? Just for a little bit?"

"I wouldn't normally ask, Mr. James," said Jacob. "I'm so thankful for all y'all have done to help me."

"It's okay, Jacob," said James. "Elmer's got a point. You have every right to go into town. I've got to go in and get my feed order. It'll be nice to have some help loading that without pulling Bill and Gabe off the new barn. We'll go in a bit."

A huge smile engulfed Jacob's face as he pulled at the collar of his shirt. "Well then, I best go freshen up."

Lou Anne sat slumped on the sofa and begged her tears to stay away. It wasn't the end of the world, just another monthly. So what if Mrs. Pearl's instructions didn't work? She and Bill could keep trying for a baby.

The tears didn't listen and fell on her cheeks anyway. She quickly wiped them away.

"Lou Anne, honey, what's the matter?" asked Dovie.

Lou Anne picked up her forgotten knitting off her lap and pretended to be busy. "Just had something in my eye."

Dovie placed her hands on her hips. "Now, Lou Anne, I didn't come out of diapers yesterday. What's wrong?"

At the word diapers, Lou Anne felt the dam break, and she started sobbing. "I'm feeling all crampy, and I just know my monthly is coming. I thought it wouldn't come this month. I did everything Mrs. Pearl told me to do. I drank raw eggs, ate hot peppers, stood on my head after relations, and I even sat on Charlotte's booth right after her as if I could catch having a baby from an expecting lady. But nothing worked, and I'm still not with child." She dissolved into tears.

"Stood on your head? Why on earth . . .?" Dovie cocked her head and then her eyes softened. "Never mind." She sat next to Lou Anne and wrapped her arms around her. "Honey, I'm so sorry."

Lou Anne was stunned. She expected Dovie to laugh at all the silly wives' tales. Dovie sat up and patted Lou Anne on the leg. "Did you know that Helen wasn't my only child?"

Lou Anne dropped her knitting again. "What?"

"Right after we got married, Simon and I found ourselves expectin' a baby. We were both pleased as punch it happened so soon. I'd never seen Simon so happy, and then just like that," Dovie snapped her finger. "we weren't expecting any more."

Lou Anne gasped. "Dovie, I'm so sorry. I never knew."

Dovie shook her head. "No one did. Not even my parents. We just kept it to ourselves, but it was hard. Even though we never met the babe, and I lost it very early, we both still felt the loss. When we didn't get pregnant after that, I figured I must be broken inside. I felt as if that first baby was my only chance, and I had messed it up."

"Dovie, you of all people know that's not how it works," said Lou Anne.

Dovie smiled. "I know that now, but back when I was your age, I didn't. I probably felt a lot like you feel now. Lou Anne. It'll be okay. I just know you'll have children."

"But how do you know that, Dovie?" asked Lou Anne. "Some women are barren. I could be."

"I guess I just have faith in God," said Dovie. "That's how I've gotten through everything, even the really tough times. I just had faith I would. I didn't know when or how, and some days it seemed impossible. But I just kept having faith that everything would be okay and in time it was."

"I don't know that I can do that," said Lou Anne. "I feel so defeated."

Dovie patted Lou Anne's knee. "I get that. I tell you what. It's okay to feel sad, or even mad at the situation. Give yourself one hour to cry or yell or whatever you need to do. Then pick yourself up by your boot straps and keep going about your day. 'Cause if we don't live, then the things we want most don't even have a chance to happen."

Lou Anne laid her head on Dovie's shoulder and let the tears fall. "Thanks, Momma Dovie."

Dovie smiled at the term of endearment. "Anytime, dear, any time."

Evalyn glanced at Joy playing in the shade on a large quilt a few feet away and couldn't help but smile as Joy giggled and cuddled the small rag doll Alice had made her. Daisy, the runt pig, slept soundly cuddled up next to the blanket in the cool grass. It took all her willpower not to put her hoe away and go cuddle with them on the blanket. She was surprised how much the little pig had grown to mean to her, and she could never get enough of Joy.

But she was already late getting their garden started, and if she didn't get the rest of the ground broken now, then they would likely have to count on Dovie's ample supply of canned goods to help them through the winter.

As much as she loved Dovie and appreciated her help, Evalyn didn't want to rely on them. She had grown accustomed to seeing Rockwood as her home and even appreciated having Robert around as a father figure for Joy. And she had to admit, she enjoyed his company more and more every day.

Joy let out a cry, and Evalyn swung around just in time to see a woman with strawberry blonde hair cuddling with Joy – Harriet.

Evalyn dropped the hoe and ran to her baby.

"What are you doing here?" she asked, snatching Joy out of Harriet's hands. "I thought you were in California. How did you find us?"

Harriet folded her arms. "Careful, is that anyway to treat your dearest friend?"

Evalyn shook her head. "I'm sorry, Harriet, I was just surprised to see you and wanted to settle Joy. When did you get back to Texas?"

Harriet rolled her eyes, plopped down on the quilt, and patted an area beside her. "Sit down, Evie, and I'll tell you all about it."

Evalyn looked around the farm. She knew Robert was in town but still couldn't figure out how Harriet had gotten to Joy without her knowing. Certain they were alone, she slowly sat with Joy.

Harriet pulled at a blade of grass. "It's actually a funny story. If you remember correctly, I left with Taff Mannford to go to San Francisco for a few days and when I got back, not only were my roommate and baby gone, but I had been evicted. Thankfully, Taff let me stay with him, or I would've been out on the street. But you can imagine my worry at seeing the two of you gone."

"You were gone for a month," said Evalyn. "I ran out of food, and I couldn't work because I didn't have anyone to watch Joy."

"Her name is Nancy," snapped Harriet. "You are the only one who insists on calling her by her middle name."

Evalyn bit her lip. "I only did what I thought was right for her."

"Without telling me?" Harriet's voice continued to rise. "Do you know how worried I was?"

"Without telling *you*?" Evalyn could feel her face grow hot. "Harriet, I had no idea where you were. How was I supposed to tell you? Besides, once Joy was here, you never gave the two of us another thought."

"Her name is Nancy," said Harriet once again.

Evalyn stood with Joy. "Her name is Joy. You stopped being able to dictate what people call her when you abandoned her. I did what was right. I came home to give her a proper upbringing, to a place where she will always feel loved and never feel unwanted."

Harriet nodded and stood. "A proper upbringing, huh? So do people know that Nancy isn't really yours? Your family? Mrs. Grant and Mr. Murphy? And how about that new husband of yours, does he know he's married to a kidnapper?"

Evalyn gasped. "You abandoned her long before you ever left for San Francisco. You never took care of her. I had to quit my job while you went running all over Hollywood, staying out for days at a time. What was I supposed to do?"

Harriet shrugged. "Here's what the law is gonna hear. I went for work in another city, thinking I had left my child in the capable hands of my best friend and roommate, only to come home and find my child had been taken. Now, you call it abandonment, and even if it was, there was no reason you couldn't have taken Nancy to my parents' house. You didn't do that. You kept her as your own which, in my opinion, makes you a kidnapper. I think I'll see what the law thinks of that little scenario."

"Harriet, people saw you around the city right after Joy was born. People know you weren't looking after Joy." Evalyn fought back. "You were sleeping around with different guys and almost never came home. I'm the one who has been taking care of Joy from day one. I fed her, changed her, bathed her … whatever needed to be done, I did it, not you. You can't take Joy from me. I'm the only momma she knows."

"Not for long."

Chapter Twenty-seven

Evalyn held Joy tightly and wept into the baby blanket, her need to finish the garden completely forgotten. She had never expected to see Harriet again, and now there was a good chance Harriet would take Joy away from her.

"It's not fair," wept Evalyn. "She never wanted you. She practically left right after you were born. I'm your true momma."

Joy reached up with a look that could only be described as concern and touched a tear on Evalyn's cheek in a comforting gesture which made Evalyn cry harder.

"Evalyn? What's wrong?" asked Robert gently, kneeling by her side. "Is Joy okay?"

Evalyn jumped at the sound of his voice. She hadn't heard his truck pull up. He put a kind hand on her shoulder. "Talk to me, Evalyn. Let me help."

Evalyn shook her head and quickly wiped her cheeks. "It's nothing. I've just had a rough day with Joy."

She cringed at her lie. She hated blaming Joy for her tears, but she couldn't let Robert find out about Harriet's threats.

Robert sat back on his heels and reached out for Joy. "Why don't you let me take her for a bit? Let me give you a little break."

Evalyn eyed Robert before glancing down at Joy. The baby smiled and reached for Robert. Evalyn handed her over with a slight nod. "She loves you like a father."

Robert cuddled Joy closely. "That's because I am her father."

Before Evalyn could stop herself, the sobs started again.

Robert handed her a handkerchief. "I'm sorry. I guess I shouldn't have said that since I don't know who her real daddy is or what happened to him. Truth be told, I'm glad he's not in the picture. It ain't right for me to say this, I know, but because he's gone I get to have a family. I feel very blessed to have you and Joy in my life."

"You wouldn't say that if you really knew me," said Evalyn, dabbing her eyes.

"Here's what I know about you," said Robert, grabbing her hand. "I know you are the best kind of mother. You're kind and caring, while also being fun, and Joy is a happy baby because of that. She hardly fusses or cries and is just as happy as a clam sitting by herself and playing." He bounced Joy on his lap. "And

Evalyn you're more than a mother, you're a generous person. Just look at the way you've fixed up Rockwood as if it were your own. The place didn't look this good even when my ma took care of it. And while gettin' this place in shape, you've helped Dovie get Jacob on the mend."

Daisy, the pig, nuzzled Robert's knee. "And look at this little piglet. She's more like a puppy than a pig because of the love you've shown her. You helped out at Quail Crossings and practically raised Elmer and Alice."

"You're just trying to make me feel better," said Evalyn.

"Is it working?" asked Robert with a grin.

Evalyn nodded and smiled back. Even with Harriet's dark cloud looming over her, Robert had made her feel as if everything would be okay. He had a knack for that, she decided. "You're a good man, too, and you're right. You are Joy's Daddy."

She squeezed his hand and gazed into his dark brown eyes. "I'm lucky you're on my side."

"Always," he said before leaning down and placing a soft kiss on her lips.

Before Evalyn could stop herself, she felt her body rising to meet his embrace and she wrapped her arms around his neck. Her heart jumped in delight and lightning zipped through her body. It was only the second time she had ever been kissed, and it was drastically different than the awkward peck she and

Robert had shared on their wedding day. This was the way kissing was supposed to feel. Bells were ringing with delight in her mind. Bells? No, squeals, she was hearing squeals. She broke free of the kiss and laughed when she saw Daisy trying to squeeze between them.

She gave Robert a wink before picking up the piglet and giving her a head rub. "Somebody's jealous."

Evalyn stood. As much as she'd like to continue kissing Robert on the quilt, there was work to be done. Somehow she had to stop Harriet from telling the world that Joy was her baby. She just hoped her once-best friend would see how keeping Joy's true identity a secret was best for everyone.

Even though Jacob kept his head down as he walked down the street from the feed store to Johnson's Drug, he couldn't help but smile. He really had grown to love living at Quail Crossings but felt alive again as he entered the store. Being able to go about his business like a normal person felt invigorating. It wasn't lost on him that this particular place was where all his trouble had started, but with the folks at Quail Crossings on his side, he felt brave. Mr. James had given him some money for helping load the feed and with what he had gotten from Mr. Pearce for helping with the barn, Jacob was determined to buy Alice a new book.

He quickly made his way to the magazine and dime novel section of the store. Mr. James had given him just a few minutes to shop while he settled his feed bill. Jacob hadn't been reading long, so he relied mostly on the pictures. Seeing a curious bunny in a blue jacket on the cover of one of the books, he knew it would be perfect for Alice.

He grabbed the book, quickly paid, and hurried out the door. James met him just outside the feed store.

"I've got great news for you, Jacob," he said, smiling.

Jacob returned his smile. "Is it that we've got time for apple pie? I sure do love me some apple pie."

James pulled out his pocket watch. "I'm afraid not. School will be out soon, but what I have to tell you is better than apple pie."

Jacob cocked his head as if thinking hard, his smile still firm. "If it's better than apple pie, then it must be good."

"Mr. Willoby came into the store while I was settling my bill. He's been traveling for a few months and said he had passed through a town about two hours southeast of here that is an all-negro community. He didn't know how much work would be there, but it seems like it would be a safe place for you to go and make a home for yourself."

"That is good news," said Jacob. "I hate to leave y'all, but I know I must go sometime. I'll leave first thing in the morning."

James shook his head. "Mr. Willoby has to go back that way next week and said you could ride with him."

Jacob's smile grew. "Really? Mr. Willoby would be willing to do that for me?"

"He's a good man," said James, "and happy to help. In all honesty, because of all that time on the road alone, he probably would appreciate the company, even if it's for just a few hours."

Jacob rubbed his hands together. "This is the best news. I can't wait to tell Alice."

"Tell me what?"

James and Jacob turned to see Alice standing behind them.

"Why, Alice, you don't get out of school for another hour. What are doing here?" asked James.

"We got out early today," said Alice.

"Well, I'm glad you're here," said Jacob. "Mr. James was just telling me he found an all-colored town for me to go to and a ride to get there. Isn't that the greatest news?"

Alice frowned. "I guess so."

"What's wrong, Miss Alice?" asked Jacob.

Alice bit her lip as the feed store owner popped his head out the door. "Oh good, you're still here James.

We just got in that shipment of chicken feed if you still want two more bags."

James eyed the street before nodding to the store owner. "Don't be long, Jacob," said James as he entered the store. "We need to get you out of sight."

As soon as James was in the store, Jacob asked his question again. "What's wrong Miss Alice?"

Alice shook her head. "I'm happy for you. I really am. I guess I just thought you'd always be at Quail Crossings, but I know that don't make sense."

"I hate to leave our friendship too, Miss Alice. But I'm ready to find a home. I'm tired of running from town to town with only a scrap of hope of finding work."

Alice forced a smile. "I really am happy for you and as much as I hate to see you go, I hope you find your home."

"Here I got you something," said Jacob, handing Alice the new copy of Beatrix Potter's *Peter Rabbit*. "I hope you like it."

Alice traced the bunny. "Oh, Jacob, I love it."

Before she could stop herself, she threw her arms around Jacob and gave him a big hug.

"Oh, you've done it now, boy."

Jacob's blood rain cold as he turned to see Frank Kelley standing just a few feet away.

Chapter Twenty-eight

Alice jerked her hands from around Jacob's neck, her cheeks hot with embarrassment and anger as she looked down Knollwood's main street to see who was watching. She wasn't sure if the fact Main Street was deserted filled her with relief or dread.

"Jacob ain't done nothin'." She placed her hands on her hips and glared at Frank Kelley, praying Mr. James and the other men would finish in the back of the store quickly.

"Looked to me like he was takin' advantage of a young white girl half his age," said Frank with a sneer. "Pretty sure even the most tolerant folks would take issue with the two of you hangin' all over each other."

"You leave Miss Alice out of this," said Jacob, stepping in front of Alice.

Frank laughed. "Oh, 'Miss Alice' will be fine. You need to worry about yourself."

"You leave him alone," yelled Alice. "Or I'll get Mr. James."

"Go ahead and get the old man," said Frank. "I'm sure he'll be interested in what I saw."

"And just what did you see?" asked Tiny, walking up behind Frank and joining Jacob and Alice.

"Why, these two in a lovin' embrace," said Frank, a smile tugging on his lips.

Alice watched the color drain from Tiny's face.

"Is this true?" asked Tiny.

"Jacob got some good news, and I gave him a hug," explained Alice. "Maybe I shouldn't have, but it wasn't like he's sayin'."

Frank's eyes narrowed. "By the time I get done, the whole town will know you're a nigger-lovin' hussy."

Tiny slapped Frank hard across the face. "How dare you!"

Frank's face turned bright red as he grabbed Tiny by the arms. "It's time you all know your place."

He shoved Tiny backwards causing her to stumble and fall hard to the ground. Someone tapped Frank on the shoulder. He turned around only to meet Elmer's fist with his jaw.

Frank immediately sank to the ground.

"I've wanted to do that for a while now," said Elmer, shaking out his fist.

Tiny bounced up and hugged Elmer, before planting a kiss right on his lips. "That was so brave."

Hearing a groan, they looked towards Frank who was getting on his feet.

"You'll pay for that, Brewer." He threatened, holding his jaw. "You'll all pay for this."

Elmer let go of Tiny and took a step toward Frank, causing Frank to turn tail and run.

"What's going on out here?" asked James, coming out of the feed store, his eyes searching their faces.

"This is all my fault," Alice cried. "I hugged Jacob, Mr. James. I wasn't even thinkin'. He's like a brother to me, but Frank Kelley saw us, and now he says he's gonna tell the whole town that Jacob and I are carrying on."

James patted Alice's shoulder. "Don't you worry about Frank Kelley. No one will believe him, but I think it's good that Jacob's getting out of town. If he wasn't safe before, he certainly isn't safe now. I think we'd better be getting back to Quail Crossings." He looked at Elmer and Tiny. "All of us."

Dovie shuffled her feet under the swing, causing it to twist slightly. Helen used to delight in twisting the two ropes on the swing as tightly as she could before lifting her feet and having the swing spin her until she was dizzy. She would giggle for hours, twisting the swing and letting it go, over and over again. Dovie's heart throbbed with pain at the thought of her late daughter and of all the years she was robbed of with her.

Dovie backed as far as the swing would let her and then lifted her feet so the swing could glide through the air. She was thankful for the breeze as it blew her tears away.

She had come into town feeling fine, even after telling Lou Anne about losing her unborn baby. Then while in the Knollwood Market, she saw Mrs. Spaulding talking to a young woman with a newborn baby. The pain had barreled into her chest faster than a tornado over the plains. Tears threatened to fall right there in the dry goods aisle, so she hightailed it to the park, hoping it would be deserted during school hours. Thankfully, she had been right and had the park to herself.

She closed her eyes as she pumped her legs forcing the swing to go higher. If she got high enough, maybe she'd catch a glimpse of her two babies, both taken from her far too soon.

"That looks like fun. Mind if I join you?"

Dovie planted her feet, causing her swing to come to an abrupt stop and launching her straight into the arms of Gabe.

She quickly righted herself and brushed imaginary dust off her skirt. "What are you doing here?"

"My plane is in Roger Murphy's barn. I cut across the park when I go to check on it." His face turned serious as he brushed a tear off Dovie's cheek. "Are you okay?"

Dovie quickly turned her back to Gabe. "I'm fine. I just got a little dust in my eye."

"Dovie, I want you to know you can always talk to me," said Gabe, turning her around.

Dovie sighed. "No one wants to hear me cry about my lost babies. It's old news; I should be past it by now."

"Babies?" Gabe raised an eyebrow.

"Simon and I lost our first child before birth," confessed Dovie. "Lou Anne has been worried about her ability to have children, so today I shared that experience with her. I thought I was fine. I mean, it was so long ago, but I walked into Knollwood Market and there was this little baby. I had to get out of there, so I came here."

"Hoping to be alone." Gabe nodded.

Dovie shrugged. "Like I said, I shouldn't be crying over them anymore. Too much time has passed, and I should be over it."

Gabe took her gently by the shoulders. "Now you listen here, Dovie Grant. No one, and I mean no one, should ever tell you that you don't have the right to cry for your babies. Anyone who has suffered a loss knows there will always be hurt and even unexpected tears. There is no time limit on grief."

Dovie hugged herself. "I guess you're right."

"Then do it," said Gabe.

"Do what?"

"Cry."

Dovie couldn't contain her smile as she threw her arms up into the air. "Well, I can't now! You've gone and made me feel better."

His smile matched hers. "Glad I could help."

"I swear you're some kind of guardian angel. It seems like you're always swooping in to help at just the right time."

"So you think I have good timing, huh?" Gabe took off his brown fedora and fingered the brim.

"You're a modern day hero, coming in and doing the right thing, just at the right mom ... "

Gabe grabbed Dovie's hand and pulled her into his arms before placing a passionate kiss on her lips. Dovie's mind whirled with confusion as she surrendered to his embrace. Goosebumps took over her body as she let his soft lips explore hers. She felt good in Gabe's arms, so safe and warm. She had missed this feeling of passion and attraction. It had been so long since... Simon.

Dovie's heart sank. She had promised to love and be loyal to Simon her entire life. She had made that vow in front of her church, parents, and most importantly God, and now here she was kissing another man. She broke away, fighting back a fresh batch of tears.

"Bad timing?" asked Gabe, a hint of a joke in his voice but also concern.

"We shouldn't have done that," said Dovie.

"Why?" asked Gabe. "Did I misread your intentions? I'm sorry if I did so. I just feel so connected to you, and that kiss felt so right. We're both single adults. We no longer need a chaperone."

"Because I'm not available," whispered Dovie.

Gabe raised an eyebrow. "I don't understand?"

"I vowed to always love Simon. I vowed to be loyal to him." Dovie felt her voice rise even though she knew it wasn't Gabe's fault. "It has only been six years. That may seem like a lot of time to most, but how do you stop loving someone you gave your whole heart to? It's hard for me to think of him as being gone forever. I can't stop loving him."

Gabe nodded. "I understand. You will always love Simon. I don't want you to ever stop. But isn't there room for another? You don't have to be alone, Dovie."

Dovie held up her hand. "I can't."

She gave Gabe a desperate look before shaking her head and running away.

Norman looked to the west and narrowed his eyes at the clouds that were building in the distance. Raising his wings, he lowered his head and hissed at the horizon. After giving the incoming storm a piece of his mind, he turned toward Quail Crossings and let out a loud series of honks. The chickens scurried under the henhouse as the cows that had been grazing near the barn, took off toward the northeast pasture. All the animals heeded Norman's warning. Unfortunately none of the residents of Quail Crossings were around to hear his call.

Chapter Twenty-nine

Evalyn pulled at a loose stitch on the sofa, cursed herself for making the small rip worse, and then sat on her hands. Why hadn't she just told everyone the truth to start with? Why hadn't she just taken Joy to Harriet's parents and explained the situation?

Joy, asleep on the sofa next to Evalyn, let out a small baby snore, and Evalyn's heart leapt with love. All of her questions had been answered with that little baby snore. She hadn't been honest with everyone because they would have taken Joy away from her and she was, without a doubt, completely and totally in love with the child.

She had prayed about what to do after Harriet's surprise appearance, and she knew the answer. She had to be honest with Robert. It was the only way to keep Joy from becoming a chess piece in an evil match of wits. Unfortunately, her lie was going to hurt others, especially him.

Tears fell onto her cheeks as she thought of the loving way Robert attended to Joy. He was her father in every way that mattered, and he would be just as devastated if Joy was taken from them. She needed an ally in this battle. She needed Robert to stand up with her and say that Joy was theirs even while knowing the truth.

"Looks like quite the storm brewing," said Robert, stomping the dust off his boots as he entered the back door. "We could sure use the rain. Hope that's all we get."

Evalyn raised a single finger to her mouth, and Robert smiled as he walked over and peeked at the sleeping baby.

"We both know that child could sleep through the sound of hungry pigs during slop time," said Robert.

Evalyn nodded at the truth. "That she can. I used to get so worried I'd wake her. The quieter I tried to be, the louder I was. Then one day I dropped a bunch of bottles while she was sleeping. I just knew she was gonna wake up screaming, but she kept snoozing. I actually went over and woke her up in case something was wrong."

"So what's going on?" asked Robert. "You've been crying again, and don't tell me it's another rough day with Joy. I know better."

"You're right, something is wrong, and it's time you know what's going on."

Robert bowed his head. "You're leaving aren't you? It was the kiss. I went too far. It's just that I've grown to …"

Evalyn stopped him. "No, I'm not planning on leaving, but I do have a confession, and you'll probably want me to leave after you hear it. You might wanna sit down."

Robert let out a sigh before sitting in a large chair to Evalyn's left.

Evalyn bit the inside of her lip before starting. "This is gonna be hard to understand, I know, but please believe I never meant to hurt you. I never thought we'd get as close as we have. You are the first man I've ever kissed."

Robert's mouth dropped open. He looked at Joy, then Evalyn, then Joy again.

"I'll explain," Evalyn said quickly. "Joy is my daughter in every way that counts. I've taken care of her from the moment she was born. I've loved her, cared for her, and made this trip home, so she could grow up in the kind of loving environment I never had and which I knew she'd never get if we stayed in California. But I didn't give birth to her."

"You stole her?" Robert whispered.

Evalyn shook her head. "No, my friend, Harriet, who I went to California with, is her mother and she abandoned Joy shortly after birth. She abandoned both of us, really. I didn't know what to do. I couldn't work anymore because I had to tend to Joy, and we were running out of money. So I made the choice to come back to Quail Crossings."

"Why didn't you tell me on the bus?" asked Robert, color still absent from his face.

"I barely knew you," said Evalyn. "I didn't know if you'd turn me in to the police."

Robert stood. "But you've had all this time to tell me and you've said nothing. You could have said something before we were married at the courthouse."

"I didn't think Harriet was ever coming back," explained Evalyn. "She ran off with a man and I never expected to see her again. I thought I could - *we could* - raise Joy as our own with no one the wiser."

"Including me. I can't believe this," said Robert pacing, each hard step causing Evalyn to flinch a little. "I thought our family was finally coming together, and now everything is falling apart."

"It doesn't have to fall apart," said Evalyn, leaning forward.

"Why are you telling me this now?" asked Robert, stopping his pacing.

"Because Harriet's back," answered Evalyn.

"And she's gonna take Joy?" Robert looked at the baby.

"She's threatened to." Evalyn slouched back in her seat as Robert's mouth fell open.

Robert rubbed his neck and shook his head in disbelief. "I could lose everything. They could take us both to jail. And Joy … poor Joy …," He shook his head again as he walked toward the back door.

Evalyn leapt to her feet. "Don't go, Robert, please. If we stand together it's her word against ours. No one will believe her."

"I need to think," he said as he walked out the back door.

Evalyn felt her heart break as she watched Robert drive away from the farm. She couldn't let it end that way. She had to make a deal with Harriet. She had to fix this whole mess.

She gently picked up Joy and headed to the truck Elmer had let her borrow. First she'd drop Joy off at Quail Crossings, and then she'd find Harriet and convince her to let them adopt Joy. No more running. No more lies. They were all coming clean, and she would find a way to save her family.

James pulled into Quail Crossings and studied the storm in the distance. It was going to be a doozy. Elmer hopped out of the bed of the truck, and James pulled him close.

"Get the rifles ready in case Frank Kelley and his father pay us a visit," James whispered, "but be quiet about it. We just need to keep Jacob safe a few more days."

James turned to Alice. "I want you and Jacob to take some blankets, last night's leftover chicken, and a lantern and go down in the cellar. Stay there until I come get you. Tiny, why don't you go with Elm? I'm gonna check on the animals."

Lou Anne walked out of the house. "What's going on? Can I help?"

"Where's Bill?" asked James.

"Checking the fence line," answered Lou Anne.

James nodded. "I bet he'll be back in before too long. I'm sure he sees the storm coming."

"Should I go find him?" asked Elmer.

"No, he'll come in before it gets too bad. Lou Anne, will you help Alice and Jacob get the cellar ready? And I want you and Bill to spend the night. Y'all don't have a cellar yet and I don't want the two of you left alone tonight. I have a feeling it's gonna get stormy in more ways than one."

Lou Anne nodded and opened the back door for Alice and Jacob to gather supplies.

"Lou Anne," James called out "is Gabe working on the barn? And where's Dovie?"

"They're both in town," Lou Anne answered.

James's mind worked overtime as he thought of what Frank Kelley might do and the storm that continued to build over them. He had to keep his family safe, but how, when they were scattered all over kingdom come? His mind turned to Robert, Evalyn, and Joy.

"Lou Anne," he shouted just as she was about to close the back door. She opened it and gave him a nod. "On second thought, I'm gonna drive over to Rockwood and get Evalyn's bunch? I'm not sure they have a cellar either. Would you secure the animals for me?"

"Sure," said Lou Anne, once again exiting the house.

Just then Evalyn pulled up in Elmer's truck.

"Oh, thank heavens," said James. "I was just about to come get y'all. Where's Robert?"

"I don't know," Evalyn said as Lou Anne approached them "but I need to go talk to Harriet. Will y'all watch Joy for a bit?"

"Harriet? I didn't know she was back. Never mind that, Evie, there's a storm coming in. Can't it wait until tomorrow?" asked James. "I prefer to have y'all here where I can keep you safe."

Evalyn shook her head. "I'm sorry, James; it can't wait. I'll be back before it gets bad, I promise."

She handed Joy to Lou Anne before getting back into Elmer's truck.

"Now, Evie, you're not thinking right," said James. "I'd feel better if you'd stay. I insist."

"I'm sorry. I really can't," said Evalyn before backing away and speeding down the drive.

James's mind fumed. After this storm was over, they were going to all sit down and have a long talk about running all over the countryside and listening to the voice of reason. He looked to the sky. "Dear Lord, help us all make it through the night."

Lou Anne tickled Joy under her chin as they sat on the sofa playing while Alice and Jacob gathered all of the supplies needed for their time in the cellar. Her heart ached with both love for her niece and longing for a baby of her own. Her stomach lurched and Lou Anne put her hand to her mouth. She was going to be ill and there was no stopping it. She sat Joy gently on the floor, then ran to the kitchen and dumped the potatoes out of a bowl on the table, just before vomiting into it.

Having lost all of her stomach's contents, she took the bowl to the sink and started to rinse it. She felt significantly better after having thrown up. In fact, she felt as if she had never been sick. Her mind ticked off what she had eaten during the day, but it was nothing out of the ordinary. In fact, there was nothing about her oatmeal breakfast and cheese sandwich lunch that should have made her feel ill at all.

Lou Anne peeked in at Joy in the parlor, who was fumbling with one of Alice's rag dolls, and then looked at Dovie's wall calendar. She started to count back days.

She was late. In fact she hadn't had a full monthly in two months. She had spotted a few times and decided that was her cycle. How had she not put this together before? She touched her belly gently as excitement fluttered through her body. Could she be pregnant? She shook her head. It was probably just a false alarm since she had just been cramping that same morning. But what if that was part of expecting? She had to talk to Bill. He would help her keep a level head.

She hurried into the parlor and caught Joy up in a big hug before swinging her around. This time next year, she could be cuddling a baby of her own. Joy laughed and Lou Anne gave her a big kiss on the forehead. Lou Anne hoped her suspicions were correct, but they had been trying for a long time. There was no guarantee that she wasn't just coming down with some illness. She needed to talk to Bill.

"You okay?" asked Alice from the doorway, holding a big quilt from the upstairs bedroom to take to the cellar.

"Never been better," Lou Anne said with a smile, the hope lingering.

"Jacob and I have just about everything in the cellar. Mr. James said he wants you and Joy down there with us. We should probably bring my dolls, you know, for Joy," Alice said, eyeballing her rag dolls on the floor.

"Of course, grab the dolls," said Lou Anne. "I'm gonna leave Joy in the cellar with you and go find Bill. Can you manage her alone for a bit?"

"Of course," said Alice, her face lighting up at the thought of babysitting.

The two gathered everything Joy would need, and after securing Joy in the cellar, Lou Anne ran towards the pasture to fid Bill.

Chapter Thirty

The wind whipped through Evalyn's hair as she got out of Elmer's truck and headed toward the Wheaton's front door. The dark clouds matched her dreary mood. She had to make Harriett see reason. Joy had only ever known one momma, and that's the way it needed to stay. Evalyn could give her a family and a steady home whereas Harriet would resent Joy for making her settle down.

Thunder rolled in the distance as Evalyn raised her hand to knock on the door. Before her knuckles touched the wood, Harriet jerked the door open.

"What are you doing here?" Harriet snapped.

"I came to talk to you about …"

"Shhh," Harriet whispered before stepping outside and shutting the door behind her. "Not here, follow me."

Harriet brushed past her at a quick pace. Evalyn glanced at the clouds and then hurried to catch up. It would probably be best for Harriet's parents not to hear what was being said until they had come to an agreement. The less anyone knew, the better.

"We have to talk about Joy and what happens next," said Evalyn.

"She should be with her momma," said Harriet, walking toward the Wheaton's shelter break of cottonwoods and Russian olive trees.

"I agree with you," said Evalyn.

Harriet stopped short, her mouth open and eyes wide. "You're gonna give up Nancy?"

Evalyn shook her head and tried not to cringe at Joy's given name. "No, I agree Joy should be with her momma, and in all the ways that are important, that's me."

Harriet's mouth snapped shut, and for a second Evalyn thought she saw relief cross her face.

"I'm her momma," said Harriet. "I gave birth to her."

"But that's all you did," said Evalyn. "You left us right after she was born. I've been there for her every minute of her life. You wouldn't even hold her a day after the delivery. The nurses said you might need some time ... that she was a big change in your life, but you would grow to love her. I loved Joy from the minute they let me hold her."

"You don't know nothing about having a baby," Harriet shot back. "It was so hard and made me so weak. I didn't have the strength to hold her or to care for her."

"Maybe so," said Evalyn, "but you still left us afterwards. Do you realize the first time you held Joy was at my house the other day?"

Harriet shook her head. "That doesn't matter. I'm her momma."

Lightning flashed, and Evalyn felt her anger grow with the electricity in the air. "Why now, Harriet? Why did you come back for her now? She's just a few months shy of being a year old, and you've never spent a day with her."

Thunder boomed overhead making both women flinch.

"Because you have what I want," screamed Harriet.

Evalyn took a step back. "Joy?"

"All of it," said Harriet, throwing her arms overhead. "You've got a husband, a house, and my baby. Taff left me in San Francisco with an unpaid rent bill. You have no idea what I had to do to get enough money to come back here. You stole my money and you stole my life!"

"I stole nothing! You threw it all away!" Evalyn screamed back. "You had your chance and you didn't want it. You can't just waltz in here and claim it for yourself now that you think it suites you."

"Watch me!" As Harriet turned to go back to the house, lightning again flashed overhead.

"Harriet, we've known each other a long time," Evalyn hollered at her. "I know you well enough to know you're bluffing. We both know you don't want what I have. You've said a hundred times that you'd rather die than live on a farm in Knollwood."

Harriet turned and smiled as she walked back to Evalyn. "I could never fool you. You're right. I'd rather die than live your life."

"So what is it you want?" asked Evalyn as a cold rain started to fall.

"Money," said Harriet, her smile turning wicked, "you give me one hundred dollars, and I'll give you Joy. I'll leave town and no one will be the wiser. What do you say, *Momma*? Do we have a deal?"

Jacob lit the lantern and sat against the cool cellar wall as he watched Alice play with Joy making her rag dolls dance around. He could hear the storm getting started and wondered where everyone else was. It didn't take him long to realize, they had sent him to the cellar, so they could protect him in case Frank Kelley or his father came looking for him. He was not going to let the good people of Quail Crossings fight his fight without him. No one was getting hurt on account of him.

"Jacob," said Alice, "You okay?"

"I was just thinkin' about Mr. Norman being up there in the storm," Jacob lied. He didn't want to scare

Alice. "I think we'd both feel better if I went up, got him, and brought him down here. What do you think?"

Alice's face lit up. "Really? Do you think he'll let you carry him down?"

Jacob got up. "Well, I wouldn't feel right if I didn't try. You stay here with Joy, no matter what, you hear me Miss Alice? Don't go leaving this baby behind for no reason. Got it?"

Alice nodded. "You're acting strange, Jacob. You know I would never leave Joy alone."

"Good." Jacob hurried up the stairs and peeked out of the cellar door. Everything looked quiet. Opening the door all the way, he got out and started walking toward the house.

Walking inside, he faced Tiny and James sitting at the table, guns at the ready. Elmer stood in the parlor by the window and watched both the clouds and the road.

"What are you doing in here?" asked James. "I told you to stay in the cellar with Alice."

"With all due respect, Mr. James," said Jacob. "I won't let y'all fight for me while I'm hiding away in a hole. My pa taught me better than that."

"Tiny," said James, "please go down and keep Alice and Joy company. I don't want her getting scared and bringin' Joy up in the open to see what's going on."

Tiny got up and hurried to place a quick kiss on Elmer's cheek. "I'm going to the cellar with Alice. Now, don't you go being a hero."

Jacob watched Elmer blush as Tiny hustled toward the door.

"Tiny," James called out, "would you fill one more jug of water and take it into the cellar with you? You'll find some jugs in the well house."

"Sure thing, Mr. Murphy," said Tiny, heading out to fetch the water.

"Now, Jacob," said James, "we need to keep you safe. A few more days, and you'll be out of harm's way."

"I appreciate that, Mr. James," said Jacob, "but I can't in good faith sit down there while y'all could get hurt up here. That just ain't right. Now, I'm gonna put Mr. Norman in the cellar with the girls. I told Miss Alice that's what I came up here to do, so I'll do it. Once, I get that done, I'll take watch."

Before James could answer, Jacob hurried out the back door and headed toward the pond. A brisk rain had started to fall, causing Jacob to turn up the collar on his shirt. He looked around the pond but found no sign of Norman.

Turning back toward the house, he caught a glimpse of white in the drainage ditch.

"Ahh, there you are, Mr. Norman," said Jacob smiling. "It's time to come get in the cellar with Miss Alice."

Jacob's smile faded as the white he thought to be Norman's feathers was actually Frank Kelley wearing a white shirt and two of his friends. The boys stood.

"You're gonna get it now, boy," said Frank, brandishing a large club while the two other boys showed their baseball bats.

"Why don't y'all just go on home?" said Jacob. "This storm's gonna get ugly. I bet your parents are worried about y'all."

Frank laughed. "My pa knows exactly where I am and what I'm doing. He ain't worried one bit."

"Listen," said Jacob, glancing at the house hoping James or Elmer would come out to check on him. "I'll make you a deal. I'm leaving town for good. You ain't never got to see my face again. I promise. You guys can go back to town and tell your pas whatever you'd like. No one will ever know the truth."

"Come on, Frank," said Paul as he looked up at the clouds. "Let's go home. This storm's gonna get bad."

"Shut up, Paul," snapped Frank. "This boy is gonna get what's coming to him."

"You don't have to do that," said Jacob. "I promise that you'll never see me again. Just leave me be."

Frank tapped his club into his palm. "That ain't gonna happen."

Before Jacob could say another word, Norman flew into the three boys and started attacking. The boys' hands flew up, blocking their faces from the beak and wings of the angry goose. As much as Jacob wanted to help Norman, he could only think of one thing- run!

Bill fought with the barbwire. He had to get the calf free before the bulk of the storm hit. The calf was only a week old and wouldn't survive if it started to hail. It seemed like every clip of the wire sent it recoiling into another knot around the calf's foot. The scared calf kept kicking his leg every few seconds which didn't help matters. Bill was just glad he got the momma cow tied up before he started working on the calf.

"Bill, what are you doing way out here? It took me forever to find you," said Lou Anne, running up to him.

"I'm so glad you're here," said Bill. "I need your help. Can you hold his leg? He keeps kicking, and this wire is already one big knotted mess."

Lou Anne stood for a moment and touched her belly. She wanted to help Bill, but was it safe for the baby? She shook her head and silently chastised herself for getting her hopes up when they didn't know anything for sure. She knelt as a chilly rain started to fall and being careful of her stomach, hugged the calf's back leg to keep it in place.

"Thanks," said Bill as he went back to snipping the wire. "I'll try to make this fast, so we can all get out of this weather. I just hope it doesn't start hailing." Lightning flashed overhead. "Or worse."

With the calf's leg still, Bill was able to cut the rest of the wire and free the calf. Bill held onto the calf, letting Lou Anne get up and out of the way, before releasing the critter that instantly jumped up and ran to his mother.

"You know, I'm glad you showed up," said Bill. "But what are you doing out here?"

"I needed to talk to you," said Lou Anne. She touched her belly feeling its warmth, even though the rain had made her shiver. "It might be too soon to say this. In fact, I'm not really sure I should say anything at all."

Lou Anne turned and Bill took her hand. "What are you talkin' about?"

Lou Anne faced him, rain dripping down her face, and stared into her husband's eyes. "I think I might be pregnant."

Bill's eyes widened with joy. He kissed his wife before dropping to his knees and cradling her belly. "I just know we are."

"Dovie, just what in the world do you think you're doing?" asked Gabe, grabbing her arm when he finally caught up with her in the middle of the Murphy's field, just past the barn that held his plane.

"Leave me alone, Gabe," said Dovie, brushing his hand off her arm.

"Come back to town with me and then I'll leave you alone," he said. "You can't be out here with this storm rollin' in. It's gonna be a bad one."

"It's just a rainstorm," snapped Dovie. "We get them all the time. I'm fine."

Gabe took Dovie by both arms. "Now, you listen to me. I've been flying a long time, and one thing we're taught is to pay attention to is the weather, especially the clouds. That storm is bad. We have to get back to town."

Dovie shook her head. "You don't get it, do you?"

"What am I supposed to get?" asked Gabe, eyes narrowed.

Dovie jerked her arms away from him. "That I can't do this, can't be with you."

"Seriously, Dovie, we've got to get to shelter," said Gabe. "We can talk about this later."

Dovie's head fell. "There is nothing to talk about. Before today Simon had been the only man I'd ever kissed. And now ... well and now I've betrayed the only man I've ever loved. I deserve to die."

Chapter Thirty-one

Evalyn shivered in the rain. "You can't be serious. I'm not paying for a baby, not even Joy."

"You will pay for Nancy," said Harriet, placing her hands on her hips, "or I will tell everyone the truth."

"Go ahead, tell them," said Evalyn, crossing her arms. "No one will believe you, and if they do, they will know you've been a horrible mother by abandoning your child. Your parents won't let you keep Joy. You've already shown you're not fit to be a mother. They'll take her from you, and you won't see a dime. You lose either way."

"So will you." Harriet sneered.

Evalyn shook her head. "No, because even if I lose Joy to your parents, I know she'll grow up in a good home, and that's all I really want for her. People will whisper, I'm sure. But when they see Joy, see what a happy baby she is, they'll know I did what was right. I'm sorry things didn't work out with Taff, but you made the choice to go with him and leave Joy behind. I didn't make it for you."

"It's just not fair." Harriet plopped down on a fallen log. "What am I supposed to do?" she cried. "I have no money, and I'd rather die than stay here. My parents already said they won't give me any money to go back to California."

"The way I see it you have two choices," said Evalyn. "You can either find a husband or find a job. We're adults. It's what we do. We don't need to depend on our parents anymore."

"There's no man in Knollwood worth marrying." Harriet snapped a twig off the old log. "Where am I gonna find work in this sad excuse for a town? All I know how to do is sew. I can't even cook."

Evalyn narrowed her eyes at Harriet's excuses. "Well, you could always take in sewing until you get enough money to move on. You've made dresses for Hollywood movies, I'm sure the ladies would line up to get a custom-made dress from you."

"Do you really think that will work?" asked Harriet. "Most of the ladies here still wear flour sack dresses."

"It will work," said Evalyn. "Times are getting better, and women are buying fabric again. Just because we live in a farm town, doesn't mean the women will be wearing rags. I'd do it myself if I weren't so busy with Joy and the farm," Evalyn sighed, willing herself to forgive Harriet. It wouldn't do anyone any good to hold onto the anger. "You can even come out to Rockwood and visit Joy. You can be the fun "aunt" who spoils her rotten, and I can be the mean ol' woman who makes her eat her peas. Who knows, you might even meet a man worth marrying."

"Oh, Evalyn, that sounds so fantastic," said Harriet throwing her arms around her friend.

"Well, it won't be as fabulous as Hollywood and it'll be hard work, but ...," Evalyn stopped, as the rain let up. "Do you hear that?"

Harriet picked her head up. "Sounds like a freight train headed right for us."

Evalyn grabbed Harriet's hand. "It's a twister!"

Lightning flashed through the sky as thunder rumbled loudly overhead.

"We've gotta get out of here," yelled Evalyn. Just as she turned, a large bolt of lightning struck the cottonwood tree next to them and knocked the girls to the ground.

Evalyn looked over her shoulder and screamed as the huge tree fell towards them.

James ran outside with his rifle at the sound of Norman's honks just in time to see Frank Kelley swing at Norman with a club that connected with Norman's wing, before Frank ran away after two other boys. James instantly knew they were probably chasing Jacob.

He hurried into the house. "Elm, take my truck and go to Bill's house. Jacob is being chased by some boys, and they are headed in that direction. I'll follow them from this end."

"I'm going with you," said Tiny as she came up behind James. She was carrying a jug of water.

"I need you in the cellar with Alice," James snapped.

"Alice is fine," Tiny snapped back. "I'm not gonna let Elm go over there by himself when there are three of them boys."

Elmer exited the house carrying two rifles. "Tiny, I can handle it."

Tiny marched over and ripped one of the rifles out of Elmer's hand. "You can handle it better with two."

Realizing Tiny wasn't gonna give up, James gave in. "Fine, go then. Y'all hurry."

Elmer and Tiny rushed into James's truck and took off. James ran to Norman. The bird was up and walking, but it looked as if he might have a broken wing.

"Norman, you stupid ol' bird," he snarled.

The rain stopped and everything went quiet. Goosebumps spread over James's flesh at the eeriness. Then he heard a heavy rumble. He slowly turned and verified his suspicions. It was a tornado, roughly a mile away.

James wanted desperately to go help Jacob and gather Elmer and Tiny, but there was no way he was leaving Alice and Joy alone in the cellar with a tornado headed their way.

"Oh, God, help us all," he prayed as he swooped Norman up and ran for the cellar.

Bill felt the tremor under his knees and took his hands off Lou Anne's stomach as he rose. He searched the western horizon.

"Do you hear that?" asked Lou Anne, grabbing his hand.

"It's a twister," he said, tightening his grip as he made out the ghostly white funnel on the ground.

The couple looked around for shelter.

"Can we make it to the cellar by the house in time?" asked Lou Anne.

"I don't think so," said Bill. "We need to go south. Go release the momma cow."

Lou Anne raced to the cow and quickly untied her. Both the cow and her calf took off in a gallop toward the south. Before Bill could grab Pronto's reins, the horse reared, snapping the reins from the fence post. He danced around, obviously spooked. Bill ran to the horse, hands raised as he tried to settle the creature. "Whoa! Whoa!"

Pronto trotted in a circle, and just as Bill reached for the reins, lightning struck near them causing Pronto to rear again. Bill stumbled back but not before Pronto's front right hoof struck Bill's face. The horse bolted back toward Quail Crossings, and Bill fell to the ground with his hands covering his left eye.

"Bill!" screamed Lou Anne, rushing to his side. "Bill, talk to me. Are you okay?"

Bill felt warm liquid flow down his cheek and knew it wasn't tears or rain. "I don't know. He struck my eye with his hoof."

Lou Anne glanced toward the tornado. It was gaining ground. She snatched Bill's bandana from his pocket and began to tie it around his head. "This might hurt, but we've got to get out of here."

Bill moved his hand and grimaced as Lou Anne maintained pressure on the eye by knotting the bandana behind his head. She grabbed his hand. "There's an old dugout house near here. Come on."

Bill stumbled behind his wife as the roar of the tornado grew louder and louder. The wind whipped at Lou Anne's dress, and he was sure he had just seen a silver mop bucket blow by. He had worked this property for almost six years and had never seen the dugout Lou Anne was running towards. He prayed she knew where she was going.

"There it is!" she shouted over the wind.

With his good eye, Bill could just make out a tiny vent hood about a hundred feet away. The vent hood was old and rusted. Fence posts and barbed wire started to fly around their heads as the tornado's roar got louder. Bill saw what looked to be new wood flying about. His heart sank as he realized that the wood could have only come from the barn they were building at Quail Crossings.

Lou Anne pulled him into the draw, and to his disbelief he saw an old wood door embedded into the small hillside. Lou Anne yanked on the door, but it wouldn't give. Bill grabbed hold of the handle and together they pulled. His ears popped from a sudden change in air pressure, causing him to pull harder.

The door finally gave, sending both Bill and Lou Anne falling backwards. Bill got to his feet first, grabbed Lou Anne, and threw her into the house. He hurried in after her, shutting the door. They both retreated to the very back of the small dugout. Bill wrapped his arms around Lou Anne, cradling both her and their unborn child.

As he looked around the little dugout house, he wondered whether it would be their saving grace or their coffin.

Chapter Thirty-two

"Elmer," Tiny said, fear creeping into her voice as she looked behind them.

Elmer glanced into the rearview mirror at the tornado and pushed the gas pedal to the floor as he shifted gears. "I see it."

The twister was close and gaining on them.

"What are we gonna do?" asked Tiny.

"I'm gonna try to outrun it," said Elmer.

"Maybe we should turn back and try to make it to Quail Crossings." Tiny hugged herself.

Elmer shook his head. "We'll never make it. Our best bet is to try to make it to Bill's house and ride the storm out there."

"Oh no!" Tiny cried as she watched the tornado rip apart the new barn. "Quail Crossings."

"Is the house still there?" asked Elmer, begging the truck to go faster.

"I can't tell," said Tiny, shaking her head. "Does Bill have a cellar?"

"No," said Elmer. "We'll just have to hope the house holds up."

"Maybe we should just keep driving past Bill's house," said Tiny. "If he ain't got a cellar, we're sitting ducks."

"We've still got to help Jacob," said Elmer, keeping one eye on the twister and one on the road. "We can't leave him to Frank Kelley and his goons."

"Do you really think Frank is still chasing Jacob with a tornado on the ground?" asked Tiny, looking over her shoulder.

"I think hate makes people do crazy things," said Elmer.

The pickup's wheels started to fishtail, and Elmer struggled to control the truck. "Hold on!"

Tiny's screams were the last thing Elmer heard as the truck started to flip.

Jacob ran as hard as he could. Sweat mixed with rain ran down his face. He prayed the weather would make the boys turn around and go home. He had no doubt that if they caught him, they'd kill him.

He felt the rumble before he saw the tornado. Looking over his shoulder, past the boys, his blood ran cold as he spotted the twister, and he realized he really would die if he stopped running. He turned his attention to the boys, hoping they would head for their truck. But all three boys were still hot on his trail. Seeing Bill's house in the distance, Jacob picked up speed. He'd rather take his chances in a cellar with the boys than take on a tornado in the middle of a field.

His legs ached and his sides cramped as he reached Bill's house. He stopped suddenly and looked around for a cellar. As thankful as he was the rain had stopped, he knew he didn't have much time as debris started to fill the air. Two of the boys headed straight toward him, and Jacob braced for their tackle. But they ran right past him and into the house.

Jacob wasn't fooled and searched for Frank Kelley. He turned to see Frank lying face down motionless on the ground, a bloody wound on the back of his head and a piece of wood debris lying beside him. "He's dead," Jacob whispered and felt sick to his stomach at the sight of Frank's body.

The twister was bearing down on Jacob as even more debris flew through the air. He started toward the porch, to follow the boys inside but stopped as his foot hit the first step. Jacob shook his head before turning and running to Frank. He knelt beside him and put his hand on Frank's back. Jacob wasn't sure if he felt relief or dread as Frank took in a deep breath.

"Get up," Jacob yelled as he shoved Frank's shoulder. "You've got to get up or that twister's gonna get you. Come on! You can beat me all you want, but you got to get up."

Frank remained motionless.

Jacob got to his feet, flipped Frank over onto his back and grabbed his hands. Tugging on Frank's arms he started dragging him toward Bill's front door. He heard it open and saw Frank's friends in the doorway.

"Don't just stand there," yelled Jacob. "Help me get him inside."

"You deserve to die?" Gabe repeated, shaking his head. "Why on earth would you say you wanna die?"

"It's not that I wanna die, it's just that I don't care if I do," clarified Dovie as the rain started to fall. "Simon, Helen, my unborn child, and my mom are all in Heaven just waiting to see me. I miss them so much. Sometimes the pain is so bad I feel like I'm suffocating."

"But Dovie, you've got all these people here that love you and depend on you," said Gabe.

"Don't you hear me? I'm surrounded by air but I'm suffocating," said Dovie, throwing her hands in the air. "Everyone would be just fine without me."

Gabe ran his hands through his hair. "I just don't understand this kind of talk. It doesn't seem like you at all. You know your family wouldn't be fine without you. What about Alice? You're the closest thing she has to a mother now. And Joy, someone needs to spoil that child rotten, and that's your job as her grandma.

And Jacob, well that boy wouldn't be alive if it weren't for you."

"I don't know what to do," said Dovie, pushing wet hair out of her face. "I shouldn't feel this way about you. I shouldn't care about you the way I do when I still love Simon. I'm just so confused."

"Well, I'm not," said Gabe. "I care for you more than I've cared for any woman in a long time. You're a strong person who doesn't take a lick off anyone, but you'd give a neighbor your last coat if it meant they didn't go cold even if you'd freeze to death. This town, your family, and I — well, we'd be downright lost without you. No one expects you to stop loving Simon. Especially me, it's one of the reasons I like you as much as I do. Dovie you have to know …"

"Shhh …" said Dovie cutting him off.

"No, I'm not gonna stop. You're talking nonsense, and I'll not be quiet until you see sense. If you'd just listen to me, you'd see how much you mean to everyone," said Gabe.

"Do you hear that?" asked Dovie when Gabe took a breath.

"What?" Gabe looked around in confusion.

"Just be still for a minute," Dovie snapped.

Gabe crossed his arms but stood silent, both of them barely taking a breath. Lightning jumped through the clouds just over their heads, causing them both to flinch.

"The church bells," said Dovie, "do you hear the church bells?"

"Yes, but what does that have to do with anything? I was trying to tell you how I feel." Thunder barreled overhead causing Gabe to look at the clouds, and a winkle of worry creased his forehead.

"What time is it?" asked Dovie as another flash of lightning lit overhead.

Gabe sighed and pulled out his pocket watch. "A little after four. We really should get back to town. I don't like the looks of this storm."

"You're right," said Dovie. "The church bells only ring at eight in the morning, noon, and then six in the evening. The fact that they're ringing now, means something is very wrong. Let's go."

She started running toward Knollwood, Gabe right beside her. As they cleared the park trees, Dovie skidded to a stop as she saw the tornado. Her blood ran cold and her legs shivered. She willed herself to stay upright as she calculated the tornado's path.

"No," she whispered. "Home is over there. There's no way it missed Quail Crossings."

Gabe grabbed her hand. "Come on, we can't stay here. We have to find shelter."

Dovie pulled back. "You're running towards it. We should go the other way, towards the feed store. That's where my truck is parked. I need to get home."

"There's no time. We have to get to the butcher shop," said Gabe, pulling on her again as the rain lightened.

Dovie reluctantly followed, praying with every step that she'd see her home again.

Chapter Thirty-three

"No! Harriet!" Evalyn screamed, grabbing her friend under the shoulders and trying to pull her free. Harriet screamed out in pain. Evalyn quickly let go and knelt beside her friend, delicately brushing the hair from around Harriet's face.

"Evie, you have to go," said Harriet, trying to push the trunk off herself with no avail. "I'll be okay, but you have to go take care of our little girl. You have to think about Joy. She needs you. You are her mother."

Evalyn started pushing on the tree with her legs as the tornado whirled toward them. "And what do I tell your mother? I just can't just leave you. Keep pushing, we'll get you out of here."

Harriet coughed hard and grasped for breath. She grabbed Evalyn's hand as a small trickle of blood escaped from her mouth. Evalyn stopped pushing on the log and folded her hands over Harriet's hand.

"You have to go. You have to leave me here," said Harriet, before another round of hard coughs. "Besides you can't get this tree off of me by yourself. Go and get my pa. I'll be right here. I promise."

"Help!" screamed Evalyn, looking around the farm. "Mr. Wheaton! Someone help."

"You've got to go," Harriet said in between wheezing gasps. She squeezed Evalyn's hand. "Please."

"It's not right to leave you like this." Evalyn rubbed Harriet's hand, knowing it would be the last time she saw her friend alive.

"You have to. It'll all be okay. Make sure to give our baby girl lots of hugs from her Aunt Harriet." Harriet coughed hard, the blood turning her lips a rich shade of red. "Joy couldn't ask for a better momma than you. She's lucky to have you, as am I."

Harriet's eyes fluttered violently as Evalyn heard Harriet take her last raspy breath. Evalyn waited for the next inhale, but it never came. Harriet was dead.

"No!" Evalyn cried as she shook her friend. "Please, wake up."

Harriet didn't move as Evalyn's ears popped. There was no time. She either had to leave her friend or risk the same fate. Evalyn leaned over and gave Harriet a gentle peck on the forehead. "I'm sorry."

Evalyn reluctantly let go of Harriet's hand and raced toward the cellar. Tree limbs flew by her head and she readied herself for a knock-out blow at any time. Thinking of Joy, she forced herself to run faster, even as her body ached. She felt something large "whoosh" toward her and fell to the ground just in time to see a corral gate fly over her head. Jumping to her feet, she sprinted to the cellar door.

Reaching the door, she grabbed the handle with both hands and pulled with all her might. The tornado was just fifty feet away, and she was afraid the wind wouldn't allow her to open the door. She fought to keep her footing as she tugged at the door again.

"I will not die today," she said through gritted teeth as she pulled with all her might. As the tornado closed in, she let out a fierce roar.

Suddenly the door flew open and strong arms grabbed her, pulling her inside the cellar. It was George Wheaton, Harriet's father. He slammed the door behind her.

"Oh, Evalyn," cried Kathleen, Harriet's mother. "Where is Harriet?"

Tears fell down Evalyn's cheeks as she fell on her knees before Kathleen and cried into her dress. "I'm so sorry. I tried to get her. She made me go. She made me. I promise I didn't want to leave. I had to."

Kathleen kneeled and lifted Evalyn's chin till their eyes met. "Just tell me what happened. It'll be okay. Where's Harriet?"

"A tree was hit by lightning and landed on her. I tried, but I couldn't get her out," cried Evalyn. "She told me to come get her pa even though we knew it was too late. She was just hurt too badly. She told me I had to go because of Joy … said it with her last breath.

But I shouldn't have left her. I should've stayed. She was hurt so bad. I should've stayed."

"Oh God," cried Kathleen, hugging Evalyn, their tears joining. "Please, not my daughter. Dear God, please don't take my Harriet."

"I'm going after her," said George, trying to open the cellar door, but it wouldn't budge.

"You can't!" yelled Evalyn. "The tornado."

Ignoring Evalyn, he hit the door again with his shoulder and it flew open. George's feet were taken from underneath him as the tornado spun around him. He barely managed to hang onto the door handle.

"George!" screamed Kathleen, letting go of Evalyn and hurrying toward her husband.

She ran up two steps, and George managed to grasp onto her with his free hand. Kathleen held onto him with both hands, trying desperately to pull him back in. Evalyn could see Kathleen losing her balance on the stairs and quickly rose latching her arms around Kathleen's waist. With all her strength, Evalyn pulled back, inching both Kathleen and George away from the cellar door.

George fell back into the cellar, the door closing behind him. Kathleen wrapped her arms around him. "Oh, George, I thought I'd lost you, too. Oh, God, I thought I'd lost you, too."

George began to weep in his wife's arms. "I'm so sorry I couldn't save our girl. I'm so sorry."

Kathleen wept with him as Evalyn sat in the corner and cried alone, hating herself for leaving her friend.

The jars of pickled beets, green beans, and other canned fruits and vegetables shook as the tornado barreled through Quail Crossings. Dust began to fill the small cellar. Alice leaned into James' arms s while they both hovered over Joy.

"Where is everyone?" cried Alice.

"I don't know," said James. "I wish I did, but I just don't know."

"What if we're the only three left?" asked Alice.

"I'm sure we're not," assured James.

"You can't promise me that, can you?" asked Alice.

James shook his head as he looked toward the ceiling. Alice wasn't sure if he was looking to God or hoping the root cellar would hold.

"You're right. I can't promise that. I'm just praying real hard that God will answer my prayers that everyone is safe," said James.

"You think He will?" asked Alice.

"That's what having faith is all about," said James, "and if he doesn't, then I'll just have to pray he gives me the strength to get through the pain. God doesn't always steer the storms away from us, but He always bears through them with us. We just have to keep that in mind."

Alice nodded. "Like He did during Black Sunday when I got lost in the duster."

"Hopefully, just like that," said James. "We were battered and bruised, but all okay for the most part."

Alice looked at Norman who was sitting close to the steps looking up at the cellar door, cocking his head from side to side at the terrible sounds coming from just beyond it.

"But what about Quail Crossings? And all our animals?" asked Alice. "We're losing our home. The home you've lived in forever. It's the only home I've ever really known."

"I can rebuild Quail Crossings, and the livestock will be okay. They know how to get out of the way of a storm," said James. "Besides home is where your family is. As long as we have each other, we will always have home."

The jars started to rattle so violently, a few fell off the shelf causing Joy to cry out. James wrapped his arms around the two girls.

"Make it stop, Mr. James," Alice cried. "Please make it stop!"

"We're gonna be okay," said James, holding her tighter. "Just hold on to me. We'll all be okay."

Alice wanted to believe his words, but couldn't stop her tears of fear from falling into his chest.

Chapter Thirty-four

Lou Anne snuggled closer to Bill and glanced toward the ceiling of the dugout. "Do you think the roof will hold? This place has to be at least fifty years old, if not more."

"I don't know," said Bill, tightening his grip as the roar got even louder. "So what do you think we should name our baby?"

"You wanna talk about that now?" Lou Anne asked with wide eyes. "I hardly think this is the time. Besides we don't even know if I'm with child."

"You must have a pretty good sense of it," said Bill. "I mean, you did run out into the pasture right before a storm was fixin' to hit just to tell me."

Lou Anne bowed her head. "I don't want to get my hopes up. I want to have your child so badly, Bill, but it could be a false alarm. We won't know for sure for a few weeks."

"Then we remain positive that it's true until we know for sure that it isn't," said Bill. "I was thinking maybe Hannah or Annabelle for a girl, and of course, Bill Jr., for a boy."

"I like Annabelle for a girl," Lou Anne let herself smile, "but I am not naming our child Bill Jr. just to feed your big head."

"Fine," said Bill "then how about Billy Dean?"

Lou Anne let out a nervous giggle. "You just don't stop do you? But I do like Dean."

"All right, it's settled then," said Bill, "Annabelle for a girl and Dean for a boy."

The walls of the dugout began to shake violently and large chunks of the ceilings fell to the floor.

"We can't die like this," said Lou Anne. "Not now, not that I'm finally ..." She didn't let herself finish the sentence but rested one hand on her belly.

Bill placed his hand over hers as more clumps of dirt fell from the ceiling. "No matter where we are, we'll be together. I love you, Lou Anne, and if we meet our maker today, we'll meet Him together, with our baby."

"I love you too," said Lou Anne as she rested her head against her husband's chest and waited to see if the roof would hold.

Elmer woke up, his body on top of Tiny's. He looked around and tried to get his bearings. The truck lay on its side, and her head rested in the mud where the window used to be. He sighed with relief as he saw her chest rise and fall with breath.

As he tried to move himself off of her, he felt a familiar pain in his left arm. It was broken. It had been broken five years ago during Black Sunday, and that was a pain Elmer would never forget.

Rising slowly and only using his right arm, he glanced over his shoulder through the back window, expecting to see that the twister had already passed them by, but it hadn't and was approaching fast.

"Mary," he said, lifting her head gently out of the mud and shaking her a bit, "we've got to get out of this truck. The tornado is coming. We aren't safe here. You have to wake up."

The tornado's growl was getting louder, and Elmer could feel the rumble of the ground shaking the truck, yet Tiny still didn't move. He surveyed the scene, wondering if there was any way he could pull Tiny out of the truck. Without the use of his left arm there was no way he could pull her out.

"All right," he said, "If you're staying. I'm staying."

As the tornado rambled towards the truck, Elmer draped his body back over Tiny's and gave her a soft kiss on the cheek.

"I'll protect you," he said as he wrapped his good arm around his girl and closed his eyes. "Always."

The truck started rocking as mud took to the sky. Elmer tightened his grip around Tiny, determined to protect her. He waited for the truck to be sucked into the sky, only to be slammed back down into the earth.

A fence post flew through the windshield and impaled the driver's seat, causing Elmer to tuck his head harder into Tiny. His heart raced as he waited for the truck to be tossed around like a ball.

The cab filled with mud, and Elmer felt it sticking to his back and legs as the tornado roared by them. The truck rocked even more violently, and Elmer curled his body even closer over Tiny's. Suddenly the noise stopped and as quickly as the mud had flown up, it fell back to the ground, coating the entire cab.

Elmer looked through the cracked windshield and saw that the tornado had passed. He waited for the tornado to get further away before he lowered himself onto the floorboard of the truck. He leaned near Tiny's face. "Mary, the twister's gone. You have to wake up. We need to get you help."

But Tiny didn't move.

Jacob and the boys looked around Bill's parlor as the tornado approached.

"We can't stay in this room," said Jacob, "There are too many windows."

"Maybe we should go upstairs," said one of the boys. "What do you think, Paul?"

"Don't be dumb, Tom," said Paul. "We usually go to the cellar, why would you want to go higher?"

"We need to find a room or closet without windows," said Jacob.

"Haven't you been here before?" asked Paul.

Jacob shook his head. "Here, let's get in this closet. At least the glass won't hit us that way."

Jacob jerked open the door to the coat closet and started pulling out boots and other random things that sat on the closet floor. The boys dragged Frank in first and then crouched around him.

"I wish it wasn't so dark in here," said Tom.

"If I were you, I'd start praying it remains dark in here," said Jacob. "'Cause if we see light that means we're dead or about to be."

The walls started to shake violently, and one of the boys cried out.

Gabe yanked open the door of the butcher shop.

"No one is here," said Dovie.

"Oh, they're here. I know they are," said Gabe pulling Dovie behind the counter. "We need to go to his cold storage room. They used double concrete blocks when they built the room to keep it cool. That's where everyone will be."

Gabe pushed open the cold storage door, and sure enough, there were a dozen people inside the room, huddled together among the slabs of meat. Dovie couldn't help but stare at the large hooks hanging from the ceiling.

"Are you sure it's safe in here?" she asked.

"Safest place in town," said Butcher Davis, "unless you're under the ground. How's it look out there?"

"Bad," said Gabe. "I don't think the twister is gonna miss the town."

As if on cue, the walls rattled and Dovie felt her ears pop. She sank to the floor as reality set in. "Oh God, the twister was coming from the direction of Quail Crossings. I don't even know where everyone is? What if they're all …?" She buried her head in her hands. "I don't think I have the strength …. Oh, dear God, please, not again."

Gabe sat beside her and wrapped his arms around her. "No matter what, I'll be right here to help you through it."

The walls shook again, and the meat started swaying back and forth. The twister was bearing down on them. Dovie buried her head into Gabe's chest and wept.

Chapter Thirty-five

"I think it's over," said George, walking up the cellar steps. "I hear birds singing."

"Seems odd that birds could sing so peacefully right after something so violent," said Kathleen, eyes red and swollen from crying.

Evalyn leapt to her feet and rushed past George, throwing the door open. She squinted as the sun shining through the end of the storm assaulted her eyes. Half of the Wheaton's house was gone and household debris, pieces of the house itself, and tree limbs lay everywhere.

"Harriet," Evalyn whispered, still trying to absorb the damage. She would help the Wheatons find Harriet and then she would go to Joy. Her arms longed to hold her daughter, and she prayed that James had kept everyone safe at Quail Crossings.

"Come on," said George. "Take me to where y'all were. Maybe she's still there and, by some miracle, still alive."

Evalyn picked her way through the littered yard with George and Kathleen following close behind. It was almost impossible to find where the orchard used to be because nothing looked as it had just moments before.

"There," Evalyn pointed and ran to the spot. "Harriet!"

Both the tree and Harriet were gone. Evalyn fell to her knees. A light rain started to fall. "I shouldn't have left her." Although she thought she had used up all her tears in the cellar, fresh ones trickled down her face as she looked over her shoulder at Harriet's parents. "I'm so sorry."

George had his arm wrapped around Kathleen who wept into his shoulder.

"We need to look for her," said Kathleen, placing her hand on her forehead. "She may still be around. The twister could've thrown her. She could still be alive. We have to look."

Evalyn looked at the broken landscape and felt no hope that they'd find her friend alive. Her eyes fell on Elmer's truck. It stood there with barely a scratch, as if it didn't belong in the chaos.

"I'll go get help," said Evalyn, rising to her feet. "I need to go to Quail Crossings and check on Joy. I just hope they were in the cellar."

"Where's Robert?" asked George.

Evalyn's heart sank. She had no idea where her husband was or if he was even still alive.

James pushed the cellar door open just as it started to sprinkle again. He surveyed the damage. The chicken coop was on the ground in pieces, as was the new barn. But the old barn and house were still standing. A few cows grazed near Dovie's flowerbed, and James let out a sigh of relief as he saw that their milk cow, Poppy, was among them.

"You can come on out," he said to Alice. "The worst is over."

James retreated to grab Norman and then helped Alice out while she carried Joy. Norman, thankful to be out of the hole, waddled around and started honking. As he did, chickens started to come out of their hiding places. It looked like most of the flock was still around, but scattered.

The livestock was the last thing on James's mind as he scanned the horizon for signs of Bill, Lou Anne, Elmer, Tiny, and Jacob. He hoped Knollwood had been spared and that Dovie and Gabe would be back soon. Alice bent to put Joy down on the ground.

"Don't," said James, "there could be nails everywhere. Why don't y'all go inside the house? She can crawl around in there without getting hurt."

"But I wanna look for Bill," whined Alice. "And where did Jacob go? He came up here to get Mr. Norman, and I never saw him again."

Pronto trotted near the barn and James's eyes narrowed. Bill wasn't on the back of the horse.

"Go inside, Alice," said James. "You need to take care of Joy for now. I'll find them."

As he watched Alice walk inside, he prayed he hadn't just lied to her. He approached Pronto and quickly grabbed the reins. Looking the horse over, he found no cuts or other injuries.

Tying Pronto inside the barn, he quickly saddled his own horse, Tex. Once in the saddle, he grabbed Pronto's reins. He leaned over and patted Pronto's neck. "Sorry, ol' boy, but I've got to take you out again. It would be nice if you could just lead me to where you last saw Bill. Dear God, I hope Lou Anne was with him. I have no idea where to start looking for either of them."

Leading Pronto out of the barn, he rode Tex toward the southeastern part of the property. Both Jacob and Elmer had also headed in that direction, so it was his best bet at finding anyone. Boards, a toaster, a washing pot, curtains, and other everyday items littered the pasture. He was sure the boards were from his new barn but had no idea where the other items like the toaster and curtains had come from. One thing he did know for sure was that someone's house had been hit.

He heeled Tex into a trot, and they made good time getting to Bill's house. He gave a sigh of relief when he saw that the house still stood, minus a few windows and bit of damage to the roof.

"Bill! Lou Anne!" James called out as he scanned the property, getting off Tex. He ran up the steps and opened up the front door. "Elmer? Is anyone in here? Jacob?"

"Mr. James?"

The voice was muffled, but James was sure it was Jacob's. He looked at the coat closet, the very closet that had sheltered Alice from the horrible dust storm during Black Sunday. He jerked the door open and there stood Jacob and two boys. Frank Kelley still lay unconscious at their feet.

Jacob hurried out, and James gave him a quick hug. "I'm so glad to see you."

"Not as glad as I am to see you," said James. "Are you hurt?"

Jacob shook his head, and James turned his attention to the boys still in the closet. They stared back at him, fear on their faces as if he were the tornado himself.

"I'm sorry for chasing you," Paul said to Jacob.

"Me too," said Tom. "You saved Frank from being ate up by that twister and probably saved us too by having us get in the closet."

"Now I see what we were doing was wrong," said Paul. "Frank made us do it. He said it was what our pas wanted us to do."

"Come on out, boys," said James. "I think that given the circumstances, we can let bygones be bygones, on one condition."

"Name it," said Paul, Tom nodding in approval as they stepped out of the closet.

"You boys start thinking for yourselves. It takes more courage to stand up and say no than it does to go along with something you know is wrong. Now, how did you boys get out here?"

"I drove my truck," said Paul. "It's parked just south of your pond if the twister didn't get it."

"I need you to go check on that truck, and if it's okay, you need to go into town and get help for Frank here," said James.

Paul started to walk out, then stopped and looked at Jacob. "I ain't seen anyone do anything as brave as when you carried Frank inside here." He turned his attention to James. "On my honor, I'm gonna make sure the whole town knows what Jacob did even though we were out to get him."

James gave a nod of approval as Paul left. He looked at Tom. "Help me get Frank out of the closet."

They lifted Frank out of the closet. Jacob quickly brushed the glass off before they laid Frank down on the sofa. Frank groaned a bit but didn't come to.

James examined his head. "He's got a pretty nasty bump, but he'll probably be okay. Not much I can do for him until the doctor comes."

He looked at Jacob. "Have you seen Bill or any of the others? Elmer and Tiny were headed this way to help you before the twister hit."

Jacob shook his head. "I never saw no one."

James looked at Tom. "You stay here with Frank. Don't let him leave, understand? He needs to lie still until the doctor comes."

Tom nodded.

"All right," said James, "Jacob we need to split up. You take the road and see if you can find Elmer and Tiny, and I'll take the horses and keep looking for Bill and Lou Anne."

James exited the house, mounted up on Tex, and led Pronto back into the pasture. As they walked along, he looked to the sky. "Dear Lord, thank you for helping me find Jacob alive and well. Please help me to find Bill and Lou Anne. This is gonna be like finding a needle in a haystack. Please lead me in the right direction."

It felt as if they had been in the butcher's cold storage room for hours even though Dovie knew it had only been a few minutes.

"I think we might be past the worst of it," said Gabe.

"The worst of it?" Dovie raised an eyebrow. "I don't think we can even begin to imagine what we're about to see out there. For all we know, Knollwood isn't even on the map anymore."

Gabe sighed. "You know that's not what I meant, Dovie."

Dovie placed her hand on Gabe's arm. "I'm sorry. I'm just really worried about everyone, and sometimes things fly out of my mouth before I can stop them. You know like when I said I deserved to die earlier." Dovie shook her head. "I didn't mean that either. I apologize for being so melodramatic all because you kissed me."

"I believe you kissed me back," Gabe said with a wink. "Does this mean I can do it again, kiss you that is?"

"It's over, folks," announced the butcher before Dovie could answer. "We better go see who needs help."

Everyone got up and headed out the door. Dovie paused at the doorway, unsure if she wanted to see what her life had become in the aftermath of the tornado. There was a good chance she had lost some family and friends, and she wasn't sure if she could bear it.

"Whatever lies out there," said Gabe grabbing her hand. "We'll face together."

Dovie squeezed his hand.

"You ready?" he asked.

Dovie gave him a firm nod, before they left the room to face what was left of their world.

Chapter Thirty-six

Jacob first saw the sun reflecting off the truck. Something didn't look right, and it wasn't just the fact that it was in the pasture and not on the road. His heart leapt to his throat as he started to run. Jacob skidded to a halt when he realized the truck was on its side. Not only was the truck lying on the passenger side, but the cab, hood and bed all looked as if they had been punched by an angry giant.

"Oh, Lord Jesus, let them be okay," said Jacob as he ran to the truck.

He stopped just short of the hood, eyes locked on the fence post that impaled the driver's side, and tried to prepare himself for what he was about to see. There was a big chance it wouldn't be pretty in there.

Jacob turned in a circle looking for help. He hoped he'd see Mr. James or Mr. Bill on the horizon. He really didn't want to face the wreck alone. He didn't want to see the mangled bodies of Miss Tiny and Elmer. He took a deep breath. No one was around and it was all up to him.

"Hello?" He held his breath waiting for a response. Nothing.

"Elmer? Miss Tiny? Hello?" he tried again and again was met with silence.

Jacob took another deep breath, willing his legs to stop shaking and move forward. No matter what condition they were in, his friends needed him. He had never had truer friends than Alice, Elmer, and Tiny, and he wouldn't let them lay in the mud, no matter their physical condition.

He carefully made his way to the front of the truck and looked through the windshield. He let out a cry of relief when he saw the fence post only punctured the seat and not a person. Maybe Elmer and Tiny weren't in the truck at all. Maybe they had taken cover somewhere. His eyes scanned down to the passenger seat and were met with a muddy face. Jacob let out a scream, as eyes blinked back at him.

"Elmer? Is that you?" Jacob cried out.

"Jacob?" said Elmer. "Oh, thank goodness. Mary, it's Jacob. We're safe; please wake up now."

Jacob slapped his knee and let out a cheerful, "Whoo-hoo! Praise Jesus!"

He ran closer to the windshield. "Are you hurt, Elmer? How is Miss Tiny?"

"I'm pretty sure I broke my arm and Mary's knocked out, but breathing. She's been out for a while and I can't wake her up," said Elmer. "Can you get us out of here?"

"You bet." Jacob nodded and hurried over to the driver's side. He gave the truck a few hard shoves to make sure it was stable and then scurried up the bottom of the truck and lying on his stomach on the driver's side door, peered into the window. The fence post was his first obstacle.

"Elmer," he hollered, "shield your face and cover up Miss Tiny. I'm gonna try to push the fence post out from this side, but the windshield might bust. I'm surprised it didn't break into a million pieces when the fence post came though."

Elmer once again draped his body over Tiny's. Reaching in with both hands, Jacob tried to push the fence post back through the windshield. It didn't budge. His angle was all wrong.

"I can't push the fence post out this way," said Jacob.

"Any other ideas?" asked Elmer.

Jacob studied the problem. "Maybe, let me try something."

Making his way off the driver's side of the truck, he walked back to the windshield. He really wished he had Mr. James and the horse or at the very least some gloves, but he didn't, so he'd have make due.

"I'm gonna try to pull it out from this direction, mind your faces," said Jacob.

He waited until Elmer had assumed his protective position. Standing on the ground by the windshield, he reached up, grabbed the fence post, and started pulling.

It didn't move. Jacob rubbed both of his hands on his pants before spitting on them, rubbing them together, and pulling again.

As the fence post started to move, splinters bore into his palm, but he kept pulling. The fence post gave suddenly, and with a loud crack, the windshield broke into thousands of pieces raining glass onto Elmer and Tiny and sending Jacob stumbling back past the hood of the truck and into the mud.

Jacob got up and quickly ran to Elmer. He delicately brushed the glass off the hood and reached his hand down. Elmer latched on to it using his good arm. The angle was awkward, but Jacob managed to slide Elmer out with little pain and only a few small cuts from the shattered windshield.

"I'll go in and get Miss Tiny," said Jacob. "I'll lift her out of the seat and then we'll just slide her along the hood of the truck kind of like we did you."

"Mind the glass and be really careful lifting her," said Elmer. "I have no idea how bad she's hurt."

Jacob gave Elmer a quick nod before sliding into the truck cab and lifting Tiny up and out through the windshield. Elmer guided her feet until she lay on the muddy ground. Jacob carefully climbed out around her.

Elmer kneeled next to Tiny. "Come on, Mary, wake up. The storm is over. Wake up, Mary."

"We got to get her out of the mud," said Jacob. He knelt, picked her up, and started walking down the road.

"Where ya going?" asked Elmer.

"Back to Bill's house," said Jacob. "That Paul kid is supposed to be fetching the doctor for Frank Kelley. She needs to be there, too."

Bill coughed and waited for his eyes to adjust to the light. A thin sliver of sun shone through the old rusted vent, but that was it. The dugout had been reduced to little more than a hole just big enough for Bill and Lou Anne to sit in.

Bill gave a silent prayer of thanks for not being buried completely and then looked at Lou Anne. Her head lay on his shoulder and her eyes were closed. Any other time, he would have thought she was sleeping peacefully.

"Lou Anne," he said gently, "wake up."

Lou Anne didn't respond, so Bill gave her a little shake ignoring the panicked thoughts that raced through his head. "Lou Anne."

Lou Anne coughed hard.

"Oh, thank God," Bill hugged her tightly. "Are you okay?"

Lou Anne nodded. "I think so."

"Did something hit your head?" asked Bill. "You were unconscious. It took me a while to wake you."

Lou Anne felt her head. "I don't think so. Nothing hurts. Maybe I fainted."

"How's the baby?" asked Bill, laying a gentle hand on her stomach.

"I think we're both fine. Really, Bill, nothing hurts." She gently touched the bandana that still covered his eye. "How are you?"

"I'm not gonna lie," said Bill. "It hurts something terrible, but right now, we've got to get out of here."

She looked around the room and got to her knees. "Where are the door and the windows?"

"Part of the dugout caved in," said Bill.

"Oh, my dear Lord." He hand flew to her mouth, then her stomach. "What are we gonna do?"

"We still have air coming in from the vent so don't panic," he said. "We can wait for someone to find us."

"But, Bill," said Lou Anne, "no one knows where we are. It was a miracle I found you and you were in an open pasture. Will they even think to look here? And if they do see it, will they know that we came in here before the collapse?"

Bill rubbed the back of his neck. "I guess we have only one choice." He got on all fours and crawled to where the door used to be. "We better start digging."

Chapter Thirty-seven

Evalyn pulled into the drive at Quail Crossings and was elated to see it was still standing. It looked like the new barn was a total loss, but she couldn't have cared less. She bolted out of the truck and up the stairs. Slamming open the back door, she rushed through the house.

Her heart leapt in delight when she saw Alice reading a story to Joy in the parlor. She rushed over and swooped up Joy, holding her tight.

"Evie!" Alice cried, jumping up and hugging her sister. "I'm so glad you're okay. Where have you been? Why weren't you in the shelter?"

"I was at the Wheaton's, in their shelter," answered Evalyn. She looked around. "Where is everybody?"

Tears filled Alice's eyes. "I don't know. It was just us, Mr. James, and Mr. Norman in the cellar. Mr. James went to look for everyone. I think Momma Dovie is still in town."

"Has Robert been by?" asked Evalyn.

Alice shook head. "I haven't seen him today."

Evalyn kissed Joy on the head and hugged Alice again. "I'm so glad you're okay, but I still need your help."

"Anything," answered Alice.

"The Wheaton farm was hit really bad. I need to go find help," said Evalyn. "I was hoping to find it here."

"Is everyone okay?" asked Alice.

"I don't know yet," said Evalyn. She knew, but there was no reason to scare Alice right now. "I need you to continue to watch Joy. Will you do that for me?"

Alice nodded. "You're comin' back, aren't you Evie?"

"Of course I am," said Evalyn. "I'm sure James will be back with everyone else soon, and Dovie will be back from town."

"It's scary being here all by myself," said Alice.

Evalyn lifted Alice's chin. "It has been a very scary day, and I can tell you've been extremely brave. I just need you to be brave a little bit longer and tonight when I get back, I'll spend the night. We'll all cuddle in bed together and feel safe, okay?"

Alice nodded. "Okay, I can do that."

"Good. Now you two finish your book and then maybe play with your dolls. I bet Joy would love to see your wooden Mr. Norman," said Evalyn. "Do you know where all Joy's things are here, her bottles, diapers, and milk?"

Alice nodded as she sat down and took Joy. Evalyn gave them both one last kiss, hating to leave but knowing she had to, and rushed out the door. She had to go to Rockwood. She had to find Robert. She just had to.

James decided to crisscross the pasture instead of following the fence line even though Bill had been checking the fence before the storm hit. Bill had enough sense to get away from the barbed wire during a storm, tornado or no tornado. Hopefully, if he found Bill, he'd find Lou Anne.

He couldn't help but be a tad upset with Lou Anne. One minute she was watching Joy, and the next minute she was running into the pasture like a loon. He was sure she was probably worried about Bill. James knew that had he been in the pasture, his wife, Sylvia would have done the same thing Lou Anne had done. But darn it, now he had no clue where she was.

The rusted vent hood of the old dugout caught his eye, and he decided to give it a look. The dugout had been used by his father's tenant farmers some fifty years ago. He remembered helping his pa dig out the soil. The whole time they worked on it, he couldn't help but think how weird it would be to live basically underground. He'd felt so sorry for the tenants and wondered if his pa wasn't being a bit unfair. That was until one hot July day when James got overheated working in the fields and passed out for a minute. After he came to, his father ran his horse all the way to the dugout instead of taking James to the house.

James had been very confused about why his father hadn't just taken him home, but the minute they walked into the cool dugout, James realized living under the earth had its benefits. After a couple of glasses of cold well water in the cool air of the dugout, he felt miles better. After the tenant farmers left for greener pastures of their own, James had used the dugout as his own secret place – a hideout for getting away from his older brothers and sisters.

As he entered the draw he wasn't surprised to see the dugout still intact, but his heart sank as he saw the mud-filled window just to the right of the door. James dismounted and took a closer look. Part of the ceiling had caved in and it appeared to have happened recently, although he couldn't say for sure how recently.

Running his hands through his hair, he looked around the pasture. Maybe he should just go back to Quail Crossings and see if Bill had already made his way back. For all he knew, they could be circling each other. Plus, Alice and Joy had been alone for a long time. He needed to check on them.

James went to mount up when he thought he heard something. He let go of the saddle and closed his eyes. He heard it again. It sounded like knocking.

He walked back to the dugout door and knocked, feeling a bit like a fool. But to his surprise, he got a knock back. He grabbed the handle and started to pull. The door was stuck, probably due to the cave in.

He hustled back to Tex and grabbed a rope. He tied one end to the door handle before tying the other end to the saddle horn. He mounted the horse and with a few clicks of his tongue, he had Tex backing up.

"Come on, boy," James encouraged. "Pull!"

The horse whinnied and danced around as it pulled backwards. James felt the rope giving and knew the door was coming lose. He gave Tex a bit of heel and yelled, "Almost there, Tex! Come on!"

Tex jerked back and the door flew open causing a muddy Bill and Lou Anne to spill out. The two hurried to their feet and scrambled into the fresh air just as the rest of the dugout caved in. The door had been the only thing keeping the small open space that Bill and Lou Anne had hid in from caving in.

"I never thought I'd breathe fresh air again," Lou Anne said, looking at the sky and taking a deep breath.

James dismounted and hurried to them, wrapping them in a hug. "I'm so glad I found y'all. Are you okay?"

"For the most part," said Bill, hugging Lou Anne again. "Pronto kicked me in the eye. It still smarts quite a bit."

"Are you okay?" James asked Lou Anne.

"I'm fine. We need to get Bill to a doctor, now," she said, trying to take a good look at Bill's eye since they had light again.

"Why don't you and Bill take Pronto and go back to your house? One of the local boys went to fetch a doctor for Frank Kelley, and they are there," said James.

"So it's still standing?" asked Bill before cocking his head. "And what is Frank Kelley doing there?"

"It's a long story I can tell ya later," said James. "As far as the house, we'll need to replace some windows and do some roof work, but yes, it looks good."

"And Quail Crossings?" asked Lou Anne.

"Still standing," said James. "We lost the new addition to the barn and the chicken coop fell over. But we're very fortunate. Alice and Joy are there now. I'll go back there to see if Dovie and Evalyn have made it back and if Jacob has found Elmer and Tiny."

"Elmer's missing?" asked Bill.

"You all were," said James, throwing his hands in the air. "Alice, Joy, and I were the only ones in the shelter when the twister hit. I found Jacob taking cover in your coat closet with the town boys that were after him. I sent one of those boys to fetch a doctor, and I sent Jacob to look for Elmer and Tiny along the road."

"I need to look for Elm," said Bill.

"You need a doctor," said Lou Anne, crossing her arms. "For all we know, Jacob has found them and taken them to Quail Crossings. We'll go to our house, and they'll be along shortly. Now come on."

James walked to Tex. "Sounds like you should listen to the lady."

Chapter Thirty-eight

Dovie and Gabe exited the butcher shop with the rest of the people who had taken shelter there. As they came onto Main Street, they stepped over the litter of boards, plates, clothes hangers, cans of Eagle Brand Condensed Milk, boxes of Oreo Crème Sandwiches, and an assortment of things that the tornado had dispersed all over town.

Dovie gasped as she looked to the north and saw that the Knollwood Market and the structures beyond it were all destroyed. Dovie and Gabe, along with the others who had taken shelter at the butcher shop, quickly made their way to the damaged area. There would be people who needed help, and even though she worried about Quail Crossings, the town was in urgent need of her nursing skills.

A boy about Elmer's age ran up to her before she had even reached the first damaged structure, stopping both Gabe and her.

"Mrs. Grant?" he asked.

"Yes," she said.

"I thought that was you. My name is Paul, and I was out at your place when the twister hit," he said.

"You were at Quail Crossings? I don't understand," said Dovie, her brain spinning at the sight of the damage around her.

"I went out there with Frank Kelley to get Jacob," started Paul. "It's a long story, ma'am, and I will gladly tell you everything, but Frank's hurt real bad and Mr. Murphy sent me in town to get a doctor, but he's busy. Mrs. Pearl said you were real good at helping people, so I hoped you'd come back to Mr. Brewer's house with me."

Dovie looked at Gabe. She desperately wanted to check on her home and family, but it felt wrong somehow to leave the destruction in town.

"Go," said Gabe. "I'll stay here and help where I can. The doctor is here so go tend to that young man."

Dovie nodded and then grabbed Gabe's hand. "Thank you for saving me out there."

Gabe shook his head. "I didn't save you."

"You did," said Dovie. "You saved me from myself."

Before she could stop herself, she gave Gabe a kiss ignoring everyone around them, then said, "My truck is just past the feed store and should be fine unless it was hit with debris from the twister. Use it to come home, Gabe"

Gabe gave her hand a tight squeeze before turning his attention to the destruction. Dovie turned to Paul. "Where is your truck?"

"I parked it over by the feed store as well. I didn't wanna drive through all this stuff."

Dovie followed Paul as he rushed down the street.

"So Quail Crossings, is it okay?" she asked, praying for a positive answer.

"I didn't get a good look at it when I left, but the house was still standing," said Paul as he opened the passenger-side door on his truck for her.

She slid in and waited for him to close her door and get in on the other side before asking. "And you saw my father, who else?"

"Just Mr. Murphy and Jacob. No one else was there," answered Paul.

Dovie slouched in the seat. She wondered about Alice and Elmer, Bill and Lou Anne. Where was everyone? Hopefully, they were all safely inside the walls of Quail Crossings.

Evalyn's cheeks felt chapped from all the crying she had done as she looked at what was left of her home, Rockwood. The tornado had destroyed everything. The house and barn were completely gone, but oddly enough, the windbreak of cedar trees still stood.

Evalyn turned the truck off and got out. She'd have to walk from here to search for Robert, as dead pigs blocked the road. Thankfully, she had run into Ben Wheaton, Harriet's younger brother, on the road and gotten him to stop. He had promised to go back to the ranch he was working at and get help to find Harriet. She would return to the Wheaton's house as well, but first she had to know if Robert had survived. She prayed she hadn't lost him as well.

She couldn't believe it was all gone. She expected to see the house debris, but it was almost as if the place had never been there. Only the rocks of the grand fireplace remained, lying in a sad pile on the ground.

Evalyn stood on the foundation of what used to be her home and turned in a circle. How could this even be? Taking a deep breath, she walked toward the destroyed barn which lay in a heap of broken boards. She prayed Robert wasn't in there.

"Robert?" she called. "Robert, are you here?"

She heard nothing. She turned in another slow circle, scanning the horizon for signs of her husband when something caught her eye. It couldn't be. But as she jogged toward it, she realized it was.

There in the middle of the road that led to the barn, sat the crib Robert had made for Joy. She traced her hand along the fine woodwork and realized it was as if someone had placed it there gently. There wasn't even a scratch on it. The mattress had been ruined by the rain, but that could easily be replaced.

She heard the screech of brakes and looked up. She gasped with relief as she saw Robert's truck pull in next to Elmer's. Robert got out and frantically scanned the property, his face a ghostly white. Evalyn wondered if it was just the shock of losing everything so suddenly, but then she realized he wasn't looking at the property, he was looking for Joy and for her.

He had no idea she had left Rockwood and was at the Wheatons' when the storm came in. For all he knew, she and Joy had been in the house when the tornado hit. His hand rubbed his jaw, and then worked its way to the back of his neck before he finally noticed her.

His hand dropped and he ran to her. Evalyn let go of the crib and ran to meet him. As they met, he wrapped her up in a tight embrace and kissed her. She held tightly onto the back of his neck as she kissed him back, thankful to feel his touch again.

He pulled away and placed his hands on her cheeks. "Are you okay? Where is Joy?"

"I'm fine and so is Joy. She is at Quail Crossings with Alice," answered Evalyn, placing her hands on his hips. "Are you okay? Where have you been?"

"After our fight, I just started driving south," said Robert. "I didn't have any place in mind to go. I needed to think about what to do next. I knew the storm was coming, but I kept driving. I'm sorry, Evalyn. I should've come back. I was so afraid I'd lost you."

"It's okay. Right after you left, I went to talk to Harriet." Evalyn let out a small cry as she said her friend's name.

"What is it?" asked Robert.

"Harriet's dead," said Evalyn. "A tree landed on her right before the twister. I tried to save her, but I couldn't get her out. She made me leave her there and told me to look after Joy."

Robert wrapped her back up in a hug as Evalyn cried into his shoulder. "I'm so sorry, Evalyn."

Evalyn pulled back. "We need to get back to Quail Crossings and make sure James has found everyone. Alice didn't know where anyone was when I found her and Joy in the house. James was out looking for them. She was scared, so I told her I would come back after I got help for the Wheatons."

"Okay, we'll go back to Quail Crossings and then to the Wheatons'," said Robert, looking around. "I can't believe all this damage and all the pigs. They didn't stand a ..."

He stopped.

"What's wrong?" asked Evalyn, and he put his finger to his lips.

Evalyn listened. What was that?

"It's squealing," said Robert as if answering her internal question. "It's coming from the cedar trees."

"Maybe some of the pigs made it," said Evalyn.

They had started toward the wind break when Daisy, the little runt pig, and Applecrisp, the goat, broke through the tree line and sprinted over to them. Evalyn fell to her knees as the pig jumped into her lap. "Oh, Daisy, I'm so glad to see you." She laughed. "I bet you're a hungry little piggy."

Robert grabbed the rope that still hung around Applecrisp's head before he bent to pat the runt's head. "Come on, Daisy, Joy will be happy to see you. Let's go."

"Could you do me a favor first?" asked Evalyn, getting up while Daisy still nudged her leg for attention. "Would you help me load the crib into Elmer's truck? I can't believe it survived the storm, but I'm so glad it did because Joy's daddy made it." Evalyn looked at Robert with soft eyes and smiled.

Robert kissed her forehead and smiled back. "Anything for my family."

Chapter Thirty-nine

By the time Dovie entered Bill's house, Frank Kelley had come to and had given his place on the sofa to Tiny, who was still unconscious. Bill sat in a chair while Lou Anne tried to clean around a nasty looking cut straight across his eye. Elmer had just walked back into the house, looking as if he had just dunked himself in the stock tank, and Jacob was bringing a basin of fresh water to Tiny's side where Alice was cleaning Tiny's muddy face. Dovie glimpsed inside the kitchen, where James sat feeding a bowl of mushy oatmeal to Joy. Evalyn and Robert were nowhere to be found.

It looked bad, but Dovie reminded herself that she could have walked in on much worse. Tiny looked the worst, but Dovie could see she was breathing and that was a good start. Before she could tend to anyone, she had to do one thing.

"Alice," said Dovie.

Alice's face lit up when she saw her and she came running over. "Momma Dovie!"

They embraced, and Dovie kissed the top of Alice's head. "I'm so glad you're okay. I was so worried about you." Dovie looked around the room. "I was worried about all of you."

"I was worried about you," said Alice, tightening her hug.

James came into the parlor with Joy and hugged Dovie. "Oh, Dovie, thank heavens. As you can see, we've got quite the mess here."

Dovie nodded. "Yes, it's quite the mess in town as well."

"Oh no," said James, "how bad is it?"

"The Knollwood Market and everything north is gone," said Dovie. "Gabe is still there helping out."

"That's why I couldn't bring the doctor," said Paul. "He's busy, so I brought Mrs. Grant here."

"Where are Evalyn and Robert?" Dovie asked.

"I saw Evie earlier," said Alice. "She went looking for Robert, but I haven't seen her since then. She said she'd come. She promised."

"Then she will," said Dovie. "I'm sure both she and Robert will be here soon, God willing. Dad," Dovie looked at James, "Did you think to bring my kit?"

James nodded. "It's in the kitchen."

"All right, let's get to work then," said Dovie, clapping her hands.

She went to Tiny first and laid her head gently on Tiny's chest. "Her breathing's good. Alice, grab the smelling salts, and we'll see if that works first. How long has she been out, and how did this happen?"

"Over an hour," said Elmer. "We were trying to outrun the tornado when I lost control of the truck and it rolled. When I came to, she was out and has been out ever since. We rode the twister out in the front of the pickup. Luckily, it missed us."

Dovie's face fell before she rushed to Elmer and gave him a hug. They had been very lucky. Dovie didn't want to think about what might have been the outcome. Elmer yelped at her embrace.

"What is wrong with your arm?" asked Dovie.

"I think it's broken," said Elmer.

"Why didn't you tell me, son?" asked James, rushing to his side.

"I wanted to make sure Tiny was okay first," said Elmer. "I can handle the pain."

Alice came in with the smelling salts. Dovie raised an eyebrow at Elmer.

"Jacob, can you make a sling for Elm before he makes his arm worse?" asked Dovie. "It'll be a while before I can make a cast. Good thing he's tough."

She turned and ran the smelling salts under Tiny's nose. Tiny's eyes fluttered open and her nose wrinkled. "What is that smell?" Her eyes darted around. "Where am I?"

"You're at Bill's house," said Dovie. "You and Elmer crashed the truck during the twister. Do you remember that?"

Tiny nodded slightly.

"Good," said Dovie. "Does it hurt anywhere?"

"No," Tiny whispered. "Well, my head hurts."

"Yes, you whacked it pretty good when the truck flipped," said Dovie. "We're just gonna keep you awake for a while. Can you sit up for me?"

Tiny nodded before Dovie helped her into a sitting position.

"Doing okay?" asked Dovie as she held up three fingers. "How many fingers am I holding up?"

Tiny answered correctly.

"Are my fingers fuzzy?" asked Dovie.

"No," said Tiny.

"Good," said Dovie. She looked over at Elmer as Jacob finished tying the sling. "Elm, you need to make sure she stays awake and alert for the next few hours, okay? If she starts acting confused or won't stay awake, let me know."

Dovie stepped over to Frank and asked him the same questions she had asked Tiny, this time holding up four fingers. Frank answered correctly. Dovie looked at Paul. "Take him home. Tell his momma to keep him awake and to find the doctor if he gets confused or won't wake up. Tonight she'll need to wake him up every couple of hours and make sure he's still alert, but I think he'll be okay." She twisted her apron. "Oh, and would you stop by the Clark farm and let them know Tiny is with us and that she's okay?"

Paul nodded at the instructions before helping Frank out of the house and leaving.

"Did he ever apologize?" Elmer asked Jacob as Frank walked out the door. "Or at least say thanks that you saved his life?"

"You saved his life?" Again Dovie raised an eyebrow. It was clear she had missed a lot this afternoon. She bent to examine Bill's eye.

Jacob shook his head. "No, I don't suspect someone like Frank Kelley ever thinks he's in the wrong or admits that he needed help in the first place."

"Well, maybe that board knocked some sense into him," said Dovie, causing Lou Anne to giggle.

"Bill," said Dovie, covering Bill's good right eye, "can you see anything out of the eye now?"

"No, it's just black," said Bill.

Dovie sighed. "This is far out of my area of knowledge. We need to get him to the doctor."

Evalyn and Robert barreled through the door. "Are Alice and Joy here?"

Dovie grabbed Evalyn and wrapped her in a hug. "Of course they are, and I'm glad y'all are here too."

Dovie looked around the room at her family. They all sat there, battered and bruised, but they were all alive. Tears escaped Dovie's eyes, and Alice came running up to her.

"Are you okay, Momma Dovie?" Alice asked.

"I am," said Dovie. "These are happy tears."

Chapter Forty

Six weeks later

They had looked for Harriet for two weeks before calling off the search. A week after Harriet's memorial service, Evalyn had come with Joy to visit Kathleen. They had just finished rebuilding the corner of the house that had been destroyed.

Kathleen and Evalyn were drinking coffee and watching Joy play on the floor when Kathleen asked, "How long are we gonna pretend that's not my grandbaby?"

Evalyn had to set her cup of coffee down due to her instant shaking. "You know?"

Kathleen's smile was warm. "Since the moment I laid eyes on her. She looks just like Harriet did when she was a baby. Harriet was missing, and you came home with Joy. It didn't take me long to realize that Harriet had abandoned her own child."

"Mrs. Wheaton, I was just so confused, and I love Joy so much." Evalyn bowed her head. "But I should've told you. I should've brought Joy to you and Mr. Wheaton."

Kathleen patted Evalyn's hand. "It's okay. We know you were doing what you thought was best."

"So Mr. Wheaton knows too?" asked Evalyn.

Kathleen nodded.

Evalyn rose, sorrow ripping at her heart. "I guess I best go gather Joy's things and bring them here now that your house is finished. I never meant to hurt y'all. I just love her so much, but I guess I always knew this day was coming."

"Sit down, please," said Kathleen. "No good can come from taking Joy out of the only home she knows. If word got out that Joy was Harriet's, it would only make Harriet look bad, and I can't stand the thought of people speaking ill of her, especially now."

Kathleen's eyes filled with tears. "Mr. Wheaton and I are eternally grateful to you for the friendship you showed Harriet and the love and care you've shown Joy. Lord knows what would've happened if you hadn't been there to take Joy in."

"I was so scared y'all would think I just stole her," said Evalyn.

Kathleen shook her head. "Now, it wouldn't make much sense for you to steal her and then take her to the very place she has family. I know my daughter. Harriet was the kind of girl who would give away her own dinner if someone else needed it, even if she was starving, and flat out tell you she wasn't hungry. She had a good heart. But Harriet was also adventurous and impulsive and selfish. She wasn't ready to be a mother that was clear."

"So what do we do now?" asked Evalyn.

"You and your husband are gonna keep Joy, and no one else ever needs to know what we know," said Kathleen. "As long as you let us be a part of her life."

Evalyn reached over and hugged Kathleen. "Absolutely."

"So how did your visit with Mrs. Wheaton go?" asked Robert as he helped Evalyn and Joy out of Elmer's pickup at Quail Crossings.

"She knows," said Evalyn.

"Knows what?" asked Alice, skipping up behind Robert.

"Alice, will you do me a favor and watch Joy while I take a walk with Robert?" asked Evalyn.

"Sure," said Alice, taking her niece and walking into the house.

Evalyn put her arm through Robert's as they walked toward the orchard.

"You were saying, she knows," Robert said as they walked through the trees, some still mangled and stripped bare from the tornado.

Evalyn nodded. "She's known from the beginning about Joy being Harriet's."

Robert stopped and rubbed his neck. "So what are we gonna do? We can still stand together and fight it. It will be her word against ours. No one will blame her for grasping at straws after losing her daughter, but they won't believe her either."

"It's okay," said Evalyn, giving Robert a gentle pat.

"What's okay?" Robert threw his hands up in the air. "Are you just gonna hand Joy over to her? It's not right. You took care of that baby when Harriett ran off. You are the only momma Joy has ever known. She can't just come in and take her because she's grieving. I'm really sorry for her loss. Really, I am, but this isn't gonna help anything."

"Calm down, Robert," Evalyn said with a smile.

"Calm down?" Robert shook his head. "How can we be calm?"

"Because Mrs. Wheaton has no intention of taking Joy away from us. She wants us to raise Joy as our own, as long as we let them be involved in Joy's life," explained Evalyn.

Robert sat on the old bench that James had made for his wife so many years before. Everyone was surprised it had withstood the tornado. "You know, you could've said that first."

Evalyn sat down with a smirk. "And missed the show?"

Smiling back, Robert wrapped her in a big hug. "What am I gonna do with you?"

"Just love me, I guess." Evalyn swallowed hard as the words left her mouth.

"I do, you know," said Robert, arms still around her. "I do love you and Joy. When I thought the twister had swept you up with the rest of the homestead, I just wanted to die too. I couldn't imagine my life without the two of you. I still can't."

Robert shifted to where he was facing her but didn't let go. "I know we already said our marriage vows at the courthouse, but I wanna tell you right now, with God as my witness, that I will love you forever- in good times and bad, in sickness and health, and for richer and poorer. Evalyn Smith, I will love you until the day I die. Do you feel the same?"

Evalyn bit her lip, but her smile wouldn't be contained. "Oh Robert, I do. I love you so much. I was terrified when I drove up to Rockwood and found it gone. I can't imagine my life loving anyone other than you. I promise to stand by you and help you, even with the pigs, for the rest of our lives together. Robert Smith, I will love you until the day I die."

Chapter Forty-one

August 1940

Evalyn smiled as she walked through the family and friends who had all come out to Quail Crossings to celebrate James's sixty-third birthday. Everyone was gathered around the pond, some trying their hand at fishing, while the younger generation splashed around in the water on the opposite side.

It had been just over two months since the tornado had torn through Quail Crossings and Knollwood. Evalyn, Robert, and Joy had moved into Bill's house temporarily while Bill and Lou Anne stayed at Quail Crossings, so Dovie could nurse his eye. The town was still rebuilding, and the shortage of wood had prohibited Robert and Evalyn from working on Rockwood. Thankfully, more pigs had survived than they thought so they could rebuild their stock and Bill's house had a barn that was perfect for swine.

The doctor had been blunt saying that Bill would probably never see out of his left eye again. With Lou Anne fighting off morning sickness at all hours, it had been easier for them to just stay where Dovie could help. There was no doubt about Lou Anne being pregnant as she started to show and felt the baby moving.

Tiny hadn't suffered any lasting effects from her head injury, thankfully, but Elmer still treated her like a fragile flower. Any time they drove anywhere, she insisted on driving because Elmer wouldn't go over five miles per hour in her presence. There wasn't much Elmer could say about it since he had his arm in a cast.

Since he had broken the same arm five years earlier, it had been slow to heal. However, the doctor assured him that the cast would come off any day now.

Evalyn glanced over to where Dovie was standing by Gabe and wondered if nuptials would be in their future. It wouldn't be any time soon, though, as Gabe had been called back to help train pilots at the Army Air Corps Training School headquartered at Chanute Field in Illinois. The United States military was getting nervous about the war in Europe. But Gabe had promised to keep in touch, and Evalyn had caught the lovebirds sneaking kisses on more than one occasion.

"There you are."

Evalyn looked up and straight into the eyes of her husband. His gaze still sent lightning bolts throughout her body, even more so after their vows in the orchard.

Cupping her face, Robert placed a lingering kiss on her lips and the men in the crowd started to whistle at the open display of affection. Even with her cheeks glowing red, Evalyn continued the kiss. After all, she was kissing her husband, and there was absolutely nothing scandalous about that.

Breaking away, Evalyn turned to the crowd. "How 'bout y'all stop ogling and come to the house for some cake and homemade ice cream?"

Robert led her to the house where tables and chairs had been set up for the small crowd to enjoy the birthday goodies.

Robert wrapped his arms around Evalyn and smiled. "How are you feeling this fine day, Mrs. Smith?"

"Absolutely wonderful, Mr. Smith," said Evalyn, "especially when I have you on my arm."

They kissed again.

"Evie," said Alice, as she followed them from the pond, "I got a letter from Jacob today. I've been waiting all day to tell you."

"How is he?" asked Evalyn. "How's Sweetsville treating him?"

"He's already got a job helping to build houses," said Alice. "He really likes it there and has his very own room at a boarding house. But after being at Quail Crossings, he ain't used to all that alone time, so he spends a lot of time in town at the city square where they play music. He's even found him a friend that's teaching him how to read and write. His friend helped him write the letter, so now we can write back and forth."

"Sounds like a wonderful place," said Robert.

"Hey," said Evalyn, cocking her head. "Where's Joy? Aren't you supposed to be watching her?"

"I handed her off to Dovie," said Alice, shrugging.

Evalyn had seen Dovie talking with some church ladies by the pond and knew that Joy wasn't with her. She looked at Robert. "I would feel a lot better if she were here."

Dovie walked up. "If who were here?"

"Joy," said Evalyn. "Alice said she was with you."

"Well, she was and then Lou Anne took her for a bit."

The guests crowded around, and Evalyn searched for Joy. No one seemed to be carrying her daughter. "Where is Joy?" she yelled to everyone.

Everyone stopped and looked at each other, but no one answered. Fear filled her body. her little girl was missing. Surely, she hadn't fallen into the water unnoticed, there were too many people watching out. Someone had to have taken her.

"Look for her," Dovie called out. "Spread out. She couldn't have gotten far. She just started walking."

The group started to disperse and call out Joy's name as Tiny and Elmer ran back toward the pond to look there, although no one could remember seeing her playing with the other young children.

"I found her," called James from the barn door. "It seems to be my calling to find folks in this family. Come here and take a look."

Evalyn and Robert hurried over. Looking into the barn, they smiled and leaned into each other as they looked upon little Joy curled up under the wing of Norman as they both napped in a pile of fresh hay.

Everyone quietly exited the barn as Lou Anne promised she'd keep an eye on her and bring her to them when she woke up. Evalyn walked next to Dovie.

"I don't think I ever said thank you," said Evalyn.

"For what?" asked Dovie.

"For letting me return to Quail Crossings," said Evalyn.

Dovie stopped. "Oh, Evie, that's what home is, a place you can always come back to. Always remember, no matter what, you'll always be able to return to Quail Crossings."

The Murphy Family

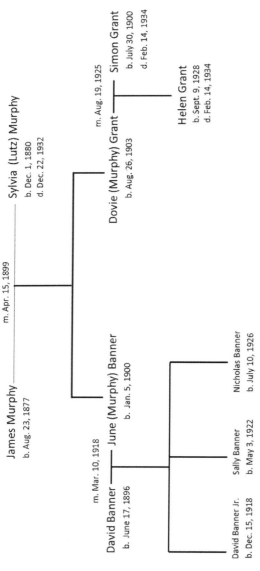

James Murphy
b. Aug. 23, 1877

m. Apr. 15, 1899

Sylvia (Lutz) Murphy
b. Dec. 1, 1880
d. Dec. 22, 1932

June (Murphy) Banner
b. Jan. 5, 1900

Dovie (Murphy) Grant
b. Aug. 26, 1903

m. Aug. 19, 1925

Simon Grant
b. July 30, 1900
d. Feb. 14, 1934

Helen Grant
b. Sept. 9, 1928
d. Feb. 14, 1934

m. Mar. 10, 1918

David Banner
b. June 17, 1896

David Banner Jr.
b. Dec. 15, 1918

Sally Banner
b. May 3, 1922

Nicholas Banner
b. July 10, 1926

The Brewer Family

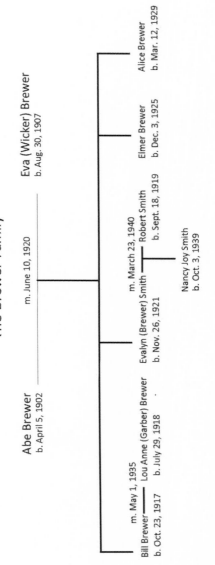

Abe Brewer
b. April 5, 1902

m. June 10, 1920

Eva (Wicker) Brewer
b. Aug. 30, 1907

m. May 1, 1935
Bill Brewer
b. Oct. 23, 1917

Lou Anne (Garber) Brewer
b. July 29, 1918

Evalyn (Brewer) Smith
b. Nov. 26, 1921

m. March 23, 1940
Robert Smith
b. Sept. 18, 1919

Nancy Joy Smith
b. Oct. 3, 1939

Elmer Brewer
b. Dec. 3, 1925

Alice Brewer
b. Mar. 12, 1929

Continue to enjoy the *Quail Crossings* series
with book three, *Missing Quail Crossings*

Also by
Jennifer McMurrain

Missing Quail Crossings

Enjoy an Excerpt from
Missing Quail Crossings

My Dearest Dovie,

I'm sure you've heard by now what has happened at Pearl Harbor. Let me start by saying I'm fine, but many aren't. I wish I could have written to you sooner, but it has been nothing but chaos here.

It has been a couple of days since the attack, and we are still pulling soldiers from the ocean. I can't believe so much carnage happened in such a short amount of time. When the Japanese hit, it felt like all we could do was take cover.

I was lucky that I was in the barracks away from the coast when the bombings took place. My buddies and I ran to help, but there was nothing we could do. Some of our soldiers were able to take a few of the Japanese planes down, but it wasn't enough. I can't put into words how I felt, other than to say I felt helpless. We never expected this to happen on U.S. soil. And now that I've had time to fully digest what has happened, I am worried.

I am worried for our young men, men like Robert, Bill, and Elmer. I worry about our girls. That they will have to send their husbands, brothers, and fathers to war, knowing they may never see them again. I can't imagine all the families getting telegrams after this one attack.

With all of this suffering going on around me, I long for your embrace more than ever. All I can think about is getting home to you and Quail Crossings. Even on the island, that used to be paradise, I long for the peace of the Texas plains.

As much as I would love to come home now, I know it is my duty to stay and continue to train pilots. We cannot rest until evil is gone from this earth forever. We cannot let this attack on our country stand.

I pray that you, and the rest of the family, are doing well and will continue to stay safe during this uncertain time. Until we meet again, my sweet Dovie, and I know we will, I will be thinking of you and missing Quail Crossings.

With all my love,
Gabe

Acknowledgments

I have so many people in my life who share their love and support with me and made this book possible. I am honored and blessed to have y'all in my life.

LilyBear House staff and author family – You guys are awesome. Thank you so much for your support. I can't imagine working with better folks.

Christina Laurie and Cheryl Trenfield – We all know I am grammatically impaired, so thanks for coming in and fixing all my flaws and making my manuscripts sparkle (even if it is in red ink).

C.D. Jarmola, Heather Davis, and Marilyn Boone – I'm not sure how I ever wrote a book without you gals. Thanks for keeping my butt in the chair and for keeping me sane during the summer of the never ending three-year old. Thanks for all the laughs, laps in the pool, and continued support. I'm lucky to call such talented, wonderful women my friends.

Brandy Walker – Everyone knows a book is not completely finished until the cover is done. Thanks for making my covers magnificent. You do magic. Also, I couldn't ask for a better sister. Seriously, it is an honor to call you my sister, and I love you dearly. Know you can move mountains.

Randy and Cathy Collar – What can I say that I haven't already said? You guys mean the world to me. You've made me what I am today. Thank you for everything, and as a writer I realize that isn't nearly adequate enough. But I did dedicate an entire book to you, so that should count for something, right?

Anna Collar – To say I miss you is inadequate. Thanks for all the memories; good and bad, the tears and laughter, the joy and pain. Thanks for always being there to listen, for all the smiles, and all the hugs (man, I miss those hugs). Until we meet again, I love you.

Claressa Carter and Rubina Ahmed – My oldest and dearest friends, thank you for always being there for me. You guys are the definition of what friends are supposed to be. Thank you for all the support, BETA reads, and for sitting with me and keeping me company when the books weren't selling. Y'all are the best.

Linda Boulanger and Darlene Shortridge – You guys have constantly been there for me to answer every question I have about this crazy publishing world. I hope you know every time you help me, I do my best to pay it forward. I'm no dummy, I wouldn't be where I am today without the two of you. Thank you.

WordWeavers – I am honored to be surrounded by such a fabulous and talented group of writers. Thank you all for your love and support. I hope you guys know that when y'all win all those awards, I'm the one who is cheering the loudest. I love you guys.

Extended Family – You guys know if I start naming names, this book would be a million pages long. When I talk about my extended family with my friends, they say we're abnormal because we love getting together and have very little drama. Well, if that is abnormal, then call me weird because I love each and every one of you. Thanks for your support.

Baby Girl – What can I say to the person I love more than anything in this world? You make me want to be superwoman. Keep on dancing and singing girl; I'm loving every minute of it (just *Let it Go!*). Remember, no matter how old you get, you'll always be my Baby Girl.

Mike McMurrain – How did I get so lucky to have a guy like you as my husband? Thank you for always being my biggest cheerleader. Thanks for being the best kind of father and making sure Baby Girl is always taken care of when I'm in my writing cave. The love you surround me with is the stuff of legends. Thanks for letting me live in a real life fairy tale.

My Readers – Wow, without you I would probably be a Pinterest professional. Thank you for all your kind words, encouragement, support, and messages on Facebook, e-mails, Twitter posts … you get the picture. Every time you leave me a message or even "nag" (in a loving way) about when the next book come out, I get the warm fuzzies. I feel honored that you enjoy my stories … completely honored.

About the Author

Having a great deal of wanderlust, author Jennifer McMurrain traveled the countryside working odd jobs before giving into her muse and becoming a full time writer. She's been everything from a "Potty Princess" in the wilds of Yellowstone National Park to a bear researcher in the mountains of New Mexico. After finally settling down, she received a Bachelor's Degree in Applied Arts and Science from Midwestern State University in Wichita Falls, Texas. She has won numerous awards for her short stories and novels. She lives in Bartlesville, Oklahoma, with her husband, daughter, two spoiled cats, and two goofy dogs.

Author photograph by Sister Sparrow Photography

Other works by

Jennifer McMurrain

Novels

Quail Crossings
Winter Song

Anthologies

Whispered Beginnings
Seasons Remembered
Amore

**Short Stories by
Jennifer McMurrain**

Thesis Revised
Footprints in the Snow
Finding Hope
Jar of Pickles
The Looking Glass

Friend Author Jennifer McMurrain on Facebook:
https://www.facebook.com/pages/Author-Jennifer-
McMurrain

Follow Jennifer's tweets -
https://twitter.com/Deepbluejc

Visit her on her website:
http://www.jennifermcmurrain.com

Made in United States
Orlando, FL
24 July 2022

20125879R00193